THE DREAM
ILLUMINATI
VIMANA CONSPIRACY

FURTHER CONSPIRACIES?!

If you would like to read further on the New Age Conspiracy to elevate Human Consciousness on this Planet and elsewhere—don't simply ask your book dealer to order the following titles—**Demand that S/He do so!** They are:

THE FUTURE HISTORY SERIES
By Timothy Leary, Ph.D.

Info-Psychology
Neuropolitique
The Intelligence Agents
What Does Woman Want?
Millennium Madness
The Game Of Life

THE ROBERT ANTON WILSON SERIES

The Cosmic Trigger
Sex and Drugs
Wilhelm Reich In Hell
Prometheus Rising
The Goddess Obsession: Book of the Breast
Coincidance—A New Anthology
The New Inquisition

THE FUTURE IS **NOW** SERIES

Undoing Yourself With Energized Meditation and Other Devices
   By Christopher S. Hyatt, Ph.D. Introduced by Israel Regardie,
   With an extensive Foreword by Robert Anton Wilson.
Undoing Yourself Too by Christopher S. Hyatt, Ph.D.
Breaking The GodSpell: Genetic Evolution By Neil Freer.
   Introduced by Zecharia Sitchin.
The Sapiens System—The Illuminati Conspiracy: Their Objectives, Methods & Who They Are!
   By Donald Holmes, M.D.
   With an extensive introduction by Robert Anton Wilson.
Angel Tech — A Modern Shaman's Guide to Reality Selection by Antero Alli,
   Preface by Robert Anton Wilson.
All Rites Reversed! by Antero Alli
The Akashic Record Player by Antero Alli
A Modern Shaman's Guide to a PREGNANT UNIVERSE
   by C.S. Hyatt, Ph.D. and Antero Alli
Monsters and Magical Sticks: There Is No Such Thing As Hypnosis?
   By Steven Heller, Ph.D. Introduced by Robert Anton Wilson.
An Extraterrestrial Conspiracy By Marian Greenberg.
   Not Introduced by Robert Anton Wilson.
The Shaman Warrior By Gini Graham Scott, Ph.D.

For a free catalog of all Falcon titles write to:
FALCON PRESS ◻ 3660 N. 3rd. St. ◻ Phoenix, AZ 85012 ◻ U.S.A.

THE DREAM ILLUMINATI

VIMANA CONSPIRACY

By
Wayne Saalman

**Introduced by
Robert Anton Wilson**

1988
FALCON PRESS
Los Angeles & Phoenix

ISBN: 0-941404-72-2
Library of Congress Card Catalog Number: 88-80461

First Edition — 1988

Cover Photography and Design © 1988 by D'vorah Curtis
Photo subject, *Angelos*, is an original bronze sculpture, by D'vorah Curtis. For information on this and other of her works, please contact D. Curtis Studios, P.O. Box 783, Sedona, AZ 86336.

Typesetting Design: Cate Mugasis

Falcon Press
3660 N. 3rd St.
Phoenix, Arizona 85012
(602) 246-3546

Manufactured in the United States of America

For Laũ ren zen

"Nothing whatever is hidden;
   From of old, all is clear as daylight."

"Meeting, they laugh and laugh —
   The forest grove, the many fallen
   leaves!"

We should understand that dream symbols are for the most part manifestations of a psyche that is beyond the control of the conscious mind. Meaning and purposefulness are not the prerogatives of the mind; they operate in the whole of living nature. There is no difference in principle between organic and psychic growth. As a plant produces its flowers, so the psyche creates its symbols. Every dream is evidence of this process.

— C.G. Jung

The most we can do is to *dream the myth onwards* and give it a modern dress.

— C.G. Jung

Introduction

by Robert Anton Wilson, Ph.D.

THIS BOOK concerns dreams of flight, and the achievement of flight. Historically, dreams of flying appeared in the collective unconscious before the reality of flight existed in technology, and it seems plausible that if we understood our dreams better we would use our technology more wisely. Our machines manifest our dreams in matter crafted to coherence, and a psychoanalysis of our culture could easily derive from an examination of how we use science to materialize our fantasies and nightmares.

Why have we always dreamed of flying, and why have we built flying machines? This question seems "eminently" worth pondering in a world where 200,000,000 people pass through Kennedy International Airport every year, flying the Atlantic in one direction or the other.

To understand the profound, it often appears helpful to begin with clues that seem trivial. I suggest that we contemplate what our children look at every Saturday morning on TV.

One of the most popular jokes in animated cartoons shows the protagonist walking off a cliff, without noticing what he has done. Sublimely ignorant, he continues to walk—*on air*—until he notices that he has been doing the "impossible"; and then he falls. I doubt very much that

3

there will be any reader of this book who has not seen that routine at least once; most of us have seen it a few hundred times.

It might seem pretentious to see a Jungian archetype adumbrated in crude form in this Hollywood cliche, but follow me for a moment.

When Hollywood wishes to offer us the overtly mythic, it presents Superman, who can "leap over tall buildings in a single bound," and a more recent hero named Luke *Skywalker*.

The Tarot, that condensed encyclopedia of the collective unconscious, begins with the card called The Fool, and the Fool is depicted walking off a cliff—just like Donald Duck or Wily Coyote in the cartoons.

A Greek legend (which James Joyce took as the archetype of the life of the artist) tells us of Daedalus and Icarus: Daedalus who, imprisoned in a labyrinth (conventional "reality"), invented wings and flew away, over the heads of his persecutors, and Icarus, the son of Daedalus, who flew too close to the Sun Absolute and fell back to Earth. Like Porky Pig walking off a cliff, Icarus's fall contains a symbolism many have encountered in their own dreams.

The Sufi order employs as emblem a heart *with wings* (and the Ordo Templi Orientis employs a circle—symbolizing both emptiness and completion—*with wings*). The Egyptian god of wisdom, Thoth, had the head of a winged creature, the ibis; his Greek equivalent, Hermes, was portrayed as more human, but had bird's wings on his sandals.

The Wright Brothers, who made flying possible for all of us, remain beloved figures in the folk imagination—but how many readers can name the inventors of such equally marvelous (but Earthbound) devices as the television, the vacuum cleaner, the computer, the laser or the modern indoor toilet? Yet while other geniuses seem "forgotten by the masses," the classic put-down to satirize any conservative who sets limits to what human art can accomplish remains "I told Wilber and I told Orville, you'll never get that crate off the ground."

I suspect that part of the function of flight consists in destroying our concept of *limit*; opening us to the insight Dr. John Lilly expressed so eloquently in *The Center of the Cyclone*:

> In the province of the mind, what is believed to be true is true or becomes true, within limits to be found experimentally and experientially. These limits are further beliefs to be transcended. In the province of the mind, there are no limits.

The poet Hart Crane, trying to describe what Wilbur and Orville Wright meant to his generation (he died in the 1930s), wrote that from Kitty Hawk onward, he sensed "the closer clasp of Mars." By 1938 people tuning in on an Orson Welles' radio program after the drama started *believed* they were hearing a newscast and the Martians were already here. A quantum jump had occurred in the limits of our social imagination. Humanity had, like the poet, sensed the "closer clasp" of Mars.

Just slightly more than 30 years later, Neil Armstrong walked on the moon, like a character in the fiction of Jules Verne, and ten years later, our instruments invaded the Martian desert already familiar to "us" through the visions of Edgar Rice Burroughs and Ray Bradbury. If this does not confirm William Blake's notorious claim that "poetic Imagination" should be considered another name for "God," it certainly suggests that Poetic Imagination may function as another name for Destiny.

Perhaps we should ponder more deeply on the fact that Daedalus means "artist" in Greek. Daedalus, designer of labyrinths, imprisoned by those he served, in a labyrinth he himself built—Daedalus, inventor of wings that took him from the Earth to Outer Space—why does he represent Art, instead of Science?

Well, to understand this we must remember that the ancient Greeks did not distinguish Art and Science as we do. The genius of an artist, Aristotle says, lies in his *tekne*, the root from which we get our word, "technology"; but *tekne* basically means skill or craft, or the ability to make things that never existed before.

In our age, by contrast, Stravinsky was regarded as "witty" or "paradoxical" (or deliberately enigmatic) when he called himself a "sound engineer." An artist who considers himself a kind of engineer? That is a hard thought for us to grasp. Yet a few moments reflection will show that as much precise structural knowledge can be found in Stravinsky's music as in Roebling's blueprints for the Brooklyn Bridge—that edifice (considered "miraculous" when it was new) which Hart Crane took as a symbol of the unity of Art and Science.

Our dichotomized and dualistic thinking has been denounced so often lately that I hardly need labor this point. I would prefer to suggest a possible common origin of both art and science. The musician and the architect, the poet and the physicist, I propose, may be best considered late evolutionary developments of the type that first appears as the shaman— and shamans in most cultures are known as "they who walk in the sky," just like our current shaman-hero, Luke Skywalker.

It should not be regarded as accidental or arbitrary that Swift put Laputa, the home of the scientists, in the sky, in order to disparage science for not having all four feet on the ground; Aristophanes put Socrates in the clouds, to similarly disparage philosophy. Outer Space seems the natural home of all descendents of the shaman, whether they be called artists, philosophers or scientists.

The ironies of Swift and Aristophanes, and the myths of the fall of Icarus and Donald Duck, indicate that the collective unconscious contains a force opposed to our dreams of flight. This appears inevitable. As Jung, the foremost explorer of the collective psyche, often pointed out, an ineluctable polarity exists in the symbols of dream and myth, a "Law of Opposites" which Jung compared to the Chinese concept of *yin* and *yang* energies Jekyll contains Hyde; love easily becomes hate; Cupid and Psyche reappear as the Phantom of the Opera and Margaritta, and also as King Kong and Fay Wray.

In the present context, the Law of Opposites means that **we yearn to soar, yet we fear to fall**. Our "inner selves" are mirrored not just in Orville Wright rising like a bird from Kill Devils Hill at Kitty Hawk, but also in Simon Newcombe, the great astronomer, who "proved" mathematically that such flight was impossible.

As I have elsewhere suggested, **neophilia** and **neophobia**—love of novelty and fear of novelty—result from the primal polarities of the first imprint of the newborn infant. In other words, what Dr. Timothy Leary calls the bio-survival "circuit" of the nervous system—the oral bio-survival *system*, I prefer to call it, since it includes the immune, endocrine and neuropeptide sub-systems as well as the autonomic nervous system—imprints either basic explorativeness or basic conservatism very quickly. That explains, I think, why some babies "chortle with delight" when tossed up in the air and caught, while others scream with terror. Infants who like this experience of flight, I suggest, already have the neophiliac imprint and those who act terrified have the neophobic imprint.

Of course, "the universe" can count above two (even if Aristotelian logicians cannot) and few of us are **either** pure neophilics **or** pure neophobics. Rather, we wobble about on a gradient between neophilia and neophobia—between joy and anxiety, between conservatism and experimentalism, between yearning to soar and fear of falling. At times we feel like Jonathan Livingston Seagull, convinced that "*a true Heaven has no limits*" and trying to fly higher and faster; other times we become the old Reaganite gulls, nervously warning that to fly too high too fast will ruin your brain and directly contradicts the traditional mores of the flock ("Just say **no** to soaring").

We contain both Orville Wright leaping into the air toward a future "where no man has gone before" and Simon Newcombe proving that Orville will certainly fall and smash himself like Humpty Dumpty.

As Joyce so poetically writes:

> *My great blue bedroom, the air so quiet, scarce a cloud. In peace and silence. I could have stayed up there for always only. It's something fails us. First we feel. Then we fall . . . If I seen him come down on me now under whitespread wings like he'd come from Arkangels, I sink I'd die down under his feet, humbly dumbly, only to washup.*

Despite the multiple dream-images here—the Irish rain falling to become the Irish river Anna Liffey, Lucifer and his hosts falling from Heaven, the falls of Adam and Eve and Humpty Dumpty, Mary receiving the divine seed from the Archangel, Magdalene washing the feet of the Saviour, the paraclete descending as a dove to bring the Apostles the Gift of Tongues, a housewife washing up the breakfast dishes—Joyce primarily invokes our deep awareness that gravity "pulls us down," our deep yearning to break free of this "drag" and soar back to our home above the clouds.

In 1988, the ancient Egyptian and Gnostic belief that our origin and our destiny reach far beyond Earth no longer seems as quaint and queer as it did in recent generations. In books like Dr. Timothy Leary's *Info-Psychology*, Dr. Francis Crick's *Cosmic Panspermia* and Sir Fred Hoyle's *Evolution from Space*, there appears a body of evidence strongly suggesting that life did not begin on this planet but arrived here from elsewhere in space. While the interpretations of these brilliant philosopher-scientists differ—Leary thinks life was planted here by advanced intelligences lovingly seeking "children" for companionship, while Crick proposes that advanced civilization created Earthside DNA as an interesting experiment, and Hoyle argues that some seeds got here by accident (on comets etc.) and some was deposited by Higher Intelligences for reasons inscrutible to us at present—their various kinds of evidence, from diverse fields of enquiry, does make a strong case that evolution is older and more universal than we traditionally think. One leaves their books suspecting that the orthodox biological view regarding Earthly evolution apart from Cosmic evolution results from unvoiced pre-Copernican assumptions about Earth's centrality and its isolation.

In addition to the sophisticated and learned works of Leary, Crick and

Hoyle, we have also recently witnessed the growth of a vast body of "vulgar" or at least popular literature arguing the proposition that Ancient Astronauts seeded this planet, not with all life, but merely with (post-Neanderthal) humanity. Instead of dissecting the flaws in the arguments of this seemingly "crank" literature, it might be more illuminating, I think, to wonder why this popular mythos provides the masses with an unsophisticated and anthropocentric form of the theories more soberly presented in works like *Info-Psychology, Cosmic Panspermia,* and *Evolution from Space.* Why do we find both first-rate and second-rate minds suddenly preoccupied with extraterrestrial evolution, while ninth rate minds increasingly embrace Pop UFOlogy?

And why, one may next wonder, does this theme also appear centrally in the most beautiful, the most "haunting" and the most often-revived science-fiction film of all time—Kubrick's magnificent *2001*?

When one idea or archetype appears in learned tomes, in tabloids, in folk-belief, in new cults, and in great art, all at about the same time, one suspects the presence of what Jung called, in his book *Flying Saucers,* "a shift in the constellation of the archetypes." In terms of current neuro-science, what Jung means, I think, is that the DNA/CNS "dialogue"—the neuropeptide "language" between genes and brain—is preparing us for a new evolutionary leap.

Later in this book, you will read a scene in which the hero says bluntly:

> **I realized that I was only as free as I thought myself to be and that there was no limit to how high we can fly!**

Here we see again that the archetype of flight carries always an umbilical connection to the idea of the **transcendence of all limits**. ("What is believed to be true is true or becomes true . . . ")

And we must wonder again if more than childish fantasy lurks in the concept of Donald Duck walking on air only *until* he "remembers" that this "is" officially "impossible" in our current reality-tunnel.

In 1904, when Einstein was starting to write his first paper on Relativity and the Wright Brothers were testing the airplane design that finally worked after many failures, Aleister Crowley, the most controversial mystic of our century, "received"—or created by Poetic Imagination—a document which he ever after believed was a communication from Higher Intelligence. In this work, called *Liber AL* or *The Book of the Law,* there is contained what purports to be a message from "Nuit," the Egyptian star

goddess, interpreted in Crowley's commentaries as the supreme consciousness of the cosmos, or the sum total of all synergetically interactive
intelligences throughout space-time. Among other things this "entity" or
corporation told Crowley:

> *Every man and every woman is a star . . .*
>
> *I am above you and in you. My ecstasy is*
> *in yours. My joy is to see your joy . . .*
>
> *For I am divided for love's sake, for the*
> *chance of union . . .*
>
> *Put on the wings, and arouse the coiled*
> *splendor within you: come unto me!*

Many interpretations of these verses are possible; you may be
astonished later, as some possible meanings that are not at all clear now
will be strongly present if you gaze back at this page after finishing the
novel before you.

Personally, after reading some of the current scientists who see
evolution as both terrestrial and extraterrestrial, I cannot look at the words
of *Liber AL* without thinking that, in some sense, the interstellar creators
who planted life here may be sending us a signal to return to our home in
the stars—that "great blue bedroom" which Joyce poetically invokes on the
last page of *Finnegans Wake* and in which the astronaut, David Bowman,
abruptly finds himself at the climax of *2001*.

Of course, the language of poetic myth, like that of dream, should
always be considered analogical and allegorical, not literal; to see only one
meaning here (or in the novel to come) means that one will "fall into the pit
of Because and perish with the dogs of Reason" (to cite Crowley again).
The content of a true archetype contains an infinity of mirrors.

For instance, my Dream Diary for 23 April 1968 records that when I
woke in the morning I remembered the following images from my night's
hermetic journey:

1. I am in a Chicago nightclub once patronized by John Dillinger.
I find that the present patrons are also a group of gangsters. They
regard me with hostility, and I become frightened. I try to leave;
they try to stop me. I open a door.

2. I find myself on the IRT subway in New York. I am riding in

the front car and watching the tunnel ahead of the train (as I did as a boy). Suddenly, I see a brick wall ahead and realize the train is going to crash into it and kill everybody aboard, including me.

3. I am out of the subway and walking in Cicero, Illinois. An angry mob surrounds me. They seem to know that I was in the recent Martin Luther King march against segregation here. I cannot escape them. Suddenly, I know intuitively what to do. I cry out, "Elohim!" and sprout wings and fly above their heads. The sky is beautiful and I feel free of all anxieties, at peace, unreasonably hopeful about everything.

When I awoke, I was thinking of Chesterton's description of the mystic experience as "absurd good news."

At the time of this dream, I was involved with Chicago friends in propagating the John Dillinger Died For You Society, a parody of Fundamentalist religions which, like all good jokes, had its serious side. I was fascinated by the way that certain outlaws like Dillinger (or Jesse James, or Robin Hood) were virtually forced to live to the full the archetypal myth of Osiris, Dionysus, Adonis, Christ—and Joyce's Tim Finnegan. I also meditated much on the way in which outlaws who did not even approximately "live" the myth subsequently had their lives rewritten in folk-imagination to conform to it. The first part of the dream-record confronts me with the dark side of the archetype, and reminds me that real gangsters are not the mythic figures imposed on them by Poetic Imagination but nasty and frightening sociopaths.

In the second part of the dream, I enter into the Underground Initiation. Although using symbols from my own life (the subway), I find myself retracing the steps of Ishtar in the land of the dead, Odysseus sailing to Hades for wisdom, Jesus and Dante descending to Hell, etc. In alchemy this was called **negrito**, which Jung compares to the initial stages of psychotherapy.

In a sense, the Underworld Journey appears the reciprocal of, and preparation for, the Achievement of Flight. Dante had to walk through Hell before climbing Mount Purgatory and soaring above the clouds to Heaven. In retrospect, I am especially delighted with the Freudian wit of the unconscious in using modern "Underworld" figures—gangsters—to represent the mythic Underworld.

In the third part of the dream, the traditional Wrathful Demons attack me, personified by the citizens of Al Capone's home town, Cicero, perhaps because the people out there always reminded me of Wrathful Demons whenever I had to associate with them. I escape by crying out a name from the Hebrew Bible, whereupon I am able to fly, like Dante or Daedalus, from the Pit to the Stars.

What I find most curious about these dream fragments is that, when I experienced them in 1968, I knew nothing about Cabala. I was puzzled on awakening about the name **Elohim** and the way I had magically used it in the dream. All I knew about that name in those days was that it appears in the first chapter of Genesis and that there is a dispute between philologists and theologians about whether it means "God" or "the gods"—i.e. whether the first chapter of the Bible is or isn't a fragment left over from a polytheistic phase of Judaism.

It was over two years after this very Jungian dream that I became interested in Cabala and eventually learned that **Elohim** is therein considered a great Name of Power—used in e.g. the Middle Pillar Ritual, which every Cabalist in training is expected to do at least once a week. The function of Cabalistic ritual in general, and this ritual in particular, was once defined by Crowley as "to raise the mind of the student perpendicularly to Infinity"—beyond all limits. This is symbolized in my dream, as in many dreams and myths, by the imagery of flight and the conquest of gravity. The 1968 dream seems to contain precognition of Cabalistic work I would be doing very seriously c. 1971-75.

Of course, if one dares to suggest that a dream contains precognition, the Rationalist immediately declares the connection between the dream image and later waking events is "mere coincidence." The "coincidence" becomes more provocative, however, when one considers that my interest in Cabala was aroused by the books of Dr. Israel Regardie, and this present novel is being published by Dr. Christopher S. Hyatt, a former student of Dr. Regardie's. Both Dr. Hyatt and Dr. Regardie have been Jungian therapists, and it was Jung who inspired me to keep a dream diary and look for "coincidences" between the dream-world and the awake-world. These links (Wilson-Regardie-Hyatt-the 1968 dream-my later study of Cabala-the present novel) seem to suit Jung's definition of synchronicity as "psychologically induced space-time relativity."

At the time I had this dream or set of dreams in 1968, I was suffering from a moderately severe depression and the general symptoms of what is now called "mid-life crisis." I had a very good job at *Playboy* magazine, with an excellent salary for the '60s, but I was approaching 40 and wanted to write full-time. (Three years later, after beginning Cabalistic work, I quit my job and have been writing full-time ever since. Although I have experienced the usual share of shocks, disappointments and bereavements, I have not suffered clinical depression again.)

The reader might find it illuminating to compare this record with a dream recounted in Joseph Campbell's *The Hero With a Thousand Faces*. In this case, the dreamer saw a **winged** horse with *one wing broken*, struggling to **fly** and falling continually back to Earth. Campbell does not even bother interpreting this symbolism, merely informing us that the dreamer was a poet forced to work at a menial job to support his family; one understands immediately.

In a sense, we have all had our "wings" broken; it remains the major function of such "hallowed institutions" as organized religion and free compulsory education to see that our "wings" are broken, or at least clipped, before we reach adulthood. How else will society have the insectoid units it needs to fill the cubicles in its hive economy?

But what if we begin to regrow healthy organs of Poetic Imagination and flight? What if we "put on the wings and arouse the coiled splendor within" as *Liber AL* urges? Is it not predictable that society will react with the fury described by Wayne Saalman in this novel? Joyce did not name his emblematic Artist merely Daedalus but Stephen Dedalus—after St. Stephen Protomartyr who reported a Vision and was stoned to death for it.

And does it not appear ultimately beneficial, in evolutionary perspective, that society should react in that manner? Those of us who have no avocation for martyrdom must learn, when we realize how much neophobia remains built into the contraptions of "society" and "the State," the art of surviving in spite of them. In a word, we must "get wise" in both the Socratic meaning of that phrase and in the most hardboiled street meaning. Neophobia functions as an Evolutionary Driver, forcing the neophiliac to get very shrewd very fast, just as stupidity provokes the merely intelligent to become also clever and cunning.

For the rest, I think this novel speaks very eloquently for itself—to those who are ready to read between the lines. As a final bit of gnomix exegesis, I offer you Proposition 12 of Aleister Crowley's masterwork, *Magick*:

> *Man is ignorant of the nature of his own being and powers. Even his idea of his limitations is based on experience of the past, and every step in his progress extends his empire. There is therefore no reason to assign theoretical limits to what he may be, or to what he may do.*

Prologue

IT WAS SUNDAY morning on San Francisco Bay and the sails were everywhere, tacking in all directions. The sun was still low to the horizon and no one seemed to be hurrying, not even the boats maneuvering into position for the day's regatta.

The Golden Gate Bridge had its tourists of course, but they were quietly in awe of the grand spectacle all about them: Alcatraz and the spans of the Bay Bridge, the white pillar of cylindrical Coit, jetties and wharves, the rolling hills with their highrise towers, the Transamerica Pyramid. It was all beautiful and a billion times photographed, and every strolling couple had at least one finger pointing at something near or far.

But soon the fingers would be pointing at a sight which had been witnessed few times on the San Francisco skyline. They would point from the sailing boats, and they would point from the walkways. Tourists would point and native San Franciscans would point alike. It would be the same everywhere. Fingers high and straight. From Baker Beach to the Marina to Fisherman's Wharf. The witnesses would not know about it in advance. They would just turn one moment and suddenly they would see something there in the sky.

And so it began. First a low buzz would be heard out on the cliffs near Dead Man's Point, its intensity growing quickly like the sounds of an orderly swarm of hornets. Then it would move out over the water at the mouth of the bay, and the tourists would turn with startled eyes as if being caught without warning by the sudden invasion of an alien squadron or as if the ghosts of suicide jumpers, lost one by one over the decades from the bridge, were suddenly rising up in unison like birds.

Fingers would hastily trace the fleet airborne parade through the morning sky as the fliers looped the magnificent massive Golden Gate like a troupe of aerial daredevils. And they would trace the smooth graceful spiral flown over zephyr-laden sails and deep blue waves. They would trace the ascent and arc of forty-four airborne men and women soaring with unitary precision, each on their own thruster rockets, each screeching brazenly toward the city downtown. And finally when the fingers would trace out the awesome sight of forty-four fliers circling the great skyscraper pyramid, round and round like an immense free-flight carousel, streaking with ecstasy while the chrome of helmets and pack parts flashed brilliant flares of reflected sunlight, never for a moment could they know that one day the eyes of the world would look back and see those same fingers tracing out a curved path straight into the ever astonished face of history.

Part 1

1

THE BUS rolled out of Katmandu at dawn. Aaron Harrison sat in a window seat and watched "the old city recede into Kingdom Come." This was his journal entry. He was just scribbling out an impression and laughing to himself. He was not fully awake. Nor, probably, were the King and Queen of Nepal. Nor the living virgin goddess Kumari. Nor the black market moguls of the midnight bazaar. But all of that meant nothing now. The bags were stowed away beneath the bus. And even as the devotees of royalty and the gods began a new day of prostrations and ritual circumambulations of Swayambunath and Balaju, even as the temple monkeys squealed for feedings of meager pilgrim food, and the birds flew up to the higher ledges on the old pagodas of Durbar Square to search the steps for any scant scatterings of grain offered to the harvest goddess Annapurna, Aaron Harrison thought only of sleep and new sweet dreams. He arranged his heavy sweater into a pillow and leaned against the window and closed his eyes.

When he and Oriana had first boarded, they had waited nearly an hour before the driver had leapt into his seat and slammed the door closed. But at last the vehicle had lurched forward on a big cushion of air. The tour bus was a virtual luxury cruiser compared to the rickety local buses, but it was also a renegade of the tour lines and no one expected any spray-haired guide to stand up and coo about the Nepalese wonders. It was just a busful of young backpacking travelers who had found the cheapest, most comfortable ride down into India. Now they were gently rocking across the valley between great Himalayan foothills as water buffalo pulled wooden plows through the soils of cultivated terraces and children played by the roadside and mothers bent to their morning laundry. And the road to Pokhara wound round in the dawnlight as if in a lazy pastoral of lost centuries.

It was hours before Aaron awoke again. When his eyes half opened he could see Oriana up front, sitting by the driver. They were spiritedly gesturing and talking. Oriana flashed smile after smile and eventually she looked back and saw Aaron watching and she smiled at him, too. Aaron returned a drowsy grin and then looked out on the now brilliantly lit landscape. The bus was winding alongside the Kali Gandaki River, its brown waters familiar from the first trip they had made to Pokhara on one of the local buses. He remembered how his knees had been cramped up against the wooden seat on that trip and how a Nepalese woman had patiently rested her chicken in a cage there as her three children romped playfully on the old ragged upholstery. But now he was sprawled out in deep cushioned luxury and no crowd of young men was riding up on the roof clinging to strapped-in pieces of luggage as before. Rugged roads were barely stirring him from his reverie. He had had an incredibly exhilarating dream, and his mind kept playing and replaying the scenes. He was searching for meaning, but more importantly, he was seeking to sustain the dream mood, the exciting euphoria of flying.

After a time, Oriana Zevallos made her way back to her seat beside Aaron. She was wearing a mix of Nepalese and American clothes: wine-colored cotton pants and a long blue tropical floral-print dress topped with a blue scarf bearing tiny red images of Buddha in a lotus posture. Her eyes had a richness of intelligence and beauty, very dark brown and very penetrating. Long, thick black hair poured down onto her shoulders.

"I was talking to Jake," Oriana explained as she sat down. "He's driven this route eight times now! God! What a job and way of life! Says he hasn't been back to the States for years. He loves it over here."

Aaron raised a brow and laughed. "I suppose so! Driving around the Himalayas all the time . . . "

"We had a great talk. He really knows this area well. He wants to own his own bus someday, but he said that he really doesn't make enough now unless he gets into the black market."

"You mean he's not already in the black market?"

Oriana drew a quick breath. "I'm not sure really." There was a pause. "I didn't really want to pry. Anyway . . . how was your sleep?"

Aaron smiled, his blue-green eyes sparkling with pleasure. "It was great. I had an incredible dream. Very long and very vivid. Another flying dream. I'm still trying to figure it out."

"Tell it to me."

Aaron leaned his head back and closed his eyes a quick moment, then began to speak. But suddenly there was a commotion at the front of the bus, and he opened his eyes to look.

"That's the Turk," Oriana explained as they watched a man making comical gestures to the driver and to the people in the front two rows. "I didn't catch his name, but he said he was from Turkey. He's such a clown."

The man was passing around a pipeful of ganja. The driver drew in a few hits then passed it back to a waiting hand. In a moment, he was laughing and running quick fingers through his long stringy hair and guiding the bus with his other hand gripped to the large steering wheel. None of the passengers reacted nervously. The Turk leaned forward in his front seat and continued jabbering incessantly. His girlfriend would smile beatifically at him and laugh with loving eyes. She was dark-skinned and wore a black beret like the Turk. They both had a wooden set of beads around their necks and a picture of their guru suspended in a locket there for all to see. The Turk's pendant hung down onto his bare chest between an open black vest. His purple silk pants made him look like a genie from Istanbul, and he smiled with a rascalish grin through a thick black beard. He would jump up suddenly and talk to the young men in the seat behind him, then just as suddenly turn back to whisper into the driver's ear. Heads would nod and laughter erupt in great volleys. Sometimes he would grab up his delicate eight-stringed Indian instrument and twang a few out-of-tune notes. Four plucks and a huge grin all around, forever in motion.

Aaron watched, then looked over at Oriana with an amused grin of his own.

"Wait until you talk to him," Oriana laughed.

"More like wait until he talks *at* me!" Aaron joked. "It looks like he never lets anybody else get a word in."

"Oh, he's alright . . . " Oriana insisted. "He's funny. But he does B.S. He tries to make you think that he's really enlightened and knows all of these important people. But at least he's not a Westerner. I'll go out of my way to avoid the same old boring nonsense."

Aaron frowned. "The driver's American, isn't he?"

"Jake? Yes. But he's hardly typical."

Aaron brushed back his brown hair, looked out the window and shrugged it off. He didn't fully understand.

"So what about that dream?" Oriana wanted to know.

Aaron smiled over at her, then looked back out the large window. He noticed that the bus was entering a small roadside village, and he saw a scattering of people all turning in the hot sun to catch a glimpse of the big modern vehicle. Many were pointing and the children were all staring with excited little gestures. Aaron laughed, his face nearly pressed up against the pane. But then he was suddenly the target of a random projectile thrown by a teenage boy from the roadside. Red water splattered everywhere over the window and he drew back in horror.

The Turk raced quickly down the aisle. "Holi Festival!" he screamed. "Balloon bombs! We are under seige!" He was like a madman and laughed hysterically. He scurried back to where a young woman sat wiping bright blue dye from her face. She had not been as lucky as Aaron. Her window had been wide open, and now she looked as if a blob of ink had hit her. The Turk began razzing her unmercifully, then he was instantly helpful and lent a hand as she mopped up. Meanwhile, the Nepalese were bent over in fits of laughter out by the roadside as other balloon bombs thwacked at the big windows. It was all fun and games, and the blue-faced girl tried hard to be a sport.

"Holi Festival!" the Turk told her over and over.

"Yeah, yeah . . . I read about it."

Then the Turk turned and hurried back up the aisle, stepping every which way over big traveler's packs and laughing. "Wild times in Buddhaland!" he yelled. "Beware the terrorists!" Aaron grinned watching him, quietly thanking the fates that he had not been hit.

The excitement lingered on for a time, even after the bus was well past the village. It was nearing high noon, and everyone was now thoroughly energetic and animated and words were flowing everywhere in a great humming blur. Finally, even the Turk was forced to settle into the general hubbub. He sat down next to his girlfriend and they engaged in quiet talk.

At last, Aaron began telling his dream to Oriana, and she sat back to listen. "It was a flying dream!" he effused in a joyous tone, "but the ending does kind of throw me. I hope that it's not meant to be taken literally!"

"Why? What happened?"

"In the beginning, I was out in the middle of nowhere when I came to a movie theater by a lake. As soon as I went in, some man hustled me off to an elevator and told me to get in. It had a glass door, and once inside I knew that I was trapped. Then the elevator took off and I was being hauled helplessly up the side of the wall. I could see the man down below pulling handles and laughing devilishly, so I began to panic. I started beating on the glass and yelling, but nobody could hear me. Finally, I just broke the glass in an angry fit and dove recklessly through the opening. My body stiffened, ready for impact with concrete, but then it all changed . . . "

"How?"

"Suddenly, I was diving down toward the lake and it was so beautiful! Its sheen was a turquoise blue, and all around I could see huge snow-covered mountains and great pine forests."

"Like here?"

"No, more like the Swiss Alps. I was as high as a cloud, and my consciousness became extremely intense. I could make out every detail with vivid clarity. Then I thought to myself: 'I'm not falling, I'm flying!' And I was! I began soaring like a bird, and I swooped all around with sheer joy. It was really great! After a while, I leveled off into an upright position as if I were about to walk on thin air. Then balloons appeared from nowhere attached to my arms and legs."

"Balloons?"

Aaron could see the humor in Oriana's eyes, and he smiled. "Synchronicity strikes again!" He laughed hard thinking back to the balloon attack. "But...," he went on, "these balloons were like buoys, and they stabilized me and I hovered over the scene as if I were on a spacewalk. Then I descended slowly and landed on the shores of the lake. The balloons just disappeared. I could still see the movie theater, so I went back to it and went inside."

Oriana nodded. "And the bad guy?"

"He was there. But a canal ran through the main lobby, and he was on the far side. I was safe, but I just had to get revenge, so I flew on over the canal and tried to take one of his tools. He was all greasy like he had been working on some machinery, and he looked awful. Very scary. Then he saw me and began chasing me. I ran for an open window and tried to fly out. I leapt with everything I had in me. But he caught my legs, and we went out together. I was writhing like a lizard. Finally, I shook loose and he fell. I took off soaring again, so free!"

Aaron's face was almost glowing. But then he grew solemn. "The strange part was the ending, though. I circled around in the sky a few times then flew back into the theater again. This time, I saw my parents there in the crowd, so I landed and went to them. My mother had a newspaper with her, and she showed me the front page. It had my picture there! And I was flying. My mother told me how proud she was. She said that everyone was awed by my ability to fly.

"But then she said that the public would be even more amazed if they knew that I was dying! I gasped. 'You didn't tell them that I was dying, did you?' I asked her."

Aaron's eyes were wide.

Oriana thought a moment. "How did you feel at that point?"

"Not worried really. I was still in ecstasy from the flying. But now that ending really puzzles me."

"What would Jung say?" She was referring to the late famous Swiss psychiatrist, Dr. Carl G. Jung. The man who had been Freud's heir apparent, but who had broken with Freud and had established his own highly renowned form of dream interpretation.

"I'm not exactly sure," Aaron began, "but flying is certainly an attempt at liberation. I mean, obviously the scary man must be a sinister shadow archetype who tries to keep me from flying free."

"Yes, but the ending talks about death. What was it you told me Jung said about dream flying?"

"Oh, that it was ultimately escapist?"

"Yeah. Does it mean that you're running from something? Are you afraid of death and you're not facing it?"

"Now wait a minute! Flying can't always be only escapist! Spirit was meant to soar free! Nobody knew that better than Jung. Some of his most profound dreams and visions involved flying."

"Yes, but to try to break from gravity is a form of denial of our earthly condition . . . "

Aaron frowned. Oriana had always been good at playing the devil's advocate role, but sometimes she pushed Aaron beyond where he wanted to go. He had wanted some form of simple excitement from her, a kind of admiration for his flying prowess, but instead Oriana was pressing into sensitive personal areas. He tried to sidestep it. "Look, Jung thought flying was great! It isn't always negative!"

Suddenly, a voice from behind cut in. "You should read him in the German!" a young woman said with a shy laugh. "You get so many other deeper meanings to his writing that you just can't get in the English translations."

Aaron turned his head quickly and saw a half-blushing face grinning proudly through braces. The girl held up a book she had been reading. It had a German title and was by Jung. When she had happened to overhear Aaron and Oriana's conversation, she had not been able to contain herself.

"The English versions really can't begin to do him justice," she went on. "There's so much more to it!"

Aaron smiled politely, but he was clearly annoyed. First, he felt intruded on. It had been a personal conversation. But then the brashness of her comment had really irked him. He smoldered at the thought that she had directly implied that he might not know his Jungian theory as well as he was sure he did. So what if he didn't read German? Did that make him only half informed? It had been the same argument his philosophy instructor had used when they had discussed his getting a doctorate years before. "Oh, you must read the philosophers in their native tongue!" True and not true, he had decided. Universal truths are hardly subject to the elucidations of any particular language. Aaron was not kind in his mind.

But Oriana jumped in and suddenly she was talking in German. Two years of undergraduate study at Heidelberg had made her very proficient. Aaron had no idea what was being said, but somehow he felt vindicated by Oriana's fluency. He smiled a smile that was half courteous and half snide, then turned back toward the front, where he noticed that the bus was arriving in Pokhara. He saw that many of the other passengers were beginning to pull up bags from beneath their seats for the brief stop-over and he became anxious.

"Have you ever been here?" the girl asked Oriana.

"We finished a trek here two weeks ago," Oriana answered. "We hiked up to Muktinath on the Jomosom Trek. It was incredible."

"This is the Annapurna Range, right?" the girl asked. "It's my first time here."

"Have you trekked yet?"

"Oh yes! We hiked up to an Everest base camp last month. You wouldn't believe the immensity of Everest! I want to climb it someday!" Her braces flashed proudly.

"Let's get set," Aaron broke in. He was impatient with the girl. He pulled a handbag out from beneath the seat. "We've only got a half-hour or so here."

Oriana nodded and began getting her things together. "Let's go eat by the lake," she suggested. Aaron stood up and waited for Oriana to go.

"Talk to you later," the girl called out as the two hurried up the aisle. Only Oriana looked back, smiling.

When they had disembarked, they found the five great snow-clad

Annapurna peaks in full glory. All at once it became a very emotional farewell to a place that they had come to love. Aaron thought back to his first view of the massive sharp peak of Maccha Pucchare, which resembled the famous Swiss Matterhorn. It had been raining when they arrived, so they quickly found accommodations and went to their room to rest. But it had not been late and eventually the storm subsided. At one point, Aaron had glanced out a window and noticed a high, sunlit cloud. He felt glad that the rain was finally breaking up. Then he looked twice, and there it was. It was not a cloud, but a mountain so huge as to be unfathomable at first. The abode of the gods! He was stunned. The true Himalaya!

Now, that inexplicable grandeur was about to be left behind, perhaps forever. When the lunch was finished and the loading begun, Aaron and Oriana lagged behind as long as possible. But Jake went to his wheel and the big engine roared, and it was time for the long, winding drive down out of the Himalayas. All of India lay ahead of them in the hot sun.

They drove on into twilight, and they drove on into darkness. By midnight they were at the Indian border. In typically slow fashion, the authorities began checking passports. Suddenly, it occurred to Aaron and Oriana that they had not gotten their entry visas in Katmandu as the others had. Now they were going to be taken into the station and grilled. Jake and the Turk hurried to their side. Soon the Turk was whispering into an official's ear, and it seemed as if joke after joke were being made. The men laughed and laughed. Aaron and Oriana sat at a table and waited. No one seemed to pay them any attention. But it was Aaron's passport the Turk was waving to the official, and it was Oriana's passport that they were handing one to the other. Then they all sat at a table and talked. The Turk chattered incessantly in Hindi, and the officials all smiled politely. The Turk treated them like old friends and perhaps they were. Aaron and Oriana never did find out what was said, but finally the stamps came out and entry was granted. In another hour a cursory check of the bus was made. It was a very casual search for drugs and contraband. The Turk talked and talked. Nothing was found, and at last the officials left.

Aaron stood out in the dark, waiting, looking up at the thick stars. He noticed a satellite which passed over, lower and brighter than any he had ever seen. He thought again about his dream and shuddered in the cool night. Was it Oriana? he wondered. Was it something wrong between them that had him dreaming escape? He knew that he loved her deeply, yet they had already spoken of splitting. It had been a perfect three-year marriage and now suddenly there was tension. Or did the dream mean something else? Flying dreams had always intrigued him. He was sure that they had something to do with the evolution of the human spirit. Still, a college professor he had once had, had argued against that. The man was the perfect picture of a gray old sage, and he was a counselor who was studying to be a Jungian analyst. When Aaron had presented the idea one evening during a class, the man had just brushed it off. It had seemed of no importance to him: just another symbol. But Aaron felt a special affinity for dream flying and from that point on, rightly or wrongly, he had doubted the professor's wisdom.

Finally, Jake was blasting the horn. It was time to go; the bus had cleared. Aaron snatched one last glance at the stars, then hurried quickly for his seat. Many of the passengers were already sleeping, some were just settling in again. But whatever their dreams that night, they were at last speeding off together into India.

By mid-morning the next day, the bus was back to a full, if tempered, pandemonium. As usual, the Turk was busy charming everyone within earshot. One minute he was the humble servant of the gods and the next he was taking credit for having inspired a world-famous rock star into making a very spiritually oriented album, an album currently hot on the charts. His girlfriend grinned and nodded. Everything was fine by her. She was an angel of love.

And so the distances were swept away in an endless myriad of reveries and chitchat, broken only by the odd ornery shenanigans of the driver or the Turk. At one point, the driver bore down on a crowded stretch of road on the hot Indian plain and blasted his mighty horn which was as loud as a train's. The Indian peasants were sent scurrying from the road in a panic: women, children, chickens, everyone and everything. Tiny crippled lepers watched in baffled wonderment. The cows bellowed in mournful disgruntlement as the big, lurching bus rolled by at an incomprehensible speed. The driver showed no mercy at all. He was hell-bent for Delhi, and if anyone got in the way it was too bad. Except for a poor goatherd who failed to move his animals fast enough, and then the great roaring, horn-blasting bus was forced to a screeching halt. The mighty Jake rose up from his seat, shirtless and tall, with the Turk laughing maniacally at his ear. He grabbed his whip and leapt out onto the road and sent crack after crack at the frightened herd. The young goatherd cowered and scowled and hurried his animals as best he could, but he did not understand. It was only a joke! Jake leapt back up on the bus and bowed for one and all and grinned wildly through his brown walrus moustache and put a cigarette to

his lips which the Turk quickly lit. There was a smattering of applause, and
the Turk giggled in pure ecstasy. He laughed and raced up and down the
crowded aisle like a madman again.

Then when the bus had barely gotten through the next small village,
the driver again suddenly slammed on the brakes and brought the great
vehicle to a grinding stop. Every head on the bus rose up to see. But when
the wide doors opened to a loud hiss of pressurized air, it was not Jake the
driver who scurried out onto the road. It was the Turk in his dark shades.
He had a sleek, long knife in his right hand. There was not another person
to be seen anywhere, just vast fields of bright yellow flowers and everyone
on the bus waited to learn what all the commotion was about. In a flash the
Turk was back, and he was laughing diabolically. He held only a few
flowers in his hand and Jake wasted no time in gunning up the big engine
and roaring off in a roiling cloud of black smoke. Then the Turk stood up at
the front of the bus like a tour guide and began to speak. "This is a poppy,"
he said, adjusting his black beret. "For making the opium." His English was
very broken, but everyone quickly understood, and a vast murmuring
went up from one end of the bus to the other. Jake grinned hugely in his
rearview mirror while the Turk took his blade and gently sliced into the
flower. As a thick fluid began oozing from the cut, the Turk explained and
pointed and lectured. He was euphoric in his rhapsody on the wonders of
the flower. Soon he was passing around seeds and parts of petals. People
examined them, then quickly and nervously passed them on to the next
person in the row behind them. The Turk talked on and on, grinning, and
sometimes he would get a short outburst of applause.

Then his girlfriend handed him a pipe which was filled with ganja, and
he dripped some resin onto the musty leaves in the bowl. A flame went up
and the Turk drew deeply and solemnly, and all at once he was a genie
again in a thick mysterious smoke and everyone watched as he made wild
faces and gestures and blew out with a crazy chortle. "Now . . . " he said in a
proud, impish voice as smoke swirled all around him, "anybody want to fly?"

2

SHE HAD the eyes of a temptress, with mascara thick as black leather circling the long, whip-like lashes. Her dress was a glittery, brilliant, seductive red, trimmed with sparkles of gold, and a thin pink veil floated with her black lustrous hair as she danced. Her red painted nails were long and tapered, the wrists sleeved in scores of thin gold bracelets, her petite bare dancing feet padded so gracefully and light that it brought Damon Burke to his knees. He was ready to worship.

But the dance was not an erotic paean to Damon Burke's private pleasure. The bright red dot at the center of her forehead meant that she was marked for another. She was dancing for a god and, in fact, she was completely oblivious of the young western admirer with his wide piercing green eyes and disheveled brown hair. She leapt and spun and arched backward as tabla drums thumped and a sitar whined and twanged through improvisations of a raga like a flock of invisible hummingbirds darting every which way through the lavishly decorated room, each bird a quivering musical note.

Then with a great flourish and a twirl, the breathtaking dancer began a series of leaps with fantastic prowess. She floated from one far end of the room to the other, then back again, and out an open door into brilliant sunshine, and she was gone.

Damon waited only a moment before he leapt up to chase the girl. His

27

heart was pounding as if the tabla and drummer had suddenly been implanted in his chest. It quickly became painful. Finally his pulse raced so intensely in his eyes that it threatened to impair his vision. He hurried out into the sun and looked hard for his dancer through squinting, blinking eyes. But she was not to be seen in the dense milling throngs peopling the bazaar. Animals bayed and bleated and sang out strange choruses of distracting cantos, while merchants called out in loud serious diatribes about the consummate quality of their produce, even if the goods were nothing more than shriveled rotting roots or dusty musky leaves. The men with wares banged on brass to draw an eye, as the old women with lotuses and incense bantered relentlessly at the passing crowd. Everyone was talking and calling out, and Damon felt as if he were on another planet. His lovestruck mind was spinning wildly as it tried to comprehend it all.

But where was the dancer? He wanted her with all his heart and now he was determined to find her. In his sudden delirium, he set out after her like a cowboy ready to rope a rebel cow. But these were sacred cows roaming and moaning, and that served only to make him more crazed. He began running through the crowd like a wild man, taking what was not his, stealing like a thief. He took silk scarves, gold necklaces, silver bracelets and great lengths of brocade. He grabbed colorful saris and long strands of beads. He stole leather belts and even turbans right from the heads of astonished Sikhs! The angered crowd began chasing after him as he worked feverishly to tie his stolen bundle of goods all into one great huge net! It was insane, but he was absolutely determined to catch the dancer.

But then as he rounded a corner amid a cloud of dust, still pursued by a mob, he saw an old woman sitting in a doorway. She wore an emerald veil across her nose and mouth, and her eyes flashed at him with a spellbinding power such as he had never before encountered. He very nearly stopped dead in his tracks, but the frenzy and the momentum pushed him on, and he suddenly reached out and snatched her emerald veil as she recoiled in the doorway and screamed out with an affronted cry. But for one instant their eyes locked, and that stunned him. Finally, he stopped and looked back. The woman's eyes were like the mesmeric eyes of a cobra, and then it was all clear to him in a flash.

The mob froze in their tracks before him, puzzled and amazed at his sudden startling stop and strange gaze.

Damon walked slowly back to the old lady and handed her the veil. For a moment there was only silence and an ominous tension. But the old woman smiled and gently put the emerald veil to her face, then laughed. Suddenly, they were all laughing! The Indians began a chant. Damon Burke grinned and held up his arms in triumph, his bizarre net dangling from the lengths of his fingers.

He began racing back through the crowd, ripping off stolen scarves and golden chains and throwing them back to the Indians. The crowd cheered and chanted and grabbed onto the great trailing tail, and they all began dancing back through the bazaar. A drum beat loudly and an electric guitar began screeching out a piercing wail. Damon Burke found himself, by magic, on the speeding wheels of a fleet pair of roller skates, streaking in cool bravado to a rock 'n' roll song as joyful as a child! He kept pulling off bracelets and bangles and turbans and saris and giving it all back to the laughing Indians. All of it. Every piece as the credits began to roll. Down in the audience, Damon Burke cheered and whooped when he saw his name on the screen as star. His girlfriend, Katerina Markovich, an immigrant to America only two years, was beside him giggling and cheering. She was clearly awed by the realism of the movie and had a thousand questions to ask, but no idea at all where to begin.

Finally, the name of the writer, director, producer appeared. It was a famous name now and the applause reflected that. The name was X. Rex Kelby.

When the lights came up, an attractive Oriental woman stood up. She was Aurora Kahele, and she quickly went to Damon and told him how wonderful he had done in his first video role. "Well, Mr. Burke," she said laughing, "it looks to me like you certainly enjoyed yourself. You were wonderful! Katerina, you should be very proud!"

Damon Burke rose up as Katerina clapped and nodded enthusiastically. "All thanks to you and Mr. Kelby," he said. "I really appreciate what you've done." He turned to Kelby at the back of the room.

Aurora Kahele, charming as ever, put her arm around Burke as Kelby waved, signing that he was honored. Aurora laughed loudly.

"Rex may not talk much, but he sure knows how to dream. That one is hilarious, Mr. Burke, and I just hope that you are fully satisfied!"

"Well, your service is all that it's advertised to be, Aurora. You and your people really know how to make a person comfortable. I couldn't have done it otherwise."

"It was our pleasure, Mr. Burke. Rex and I are so pleased that you came to us." She quickly gestured to an assistant. "Rachel, would you take Mr. Burke to the copy room now and see to it that he gets processed correctly?"

"Thanks, Aurora," Damon said. "I want you to know that I intend to make another as soon as I'm able. Mr. Kelby, I hope you'll think of me for one of your future scripts . . . "

Kelby nodded politely. "I already have one in mind, set right here in San Francisco. I think you'd like it."

"I'm sure I would! But after this strange Indian madness, I mean . . . how do we top that! This was fantastic!"

Aurora laughed loudly. "We're so glad you're pleased," she said. "Rachel... will you see to Mr. Burke, now?"

"Certainly," Rachel smiled. "Then I'll be back to see about lunch for you and Rex."

Aurora walked to Kelby as most of the others left the room. She sat lightly on his lap. "This is going so much better than we had ever hoped for, Rex. You really came through on this one!" She kissed his cheek gently and laughed.

"We're exceeding our wildest dreams, right?" Kelby said with punctuated mock seriousness.

Aurora giggled. "That's saying a lot in your case, Rex! Your wildest dreams are already legendary!"

"Please, Aurora . . . " Kelby joked. "Not in front of our guests . . . "

Aurora turned and smiled at the patient couple sitting near the front of the small theater. They each shyly smiled back, then looked away. Aurora kissed Kelby on the lips, then jumped up. She hurried around to where the couple sat and smiled hugely as she held out her hands. "Well, how did you like our little show?"

"It was fabulous!" the man roared. "We were really impressed!"

"So, have you made up your minds yet?" Aurora was of Filipino/Hawaiian descent and had a way of rolling words off her tongue. It gave everything she said an exciting, upbeat spaciousness. "We can go with autobiography, a rock video format, dream montage, comic or serious dream drama . . . "

"Oh yes . . . " the woman laughed. "We've studied your brochure and thought we had our minds made up until we saw this video! How do you do it?"

"What you saw was created almost entirely from Rex's Holodrama Simulator. We have thousands of images in our computer, and we just work out the action and put you or whoever right into the middle of it."

"And you could do that even if we wrote the script?"

"Absolutely!"

The man looked at his wife and thought a moment. "Would we be able to go over a few possible scripts with Mr. Kelby?"

"Oh sure . . . " Aurora was up in a flash. "Come along . . . "

Kelby was quietly writing in a notebook.

"Bill and Nancy, I would like you to meet X. Rex Kelby. Rex? Could you hear us talking?"

Kelby smiled through his lean, angular features. He had the look of a Nordic sea captain, tall and gray with a youthful clean-shaven face. There were very distinct lines etched into his every expression. He looked up now with a pleasant subtle grin and nodded. "Yes, I heard, Aurora, and I've been perusing my notebook here to see if anything comes to mind." He was used to all of his customers asking to read potential scripts, so he would automatically begin leafing through his notes as soon as Aurora approached the next client. He would then sit quietly in back and try to get a feel for the kind of person or people they were and pick out a few pieces that he deemed suitable. "Please have a seat," he said, gesturing to the couple.

When everyone was comfortable, Aurora asked the couple again about the kind of video they preferred to make.

"How about something funny that we can be in together," the woman suggested.

"All right . . . " Kelby said. "Aurora, read them this one." He handed her a typewritten copy. The dream had been written for oral presentation.

Aurora smiled. "Oh . . . *Strange Kingdom*," She laughed. "I remember this one."

The couple looked intrigued.

"Well . . . it takes place in a remote kingdom amid great tall mountains. Now, imagine that Bill is walking down a road to an old mysterious castle. He goes inside and walks warily down the dark corridors of the castle . . . " Aurora's black eyes were wide and dramatic. The couple smiled at each other with anticipation and amusement. "Then suddenly he comes to an open window on a top floor, and outside in the dark sky is a huge full moon shining through a thick mist. He stops and stares. He's spellbound by the tremendous luminosity which seems to grow right before his eyes. Then, the thick mist starts to crackle as if some kind of electrical energy is shooting through from the bright moon. It sizzles and sparks flare up in brilliant colors! It totally dazzles him. In fact, that energy seems to reach down and begin to overpower him! Then he falls to the floor and is nearly paralyzed there. His eyes are filled with fear as he watches the sparks crackle through the mist. It's totally frightening. He just lies there, and the rainbow mist curls and spirals through the window.

"But then Bill fights with all of his might and breaks free. He crawls away from the window and is finally able to get up and race down the corridor. He runs outside and hurries down the road. He keeps looking back to see if any demon or shadow figure is following him. But after a time, he realizes that no one is following and he relaxes and slows down.

"Then he comes across a beautiful young lady by the side of the road." Aurora looked at Nancy and winked. "This is where you come in . . . "

The girl smiled and rubbed her hands together excitedly as Bill's eyebrows went up and down in rapid motion. Aurora shot a quick glance at Kelby and laughed.

"But . . . there's a problem."

"Oh, no!" Nancy whined.

"Yes. A big problem. Nancy is dressed very sexy, see, with her tummy showing."

"Sounding better and better!" Bill roared heartily. He had a thick Boston accent.

"But . . . " Aurora cautioned, "there is a problem!"

"You mean I can't just ravage her right then and there?" he joked.

"No . . . because she is dying."

"Dying!"

"Yes, dying. The girl has an actual hole in the side of her tummy. It is not gory or bloody, but just dark and threatening, and the man knows that the girl is dying. He kneels down and holds her and feels great sadness overcome him. He finally finds the love of his life and she's dying.

"So . . . what to do? He starts to lift the girl to carry her somewhere and try to save her. But suddenly a strange noise fills the air. It's a motor, and it gets louder and louder. Bill, you smile, thinking that help is on the way. You leave Nancy in the grass and turn, ready to wave down the car or whatever is coming. But it's not a car or truck, it's a huge old steam locomotive tractor. And it's driven by a madman! He looks completely crazy, and he's steering a totally erratic course. In fact, he's bearing down on the two of you and you wonder if he'll run over you! You both grow petrified.

"Then, just as he's almost on top of you, that huge old tractor rises up and flies! The madman laughs wildly. You notice that he's got a butterfly net and he's actually chasing a butterfly! It's one of those beautiful monarch butterflies, and it flutters every which way as the man chases it on his flying tractor, which puffs and belches hot steam and whistles dumb noises. It's hilarious and ridiculous, and you both laugh like crazy. You watch the preposterous chase as they loop around in the sky and wonder what's going to happen. Then they come around and they're heading right at you again! Bill, you lift Nancy up in your arms as if to run. But you can't tell where they're going, the way they fly so crazy, see? Suddenly, they're right over you, and the butterfly zooms straight into the hole in Nancy's side! Then wham! Blank! Nothing! The dream is over, the video ends."

Bill and Nancy laughed themselves breathless. "You dreamed that?!" the man asked Kelby incredulously. He had never heard anything like it.

X. Rex Kelby smiled enigmatically. "Absolutely authentic," he assured him in a matter-of-fact tone.

Aurora giggled. "Yes, it's true. That's a funny one. He's had all kinds. Have you never seen any of his other works?"

"We've seen a few on TV, I remember. But at the time we just didn't pay that much attention. You know how it is with new things. Then, suddenly, it's like all the craze, and U-Star Video studios popping up everywhere . . . "

"Yes, yes . . . " Aurora giggled. "Then the first annual X. Rex Kelby Video Fest, which was really pretty small. But last year was huge."

"We'd really like to attend this year."

"Well, you could have an entry!"

"Kelby smiled. "I wish I could say I love all of the attention this is getting me. I mean, I do and I don't. I prefer privacy . . . "

"You're in the spotlight now, Mr. Kelby," the girl giggled. "A real celebrity."

"Oh, please . . . !" Kelby argued.

Just then an assistant entered and passed a note to Aurora. "Okay," was all she said after she'd read it. "I'll be right out." The assistant nodded and left the room.

"I've got an important call from one of our New York people. Would you please excuse me? Rex, could you read Bill and Nancy another script or two or shall I call in an assistant?"

Kelby shook his head. "No . . . they can read here themselves for awhile. We can amplify and answer questions when you get back."

Aurora was already half way out of the screening room. "Sounds fine," she called back. "I won't be long."

Kelby handed the couple four pages and asked them to read. "I'll answer questions if you need me to. I'm just going to be reading this." He held up a book.

The young man frowned slightly. "What language is that? Vedas? Is that how you say it?"

"Yes, that's close. It's an Indian text. Among the oldest writings in existence."

The couple smiled and nodded, but Bill shook the script pages nervously. "We better start reading these," he said, shaking his head.

Kelby opened up his book and began reading, too.

It was twenty minutes before Aurora returned. She had gotten bogged down in financial detail with one of the company's managers in a second phone call, this one from Los Angeles. Meanwhile, the assistant, Rachel, had returned and had helped the couple make their choice. They had already left the room when Aurora returned. Kelby was sitting quietly reading a second book he had with him.

"That was Parker in L.A.," Aurora told him. He's having a little trouble with the ledgers down there, but I think I straightened him out."

Kelby looked up and studied Aurora's face. He smiled confidently, knowing that Aurora was a superb business person and that every possible problem was well attended. He said nothing for the moment. His mind was elsewhere. There was a look in his eye that Aurora knew well, and she grinned widely when she noticed.

"What is it, Rex? I can tell . . . "

Kelby smiled, his eyes racing back and forth. "It says here, in this other book I picked up with the one on the Vedas, that thousands of years ago there were flying machines described in the Hindu epic, the Mahabarata, which is part of the Vedas. So I've been studying a translation. This was written down around 1500 B.C., based on oral accounts much older. Everybody just took it as fantasy about flying gods, but in modern times with our knowledge of rockets and jets, these descriptions make perfect sense. The flying machines were for real!"

Aurora was not so easily convinced. "You're going to tell me that they had airplanes and rockets way back then! That's pretty far-fetched, Rex!"

"I know, I know . . . " Kelby muttered. "But, nevertheless, here they are, described in detail. They were called vimana, and they were fueled on mercury. People even fought wars with them over India."

"India," Aurora said dryly. "They can't even run a decent airline today!"

"Yes, but these were the gods! It says here that Rama on his return from Lanka was given a vimana as a gift from his wife Sita, after he rescued her."

"You know what kind of flying thing I'd give you if you rescued me!" Aurora laughed, looking at Kelby seductively.

Kelby drew back and snorted. "Aurora! This is a serious ancient book!"

"Yes, yes, go on Rex. I can run your business, but sometimes these wild ideas of yours are even too much for me."

"They're not my ideas, Aurora. This part is in the Ramayana. It says that the vehicle had window apartments and excellent seats . . . "

"Apartments? What is it, a flying building?"

"That's just the translation. Compartments is probably the right word."

"But, Rex, how is this possible? Spacemen again?"

"I guess. Why not? Look at all of the evidence."

"Rex, if Dr. Rayburn knew that you were studying these books instead of your textbooks, he'd probably kick you out of the program."

"But there are engineering descriptions in these books! Look! Here are pictures of an ancient model of a plane with delta wings!"

"You're not getting a doctorate in archeology, Rex."

"Aurora, my thesis is completely based on aerodynamic engineering. This is all a part of it!"

"Spacemen are not a part of it."

"I have to study the literature. That's part of the research. And these are the oldest books known to man."

"Full of aliens?"

"You're an alien."

Aurora looked shocked. "From another country! Not from another world!"

Kelby winked and grinned. "I'm not so sure, Aurora."

Aurora ran a hand through her long, glossy black hair and turned up her lip like a child. But suddenly Kelby wasn't looking. His mind had grabbed at an idea, and his eyes were racing back and forth again.

"Hey, that's it!" he said excitedly. "That's what I'll call my research model."

"What?"

"Vimana."

"I'm telling you, Rex. Dr. Rayburn will say you're crazy!"

"No he won't. He's not as narrow minded as you make him out to be. It's you I worry about!"

"Rex! Stop teasing!"

Kelby laughed long and hard. He felt great. "Give me a kiss, Aurora. I want your body, and I want it now!" he demanded. Aurora giggled and plopped petitely onto his lap. They began kissing like teenagers.

But X. Rex Kelby was not thinking about sex. He was deeply involved with his research project at Berkeley. It was an updated version of the military's old rocket packs: single-person propulsion units, which had been researched for use in combat. Modern computer applications and microchip miniaturization as developed by countless scientists and applied specifically to propulsion units meant an incredible leap forward in the field. Now Kelby had turned his prodigious engineering talents to creating a whole new model which he not only planned to use for his doctoral project, but as a viable, patentable device. He had already produced a test model. Research would have gone much more quickly had not his business venture suddenly caught the public fancy.

The Holodrama Simulator was a revolutionary device in its own right. Kelby had become famous for it, and the U-Star Video company was an overnight success. Kelby had cleverly promoted his studios toward the everyday man and woman, not to professional actors and actresses. He made it appeal to even the shyest of people. Anyone could star in their own computer-modulated show, buy a copy and show off to all of their friends on the home VCR unit. It was becoming a national craze. And X. Rex Kelby was becoming a hero and a very wealthy man. But above all, he was a dreamer, both literally and metaphorically. He turned his nightly dreams into scripts, and people paid large sums to obtain the right to use one. Dreams were his reverie and his mysticism. His other passion was flying, and he meant to revolutionize that field, too. The single-person propulsion unit was the new gleam in his eye; and now he had it, the enchanted name: Vimana.

3

VARANASI was ablaze with gusts
of summer wind, and Aaron Harrison was sweating profusely. He poured
cool water onto his scarf and wrapped it around his neck without wringing
out any of the excess. It dripped down his chest and back, and for a
moment he was cool. A street vendor offered him a soda from his icy
bucket, and Aaron bought two. He drank down the first in a matter of
seconds, then eased into the second. Oriana watched and shook her head.
She seemed to be handling the heat a little better.

"I wonder what that must look like to these people," she laughed. "A
couple of Americans get off the train and the first thing they do is drink,
not one, but two colas." The Indians had formed a small circle around the
two and were looking on with varying degrees of interest. Aaron smiled
and viewed the faces. They all smiled back.

"This is survival, Oriana. This heat is like being in a blast furnace.
Watching those Indians on the train all passing their jug around and
gulping down big slugs of water was unbearable. I wish to hell that we
could drink the water!"

"Water not dirty," one of the listening Indian men said as if offended.
"Gangi water, holy water."

"I'm sorry," Aaron apologized. "I didn't mean to say . . . "

"Water no make sick. Only unholy people get sick."

Oriana smiled broadly at the Indian. "I'm Oriana," she told him and offered her hand. "What's your name?"

The Indian immediately burst into a giant grin and turned from Aaron. "I am Saba," he said through red-stained teeth. "Where do you go? I will take you."

"Anywhere," Oriana laughed. "Do you know a good hotel? Cheap?"

Suddenly, James was there, an Englishman the two had met on the train. He was with Rick, the American he had shared a compartment with overnight.

"We've got word of a hotel near here where a lot of travelers stay. It's supposed to be good."

Saba perked up as if he had just lost the control he had gained for mere seconds. "Where, where?" He demanded to know. "I will tell you if good."

"Just past the Mayfair," James explained. "The Riverflower Hotel."

"Yes, yes," Saba nodded and bent quickly for Oriana's pack. "Let me carry," he insisted. Soon they were all walking down a dusty side street with Saba talking and pointing with his free hand.

A half-hour later the four had all checked in and had placed their packs in their rooms. Aaron and Oriana headed back to the courtyard which was the coolest part of the hotel. None of the rooms were air conditioned. Even the innkeeper was sitting outside his door looking out onto the courtyard. Through the far arched doorway to the street, they could see James and Rick getting into a bicycle rickshaw. Saba was busy talking to the rickshaw driver with rapid hand signs. Aaron and Oriana nodded to the innkeeper and passed on by.

"Where are you going?" Aaron asked.

Rick was dressed as if he were leaving on a safari. He held up a whip and laughed. "We're going down to the ghat." His blue eyes glistened wildly.

"What's the whip for?" Oriana asked as if talking to Aaron, but saying it so that Rick would hear. Her tone was disapproving.

"For the dogs," Rick laughed through his beard. "I hear that once a dog tastes human meat they get it any way they can. And they've got rabies!"

James sat with a wry smile and looked away.

"Come on!" Aaron laughed. "They burn those bodies on the pyres. They don't just leave them lying around."

"Yeah," Rick said. "The rich are burned. The poor ones can't afford the firewood. They get eaten by the dogs or if somebody throws them in the Ganges they bloat up and float away downriver." He pantomimed convulsions and grinned. "They won't get me," he said, holding up his whip. "I didn't bring this all the way from L.A. for nothing."

Suddenly, the rickshaw lurched forward. "Ready?" Saba wanted to know. He was impatient. James turned to Oriana. "Should we have dinner together, then?"

"Sure," Oriana smiled, "meet us back here around four."

And they were off, Saba jabbering to the driver and pointing as the dust flew up slowly all around.

Aaron and Oriana decided to go to the main bazaar and save the ghats for dawn the next morning. It was still early, and they caught a bus. Soon they were deep in the bustling market throngs. Goats were led along on ropes, and cows wandered freely. Children raced around with flowers and food and mischief in their eyes as vendors yelled out from behind wooden carts in a smoky haze. It was fabulous chaos. The Americans pushed on through in no particular direction. They did not intend to buy. They just wanted to move with the curious sights and clatter.

After they had been wandering for a few hours, all at once Aaron saw a hand slipping stealthily around a teen boy's back, making its way slowly into his shoulder bag. Aaron, six feet in height, towered over the small thief, and he just gave the boy a hard shove. He looked wide-eyed at Oriana, but in the noise of the bazaar he decided it was worthless to even try to tell her what had just happened. At least he beat the thief at his own game, he figured, and laughed to himself.

Then Oriana was tapping his shoulder and pointing ahead. There was a small gap in the crowd and a familiar face had stepped into the space. The man was nearly naked. His pale skin was wet and shivering, his hair long and curly brown and his full beard glistened. The blue eyes looked dazed. Necklaces hung down and glittered in the bright sun. He looked very ill. The eyes almost rolled. Aaron and Oriana both hurried forward, wondering if he would collapse.

"Mauricio!" Aaron called out. The man smiled and wanly pressed forward. Both Aaron and Oriana gave the Brazilian a hug. "Look at you," Oriana said in disbelief. "Are you sick? What happened?"

Mauricio grinned. "Very sick," he said. "I just come from the Ganges. Maybe the holy water heal me."

Aaron stood back and looked Mauricio up and down. *My God,* he thought to himself, *he looks just like Jesus Christ come down from the cross!* The man wore only a loincloth and was sweating with fever.

"I got sick in Katmandu," he explained. "I had been drinking the water right along. Then suddenly . . . this."

"You've lost a lot of weight," Oriana said.

"I was sick, too," Aaron complained. "What luck. Our last week in Katmandu and I came down with it. We'd just gotten back from the trek. Probably got it up in Muktinath where we last saw you. Maybe you picked it up there too."

"No, it was later," Mauricio explained. "I was staying in Pokhara after the trek. At least I had a great view of the Himalayas from my sickbed. But . . . I decided to move on anyway. I took a bus here. It was rough."

"We went to Delhi first," Oriana said, "after the Taj Mahal in Agra. Then here by train. Aaron got sick again in Delhi, and this heat is killing him."

"Come on, Oriana!" Aaron complained. "I'm beginning to feel like a pathetic wimp, the way you talk."

Mauricio mustered up a laugh. "I've got to go now," he said. "I am weak."

"Can we help him, Aaron?" Oriana asked, nearly whispering.

Aaron shrugged. "You're the doctor, not me."

"You are a doctor?" Mauricio looked surprised. "You never say."

"Not a medical doctor," Oriana explained, almost shyly. "I've got a Ph.D., but . . . "

"You never say," Mauricio said again. "All those times we talk, walking in the mountains."

"Well . . . anyway . . . " Oriana said evasively, "You need bed rest now. Better not let us hold you up any longer. We'll get together again and talk."

"Yes," Mauricio grinned. "And if I don't see you, you have my address in Brazil. Write me. Maybe I come to the States some time."

They watched him pick his way slowly through the crowd with bare skin shivering. His blue loincloth was limp and damp on his hip, and he carried his shoes and bag like a street bum.

"He looked so big and strong in the mountains," Oriana said with a shake of the head. "That bright blue poncho fluttering in the wind, and he never did need a coat. Isn't that incredible that we ran into him again?"

Aaron just watched. He was thinking about Jesus Christ again and how striking Mauricio had been standing pale and sick in the midst of this bustling bazaar.

Dinner with James and Rick was at the Tanjore, and as soon as they were seated, Aaron, Oriana, and James began to chide Rick about the whip. "The dogs wouldn't even sniff him," James joked.

"Wait till you see 'em burning bodies!" Rick said excitedly, completely unfazed by the kidding. "The heads swell up and burst. And you can smell the meat cooking. Sometimes they take a heavy stick and bash in the skull!"

"That's to release the spirit," Aaron commented. "I've read about that."

"Nice table talk," Oriana complained.

Rick didn't care. "I snapped off a lot of photos," he said. "One man got mad at me and started yelling at me in Hindi. I just put my hand on the whip hanging on my belt. You should have seen his eyes!"

A long hot night followed. Aaron and Oriana went back to the hotel room and switched on the lights and the ceiling fan, but they had no sooner gotten into bed when all at once the electricity went off.

"What now?" Aaron asked perturbed. "We'll sweat to death."

Oriana hushed him. "Let's go down and check it out," she said. "Probably happens all the time."

They groped along the second story balcony, and the two could see people leaning on the rail in the darkness. They had their damp scarves around their necks, and Oriana suggested that they go down to the water pump and get them freshly wet. Soon they were there. A few Indians were standing quietly in the shadows, and suddenly a voice came at them.

"You need water?" the voice asked. "Let me pump," he said eagerly.

It was Saba. "Always ready to lend a hand," Aaron commented sarcastically.

"My pleasure," Saba said, completely enthused. He began to pump vigorously.

Oriana put her scarf under the water and patted her face with it.

"You are very beautiful," Saba said. "Everybody say you look Indian with your long black hair."

Oriana laughed. "Thank you," she said modestly. "But, this is from my Italian side. Do they really think I look Indian?"

"Oh, yes," Saba said. "All my friends want to meet you."

Dark figures moved slowly out from the shadows. They had not understood the English, but Saba's sweeping hand gesture had brought them forward like a stage act.

"You need smoke? Hashish?" he asked. "Make you feel better in this heat."

"How long's the black-out going to last?" Aaron asked. He was wary of all the figures in the dark. "We need our fan to work!" he added nervously.

Saba paced back and forth quickly. "I have the best hashish . . . " he whispered to Oriana.

Oriana could see Aaron reacting nervously in the dimness. "We had

better not, now," she told Saba. "Maybe tomorrow. We're tired. It's been a
long day."

"See you later, Saba," Aaron said in a friendly but firm voice.

The dark figures pressed in a few steps.

Oriana was light and cheerful. "Bye, Saba," she said and then hurried
away toward the hotel courtyard. Aaron dipped his scarf in the bucket and
quickly followed after her. He wasn't sure what might happen next.

Saba gestured for the others to follow him. "Wait," he yelled. "We come
to your room!"

"No," Oriana said firmly.

"Tomorrow!" Aaron insisted.

"Damn!" Saba whined as he turned away disappointed.

"Bye, bye," a voice said from the shadows.

Back on the balcony, Aaron and Oriana stood outside their door looking
out on the courtyard and up at the stars. Varanasi was very quiet for the
huge city it was.

"It's so nice to see Orion again," Aaron said with quiet excitement, "I
really missed it in Australia."

Oriana wiped her face gently with the scarf. "Yeah, well now we get to
miss the Southern Cross."

"And the Magellanic Clouds."

They kissed. "I love you," Oriana whispered. "Maybe we should go in
and make love."

"In this heat!"

"You wouldn't refuse?"

"Me?" Aaron laughed.

"I love you," Oriana said again.

Aaron smiled. "I love you, too."

"Why do you think we're arguing so much now? Are we bad travel
partners?"

"No, no," Aaron insisted. "It's just culture shock. We still haven't
adjusted. We're in the old kingdom now. We'll be okay."

"You have so much potential," Oriana said after they had gone back into
the room. She was thinking about the tension she and Aaron were having.
"I hope that you don't give up."

Aaron sighed, as if it had been unpleasant to hear her say that.

"You know why I always say that, don't you? I mean, it's a positive
thing. You're growing."

"But I don't want to always be *becoming*. I'm content just to *be*. To be who I
am."

"Don't be defensive . . . "

"I'm not!"

Suddenly, the light came on and the fan began slowly whirling its long wooden blades.

"Oh, thank God!" Aaron hooted. Oriana laughed. "Now we'll get through the night!"

They shut out the light and lay almost naked under the fan, mopping their bodies with the wet scarves and slowly kissing, barely touching anything but lips, it was so hot. Soon they were making love, and afterwards the blades above them lulled them into a deep blissful sleep.

The next morning, they arose before dawn and joined a small tourist group for a ride to the ghats. Boats had been arranged, and the group split into two small sets.

The Ganges River was completely placid. As the boats pushed off, Aaron and Oriana watched the ancient sight of yogins flexing, vendors sipping tea, beggars sleeping and washerwomen dashing their clothes against the rocks on the bank. Many were already dipping in the cool water, doing ritual *puja* and cleansing their minds of impurities.

Aaron took photographs. The light was a rosy glow in the east. The oarsman took the boat a short way downriver, then turned around and headed back by the main ghat. Four bearers held a corpse aloft and made their way to a pyre. The burnings would begin as ever.

"This looks like a medieval city," Aaron said, and Oriana agreed. It was an awesome sight.

By the time they disembarked, the ghat was in full stir and the chanting was loud and sonorous. Holy men seemed to beckon at every turn.

4

X. REX KELBY was deep in dream at his home on a high hill overlooking San Francisco Bay. He was dreaming that he was walking down a street in the city and that he came to an old Victorian mansion with four witch's hat turrets, and it was painted in blues and reds with bright gold gilding. The house was awesome, but it was the sight he saw inside the large picture window that stopped him in his tracks. For there he saw an incredible golden statue of a man and a woman, each with wings. They were facing each other and curving gracefully into a perfect counterpoint dance of flight. They each had one foot on a great golden sphere, an earthly globe of tremendous size. When Kelby went inside the house, he met a woman, a woman he had never seen before but who was more familiar than any person he had ever met. They became lovers at once and, after a time, they flew away together out an open window. They made love in the bright rays of day, flying through a soft wind and reveling in the ecstasy of a sensuous kiss that went on and on.

It was a different form of exhilaration that fueled the reveries of a man named Jack Katz. He was Aaron's old travel partner from years before, and now he was sprawled out on a blanket in his backyard in Almaden, a country town south of San Jose. He had been out all night again, and he was still sipping his bottle of cherry brandy. He had his shirt off and lay in the morning sun with half-open eyes on a book. He began falling asleep as he read. Tamara sat in the kitchen feeding their three children. After a while, she brought the smallest out and laid her on the blanket. Jack looked up and smiled.

"You wouldn't believe it, hon," he said as he propped the baby girl up against his massive bare torso. "Me and Ben and Dusty outdrank everybody in the bar last night. Then we went on up to Erica's and I put Ben and Dusty away."

Tamara was silent.

"The stars were so good up there," he said excitedly. "Ben and I tried to find Sagitta."

"Yeah, I'm sure it was a regular astronomy expedition!" Tamara's tone was sarcastic.

Jack bristled slightly. "You're waiting to get at me, aren't you?"

"No, no . . . " she quickly said. "Not anymore."

"Well, we did talk this all out."

"I know."

Several minutes of silence passed.

"Why don't we get the kids together and go up to Ben's and do some archery?"

"I'm sure he'd appreciate that."

"What do you mean?" He knew that tone.

"Don't you think he's asleep? You said you put him away, Mr. King of the Mountain."

"Hon, you wouldn't believe it! I was the only one who could guzzle a full pitcher without stopping."

"Plus tequila, I suppose."

"Plus two or three other things," he laughed.

"Jesus, Jack . . . " Tamara said with a shake of her head.

"I brought you a little something, too . . . "

Tamara's eyes immediately subtly flashed and she smiled. She drew deeply on the cigarette she had just lit.

"Hey!" Jack sputtered all of a sudden. "Let's go up to the reservoir and take the kids canoeing."

"I thought you were going to fix the truck today! You could still work for the Tacketts this week and get a little of that job done."

"Yeah," he whined, brushing his long blond hair off his face. "But I can get Charley down here this afternoon to help me. So we could still go canoeing."

"Alright," Tamara decided after a moment. "I'll go up with you and watch."

"Why just watch?"

"Don't start that, Jack."

"Hon . . . "

"I'll get the boys ready."

Tamara stood up and started for the back door, then stopped. "Did I tell you there's a letter for you?"

Jack frowned. "No! From who?" He felt annoyed.

"Aaron."

"Aaron! And you didn't tell me all day yesterday!"

"You weren't home all day yesterday!" Tamara barked, knowing she had the upper hand.

"I called three times," Jack argued as he sat up frowning.

"Well, get it!" he demanded. He took a long drink of the cherry brandy from the bottle.

In a minute she was back with the letter. She threw it down at him and half grinned.

"Where the hell are they now?" Jack laughed. "Boy, hon, you should have seen Aaron and me when we were traveling together . . . "

Then he had the letter open. "They're in Delhi," he said aloud as he read. "And they stopped at the Taj Mahal on the way down. Some emperor built it for his wife when she died."

"I'm sure you'd do the same for me," Tamara cackled.

Jack ignored her. "Oh my god . . . " he said. "Aaron says they were wandering around Delhi and they got on some back street where they saw two lepers without legs wrestling on a dirty pile of straw!"

"Nice," Tamara blurted out with a sharp smoker's cough. She rasped hard two or three times, then began laughing. "Nothing like the beauty of India," she cracked.

"Yin and Yang, babe. You got to take the . . . "

"I know. Keep reading."

"They're going to Varanasi next."

"Where's that?" she asked. "As if it would mean anything to me if you told me."

"Varanasi used to be called Benares. It's the old holy city on the Ganges River. The British used to call it that. Aaron says some people, Westerners, now call it Banaras. But Varanasi is the real name. That's the ancient name."

Tamara drew on her cigarette.

"After Varanasi they're going on to Calcutta and Darjeeling."

"Well, I heard of Calcutta anyway."

"He says here that when they were in Old Delhi, he saw that mysterious iron column that never rusts. It's at a temple called . . . I don't know if I can pronounce this . . . Qutab Minar." He made a face. "Anyway, this thing is over two-thousand years old. They don't know who made it or anything."

Tamara shook her head. "I don't get it. What's the big deal? A piece of iron and it never rusted. So what?"

"They don't even know what kind of metal it's made from, Tamara! It's a strange kind of alloy. Probably people from another planet made it." Jack looked away abstractly. He loved the idea of spacemen coming to earth in ancient times.

Jack had always been a dreamer. He had grown up in Colorado, the first son of a girl who had become pregnant at thirteen. He had never known his father. But his mother had come through with the help of her parents, and Jack had had a loving home for three years. Then his mother had moved out with him. She had always been ahead of her years, and she had continued to mature quickly. At sixteen she had wanted her independence. There had been a relative in Los Angeles who had offered to put her up until she had found work. So Jack had come of age in the coastal city, and he became even more fiercely independent than his mother. She eventually married and gave birth to another boy and a girl. She let Jack do as he wanted. He grew quickly into a tall, muscular boy and ran with the more wild of his schoolmates. As a teenager he joined a rowdy local motorcycle club with boys his age. It has been all fun and games, and Jack had always been big enough that no one could push him into violence.

The wild times went on and on. Jack supported himself by working at odd construction jobs. One morning he had gone to the union hall hoping to get some daywork and while waiting he happened to notice a young brown-haired man reading diligently at some book. He could only make out one word in the title from a distance so he moved in closer and sat down two chairs away from the man. Suddenly, the man turned away ever so slightly. Jack then tried bending down to read the title, but again the man lowered his book as if to purposely thwart his efforts. But Jack was persistent. He bent lower still until his long hair was nearly sweeping the floor. The man refused to turn his head and acknowledge Jack. Finally, Jack read it. It said "The Wisdom of the Mystics." Jack was fully intrigued. Finally, he could stand it no longer and he spoke.

"Do you read many books like that?" he asked.

Aaron Harrison turned his head slowly and studied Jack's serious face. He grinned ever so subtly, thinking to be cautious. "Mmm . . . " he shrugged, non-committally. "How about you?"

Jack grinned hugely. "All the time," he boasted.

Aaron laughed. "Oh, good," he said. "I was almost afraid to let anybody in this place know what I was reading!"

"So that's why you made me practically crawl on the floor to read your damn title! God, I couldn't figure out what you were hiding!"

"I didn't want anybody to think that I was a weirdo! You can't always guess what these macho men might think of a book like this."

Jack laughed, then turned serious. "Have you ever read any Zen Buddhism?"

Aaron quickly shook his head no. "I'm not interested in joining any religion right now." He immediately felt nervous. But Jack roared with laughter while Aaron looked on dumbfounded. He had no idea what was so funny.

Finally, Jack's laughing subsided. "Zen is not a religion," he explained almost smugly. Then he grinned deviously and sat back in his chair as if he knew a great secret.

"So what is it?" Aaron asked, slightly incensed at the impishly arrogant smile of the stranger.

Jack looked around suddenly. "We aren't going to get called today," he said matter-of-factly. "Why don't we get out of here. I've got some smoke in my car. Let's go talk."

Aaron felt slightly reluctant for a moment, then became enthusiastic. "Sure," he said. They introduced themselves and jumped up to leave.

For a solid year after that they became inseparable, sharing wild urges and especially books. Aaron had temporarily dropped out of his under-graduate philosophy program for the express purpose of finding meaning in his life, but when he left Ohio on that cold January day with his college roommate, he never would have dreamed that a man like Jack Katz would be the one to inspire him to new realms of learning.

By the time Tamara came into Jack's life, Aaron had been long gone to Australia. "I can't wait to meet those two," Tamara said now as Jack read on from the latest letter.

"Here it says they met a sitar player who lost all of his hair, eyebrows and all. Some man poisoned him trying to kill him."

"Poisoned him!"

"Yeah. There was a national competition to find the best sitarist in all of India. Some guy got jealous and poisoned this man. Now he's bald as a vulture, and he plays for tips at a huge carpet gallery."

"Nice . . . first lepers, now this."

"Wouldn't want to go there, huh?"

"No thanks," Tamara laughed. "I'll stay here where I can drink the water."

"Maybe I could go . . . "

"No, no. It's bad enough you stay out all night. India's in another century. We got kids to raise."

By noon, Jack and Tamara were up at the reservoir. Jack had the boys in a small canoe, and Tamara sat on shore with the baby. She was waving at the boys, and they were grinning back at her. Fishing poles were stacked together at the front end, and Jack paddled slowly, occasionally drinking from a beer.

An hour later, they were catching fish. Jack would explain very carefully to the boys how each step was done, and they would grin timidly. His full, deep voice would carry out across the water.

Then, all at once, he was whooping and rocking the boat. Tamara looked up, expecting to see Jack holding a large fish, but instead he was pointing at the sky.

"What is it?" She yelled out at him.

"Look, hon, by the ridge!"

Tamara squinted and made out a colorful form looping out high above the water.

"It's a hang glider. Can you see him, boys?"

The hang glider swooped through two coils and then darted far out over the water. In seconds, he was riding a brisk wind across the lake. When he saw Jack and the boys waving, he looped around above the canoe and somewhat clumsily waved back. Jack was whooping with a voice that boomed out in all directions, even echoing off the far ridge wall. He would swig from his beer and then let loose volley after volley as the boys cheered.

"I've gotta do it, hon!" he yelled. "I'm gonna row over and talk to 'em."

"Jack!"

"I won't be long."

"Sure . . . " Tamara mumbled to herself. The hang glider was back now at the ridge, sailing along beside the cliff in the bright sunlight. A party of people could be seen together on top of the ridge in a clearing. Jack headed straight for them, then curved over to where an old rock slide had left a stony slope that could be climbed. Soon, he and the boys were struggling up the slope.

Tamara watched with a hand shielding her eyes from the sun. She wore a worried look on her face as she watched Jack nearly dragging the boys up the incline.

Finally, they were on the ridge top and Jack began talking to a man in the group. He knew two or three of the people there. They were locals. He was given a fresh beer and soon another "whoop" splashed down across the water. Tamara laughed and shook her head.

Meanwhile, the hang glider descended down onto the clearing and the pilot made a skilled landing. The crowd let loose a fractured cheer, and the flier grinned through his face mask and reigned in the kite and secured his footing.

"Boys . . . " Jack was saying. "You know how we fly our dragon kite?" The boys nodded and grinned and jumped up and down.

Then Jack went to the flier and began a conversation without introduction. His excitement and size nearly overwhelmed the quiet small man who had no intention of letting Jack use his glider.

"You have to take lessons . . . " the man argued. "This can be dangerous."

But Jack was persistent as always. He began offering any enticement he could think of to persuade him.

"You'll never fit into my suit," the man argued.

"I don't need a suit!" Jack laughed.

"And no helmet?"

"Well . . . that might fit."

Then one of Jack's friends told the man to let him try it. "If he racks up your glider he can take care of you, Vinnie. He's got a real reputation in this valley."

"What if he kills himself."

"Not your fault . . . "

"That'll be my karma," Jack insisted. "Nothing on your head. Anyway . . . I won't crash."

And so it went until the man gave in. Soon, Jack was getting instruction, and he calmly sipped at his beer and nodded and repeated the basic directions he was supposed to follow.

Finally, he secured the helmet and began pacing forward toward the edge of the ridge. The man walked slowly beside him, quiet and nervous, while Jack's friends cheered him on.

"What's funny," Jack boasted through the helmet mask, "is that two nights ago I had a flying dream and damn if it isn't coming true!"

The glider owner gulped. "Didn't die in that dream did you?"

Jack roared with laughter. "Heck no! I flew right up into the sun, smooth as an eagle on a fat north wind."

And with that he kicked off at the edge of the cliff as if he were leaping for eternity.

5

AARON and Oriana spent a long day wandering around Varanasi. By late afternoon they were pricing and studying Indian carpets at shop after shop. They were becoming hot and exhausted and a little frustrated at not having found just the right carpet to suit their tastes and budget. An early summer wind was stirring up dust, and they had strayed deep into an area of Varanasi they figured to be out of the way, looking for some little backstreet shop that would offer the perfect bargain. Now it would take hours to get back to the hotel, and that prospect alone made them both irritable.

Finally, they just stopped in the street and squared off. "What do we do? Eat somewhere close by and regain or energy? Walk back to a main street? Splurge on a taxi?"

The day had been a tough one from the beginning. They had already had a serious clash by the time breakfast had been served. For over three years every action had been locked onto a common goal: traveling through the Orient. Now it was happening, and the constant uprootedness in the lands of exotica produced effects they had not imagined. Oriana found it hard to adjust to the living conditions. Aaron had been used to an almost meditative quietude. Now there was constant chaos.

They stood on the street looking at each other, almost pleading for the other to make a decision, any decision, and get them, preferably by magic, out of there.

Instead, the unexpected happened again. A diminutive elderly Indian man was suddenly busy beckoning in broken English. He wore a beige shirt and pant outfit which was right at home in the swirls of dust on the street. His hair was short, and he wore silver framed glasses.

"You must come," the man said, and offered Aaron a card. "He wants you."

Aaron reflexively jerked back his hands. "What do you mean he wants me?"

"You . . . "

"No . . . come on," Aaron laughed. "You don't mean me specifically . . . "

"Yes, you. Shastri is waiting."

Aaron looked at Oriana. She rolled her eyes ever so slightly and looked away. Finally, he took the card. It read: Pandit Shastri Pantanruja, Gold Medalist Astrologer and Palmist.

"We must go . . . " the small stranger insisted.

Aaron was intrigued, though he knew the man would have said the same thing to any Westerner he ran across on the street. He was just drumming up business.

"What do you think, Oriana?"

"You must come," the man said again. "Shastri is waiting."

Oriana's eyes bore the look of exhaustion. "Whatever you want," she said resignedly.

"What do *you* want?" Aaron asked with emphasis. "Isn't stuff like this why we came here? And after this morning I think it'd do us good to talk to an astrologer. Plus he's a palmist. He's psychic. Maybe he can tell us why we're fighting all the time."

"Go if you want," Oriana said in a biting tone. "I'm thirsty and I need a drink." She charged across the street and into the open door of a small restaurant. Aaron followed at once and left the man standing bewildered on the street. She quickly purchased a soda and began drinking as Aaron apologized. "I just thought it would be fun . . . " he explained.

"It's a two-bit hustle, Aaron. They prey on Westerners for their living."

Aaron looked at the card again. "But he's a gold medalist. It says he graduated from the University of Benares."

The man continued standing bewildered on the street as people passed every which way by him. He kept looking through the open door, cocking his head and adjusting his round, silver spectacles.

"Let's do it, Oriana. We need some answers about us. This is Varanasi. I doubt very much that he's a quack like you find in L.A. with a big sign out front of the house. This is the Holy City."

Oriana drank more of her soda and thought. She was not the one usually dragging her feet on new adventures. She was just very tired.

"Okay," she said at last. "Let's do it."

Aaron smiled and waved at the man. He stepped forward two paces and cocked his head. In a moment they were on the street beside him.

"Where is he?" Aaron asked.

"By the Golden Temple," he answered. "Not far."

Soon they were winding through narrow alleys filled with people. Flower and incense vendors were thick along the walls, and small grills were everywhere frying up curried meals as twilight slowly descended through narrow gaps in the tightly clustered blocks of buildings.

Finally, they were all entering through a small door off an alley. The little man bowed and gestured toward the gray-haired man reclining on a mattress just inside the door. The room was barely larger than the mattress, with walking space on two sides only. The gray-haired man grinned up at Aaron and Oriana. He wore a white tee shirt and white cotton pants. His feet were bare, and a three-day stubble adorned his youthful-looking face.

"Welcome, my friends."

Aaron nodded and introduced both himself and Oriana.

"I am Shastri," the man laughed, "and you have met my helper Timo." Timo smiled humbly and backed out the door. "I go now . . . " he said.

Shastri waved. "A very good man," he said proudly. "And this is Hans, my German friend. He study with me."

Hans had curly dark hair and a full beard. He was young and spoke only a little English.

"Do you mind if he stay?" Shastri asked. "I am teaching him old secrets."

Hans grinned broadly and the two broke into a huge laugh. Oriana said something in German, and Hans arched his eyebrows approvingly. Everyone felt instantly at ease, though enroute, Oriana had cautioned Aaron to be on guard, especially for overcharging on services rendered. Now in the casual gaiety of the tiny room with its sweet incense, Aaron was not able to bring himself to discuss the charges for a reading.

Shastri was quick to hand Aaron a pad with pen. "Please write your name and birthdate," he commanded with a laugh. "We do you first."

Aaron smiled agreeably. He was ready.

"Indian astrology uses fixed signs," he explained, pulling out a thick book of charts. "In the West, everything is relative to movement of the stars, and exact place of planets and stars at time of birth. Ours is different."

In a moment, Shastri was pointing at aspects on a chart and he and Hans would nod and laugh. Then he took Aaron's hand and studied one palm. Again he would point, and he and Hans would nod and laugh.

"You are very smart," he said finally. "You paint *de* pictures. Right?"

Aaron nodded affirmatively.

"You play *de* music."

Another nod.

"You write *de* books!" Shastri laughed. "You will be very famous!" He did not waste time.

Aaron smiled and felt excitement rushing up his spine. It was as if all his hopes and dreams were about to be given sanction by a bona fide Indian mystic. He could not believe the luck. Even if it was all phony, he reasoned to himself, from this moment on he owed it to himself to try for the best he had in him.

Shastri was giggling like a schoolboy. "You will write *de* books! What do you study?"

Aaron explained his deep interest in dream interpretation. "Will I be a psychologist?" he asked. "I want to write about dreams, like Jung."

"Like Jung?" Shastri said. "Swiss doctor? Very famous?"

"Yes. He worked with Sigmund Freud. You probably heard of Freud."

"Yes, yes," Shastri laughed. "I have met Jung. He came to India!"

"But he's dead now."

"I was young then. Student at University. Long ago. But he come and visit my teacher."

Aaron looked at Oriana with stunned joy in his eyes. Oriana's eyes were twinkling a rich chocolate. She knew how important this was to Aaron, but she sat back slightly aloof as if a shade of doubt were necessary under the circumstances. Aaron wanted to believe and practically wallowed on the star charts.

The reading proceeded with greater detail, with Shastri commenting and Hans nodding. "See the chin," he would say. "Strong chin. Likes *de* sex!" and both would laugh uproariously. "You like *de* sex too much, me thinks!"

Aaron would shake his head and grin boyishly, then nervously twirl a few strands of hair on the end of his moustache.

It continued on and on. Most of the details were right and convincing, but there were errors too, and Aaron had to weigh that in. Over all, though, he was exceedingly impressed and satisfied. He felt great.

Then it was Oriana's turn. Like Aaron, she revealed nothing except to respond to questions in the simplest terms.

"You will write *de* books too!" Shastri laughed. "You are brilliant mind."

Hans gushed looking at her. He was awed by her beauty.

"I'm going to be famous too, huh?" she said in a chiding tone.

"Oh . . . Aaron will be too famous, me thinks!" Shastri laughed. "You not famous like that. You scholar."

Oriana looked over at Aaron and raised her brows. *There's no way he could know I have a doctorate,* she thought to herself. *This is spooky.*

Shastri launched into details. "You are very close to your mother," he began, "and you want to be just like her!" Oriana smiled but chose to remain silent. Shastri talked on and on. Again, there were hits and misses. But again, like Aaron, Oriana was impressed. He seemed to really know her.

Finally, Aaron pulled up close to Oriana. In all the excitement, they had not talked about the two of them as a couple. In fact, neither had revealed that they were married. Aaron decided to seize the moment. With all the good news flowing out, how could they lose?

"What about us, Shastri?" he said. "We're together. We're married." He took Oriana's hand and then put Shastri's hand on top of the two together. "What do you feel about us?"

"Oh . . . ! ! " Shastri laughed. "You are not right for each other! All wrong!" He was almost rolling on the mattress with giggles. "Not right," he said again.

Aaron and Oriana both grew solemn and stunned for good reason. His words struck hard, and no amount of laughing could soften the blow.

"I am sorry," Shastri said in a more controlled voice. "But you are just not suited for each other."

"We've been married for three years!" Aaron said in a disbelieving tone. "Are you sure?"

Oriana was stone quiet. She knew that it was not completely unbelievable Events of late had seriously strained their relationship.

Shastri grinned and laughed again. "You should not make snap judgment. Maybe you travel separate for awhile. Wait until you get back to United States to decide for sure."

Oriana looked around and was more than a little put off by the smile that Hans flashed at her.

"Something's wrong," she said finally. "This is too much. We've got to think about this. . . . "

"Of course, of course . . . " Shastri smiled. "Tomorrow you come back. Both of you. I talk to each alone, okay?"

"Well . . . "

"It's alright with me," Aaron said after a moment. "We can sleep on it and see what we think in the morning."

And they stood up to leave.

Finally, the subject of money came up. "You need to buy a special charm," Shastri said. "Both of you. This will help."

The astrologer handed them each a red cloth bracelet with a tiny capsule sewn in the lining. A special prayer had been printed on a small roll in sanskrit and was inside the capsule.

"How much do we owe you now?" Aaron asked after they had each put the bracelet on.

Shastri quoted a figure. Oriana frowned and headed for the door. Aaron counted off bills, then smiled and shook Shastri's hand. "Tomorrow," he said agreeably.

"Yes . . . tomorrow," Shastri laughed.

Then they quietly left. They hurried out of the alley to a larger street nearby and flagged down a trishaw. Soon they were rocking and bumping down an old Varanasi street. The mood was one of both sullenness and excitement. After all the tension of late, Aaron sensed a new possible freedom and a destiny to match his greatest dreams. Oriana was somewhat angry. She was seven years older than Aaron and had already known success in her field. Now some giggling guru was advising that she and her husband split up, that they were all wrong for each other. It did not make sense. They had had a perfect five years altogether . . . until now. *Why now?* she thought. It was all too sudden.

In the morning, they each went alone to see Shastri and both felt great ambivalence about his advice, which had not changed. The astrologer continued to insist that the two of them were just not right for each other and counseled them both to begin a trial separation. He even mentioned to Aaron about a young blond woman in the future and about a child. He showed it all on star charts.

When Aaron went down to the ghats on Shastri's insistence, to bathe in the holy Ganges, he was fairly convinced that the astrologer was right. They were very different types of people, and they had always regarded their romance as a miraculous fluke. But the love had been real and each still cared enormously for the other. But the bottom line revealed a sad truth.

They were now each dragging the other down. Traveling had made it all different, and each had separate dreams to fill.

And so it was one cautious step down into the green river for Aaron, where he felt a fine slime of mud rise up between his wary toes. Step two was less muddy and he had felt encouraged. Then on the third step there was no mud at all, and he hurried on into the ancient holy waters where the dying go to have their ashes scattered. And after puja he was enlightened in a simple way that he had never imagined. As he sat with an old gray bearded, long haired yogi on the upper ghat, he suddenly knew what it meant to feel a lightness of burden. He had been told to go in peace a free man, divested of all responsibility except to his own needs. A new-found liberation swept over him in a way which made him feel as if he might float off into the sky. It would be many years later before he would realize how incredibly selfish he had been on that day and how enlightenment means a going beyond the self, not a reveling in it. But for now, as the old sage dabbed a red paste on his forehead, Aaron Harrison felt very blessed indeed. Shastri's words echoed in his mind. *You will be too famous!*

6

THEY HAD a bad fight that morning and an even worse one the night before. But he was not prepared for what he saw when he got home from work that day. Namely, everything he owned racked, stacked and strewn over the small front yard. Obviously she had help and she was very serious.

Eric Harrison parked his car and got out slowly. He thought how bizarre it looked to see all of his possessions, collected piece by piece over the years, all helter skelter on that absurd incline which passed for a yard. A yard he could mow in minutes. He knew, though, that it would take him much longer to clear it of virtually everything he owned.

All at once, Lynda Matthews was on the porch with her neighbor Ted, and they were struggling with a large rocker. When she saw Eric in the driveway, she glowered through thick mascara and her arms tensed up. She easily pushed the big chair down the stairs and nearly made her helper trip. His face flushed with anger momentarily, but he kept silent. He did not relish the position his neighbor and cousin had put him in.

"I see you've made up your mind," Eric yelled across the yard.

"That's obvious," she quickly retorted. "Now get it out of here."

Eric felt the burn crawling up his back. "This is stupid!"

"You should know."

"I can't get a truck out of nowhere. Where am I going to get a truck?"

"The same place you got all of this other stupid stuff, I guess."

Eric huffed loudly. "That makes sense."

"Nothing makes sense anymore!"

The rocker was set clumsily on the sidewalk with Ted puffing hard. "I'm going now," he told the girl. He hurried down the sidewalk toward his house. As he passed Eric, he mumbled something that was half apology and half warning. He knew all about the verbal violence of the past few days. He knew every detail: the jealousy, the drinking, the pushing. The only thing he hadn't known was when Eric would get home this day.

Eric stepped forward toward the fleeing neighbor. "Just get lost," he barked. "I never could stand you anyhow!" His temper was gone, and he was ready to be cruel. His short blond hair was on end.

Lynda frowned hard and marched up the steps with rigid lividness. She went inside and slammed the door.

Eric charged in after her.

Suddenly, he was forced right back out the door. When he tried standing his ground on the porch, she let out a scream and shoved with all of her might. Eric went down. But not all the way down. His wrist was caught in the wrought iron railing. It snapped.

Lynda knew it was serious and helped him up from where he was trapped, half off the porch. But her anger still had the best of her. "You know where the hospital is. Walk!"

Eric bit his lip and turned to go. "Call my Mom," he yelled.

"Figures!" Lynda snapped.

"I mean so that she can get ahold of my Dad at work and he can bring the truck over! I'm going to the damn hospital, now. Go to hell!"

"Anything to hurry this up and get you out of my life!"

Eric felt dizzy, but he struggled on. The hospital was just across the park. His wrist was swelling quickly. As he walked, he thought about the tumultuous romance of the last two years: a hot bed, but even hotter bedlam. The hope was gone. Still, as he walked, he felt intensely sorry that it hadn't worked out. She had left her husband for him. That weighed heavy. And he genuinely loved her sons. But two hotheads together hadn't a chance except in hell. And he couldn't take that any more.

Then, as he got closer to the hospital, his thoughts turned abruptly. He thought back to a sweltering summer night from the year before. He and Lynda and the boys had been out in the yard trying to stay cool when they had heard the sirens screeching. A strange frostiness had crept up his spine and he had paid more attention to the sirens than he normally would have.

Then, from across the park they heard the screams. It was a man, and he had been shrieking at the top of his lungs. The agony howled out across the wide park lawn like a specter screaming from the Inferno. In a moment, the wailing voice was hurried into the infirmary and it was gone. But that piercing wail had haunted Eric all night. In the morning they heard the news on the radio. It was his best friend, John. He had been riding his bicycle with his wife and child when a truck crashed over him as he rode at the side of the street. His whole chest had been crushed in. He lived only an hour. But that hour must have been an eternity that seemed never to end, and afterwards, Eric had sweated that same hour many times himself in a half sleep. Once, he fully believed that he had even seen the dead man walk in through the open bedroom door, then disappear.

And now he was unnerved again. His wrist was probably broken, and everything he owned was waiting for him on the lawn. It all seemed like garbage. He wanted to leave it all. Just get out of town and never come back.

But that night as he sat at his parents' home in the country, his arm in a half cast, his mother reminded him of the litigation still pending against him. At the height of their romance, he and Lynda had gone to an auction and bid on ten acres of land with a large house and barn. Eric wanted to live in the country again, and he loved fixing up old houses. But he had gone out on a limb and bid on the estate before he had secured a loan. He and Lynda were planning to sell both of their houses. They had just moved in together in her home and thought that they could easily arrange things with the bank. But then his buyer fell through and the bank turned him down for his loan. When he told the farm owner that he had not gotten his loan, the man went straight to his lawyer. His whole life had become crippled by the numerous court and lawyer sessions. When he finally sold his house, he had to put the money in his parents' bank account so that the farm owner could not get at it. His large down payment was as good as gone. In the following months, he and Lynda had fought repeatedly. It got so bad that finally he was forced to leave his job where the two had met. He was a photographer and dark room expert at a local printing shop. The dark room was his den of passion, and many a new girl had been caught in his shadowy fingers. So it had been with Lynda. But instead of a quick flash and four months on a whirlwind, this young lady had taken him seriously. She left her husband, despite Eric's known reputation. She made a big mistake. Eric always became tired of people. Man or woman, it didn't matter. He would run with some new friend for months then suddenly drop them as fast as he had charmed them. He had always demanded absolute loyalty from his friends and lovers, but he could return the same for only a limited time. The ones who understood that, his few true friends, would know when to back off and leave him be. Eventually, he would call. But force it . . . and he would never speak to you again.

People either loved or hated Eric Harrison. Normally, he was extremely shy and nice. But when he drank, he could be brash and obnoxious. He wanted a good time and always wanted to go home with the girl. He could lash out at any man who got in his way. His mouth and stockiness had saved him from many a death. Yet, he had almost never been in a real fight.

Lynda had given him a real fight. And they had both lost.

A few days later, a call came. It was an old drinking buddy named Randy Mack. He had just hit town for a few days to see his parents. He was living in Colorado, and as always, got carried away in telling Eric how well he had been doing at a house construction job there. When Eric told him his woes, Randy said he'd be out in half an hour. He told him to have his bag packed. Eric thought a minute, talked to his mother, then made up his mind. "Come and get me," he said. "Let's get the hell out of here!" He could always come back for court if necessary, he figured. But with the pace as it was, he would not be summoned for a year.

It was like a prolonged beer run . . . every state, every day the same. Drink and drive. Endless wisecracks. Randy Mack always talking, writhing, mocking. He was handsome and streetsmart, but actually more of a dandy than a punk. And he could outgun Eric for the new girl in town. He had at least one illegitimate child. Now he was dazzling women out of state. And to have his old drinking buddy with him made the action all the hotter. The rivalry was a friction that sparked every party. If anyone were caught in the middle, they would be steamrolled.

So they rolled on across the vast midwest in a near frenzy. Both were free again. In fact, being on the road made them both freer than they had ever been. But for the way they were, they were too free. It was dangerous. A TNT of hiss and liquor. And too much swagger.

Grand Junction was not as Eric had hoped. It was scenic, but not like the best Rocky Mountain towns and cities. Located near the border of Utah, it shares that state's red bare sandstone beauty. But it is hot and parched, and they were building houses right up on the stone ridges. The growth was phenomenal. Randy Mack was working for young men who were making fast fortunes. Eric had a job with him in a matter of days. Despite his wrist in the cast, he was able to put in full days at hard labor. And party at full throttle, beginning as Randy quickly showed, on the job, preferably in the mornings.

If it got too crazy, that was unavoidable. Huge parties would spring up almost nightly. The women came and went with Eric and Randy jousting for the prettiest.

Then one night, Randy was romping and rolling on the bed with a girl he had met named Kate. Empty bottles were everywhere, and the two were snorting cocaine. Eric came in by accident.

"Eric!" Randy yelled out. "Get over here and meet this girl."

Kate looked startled.

Eric laughed shyly but was immediately enticed. "What the hell you mean, buddy?" he asked, pretending not to know.

Kate pulled the sheets up around her bare shoulders and giggled groggily. "I need help, Eric. I'm too far gone." Randy was like an old drunk.

Eric ambled nearer to the bed, rolling a beer bottle between his fingers. "Maybe your girl doesn't want to be introduced like this . . . "

"I'm not his girl . . . " Kate said, pulling at her thick brown curls. "And he does need help."

Randy laughed hard and rolled across the pillow as Eric sat down.

"I'm Kate," the girl said. "Want some coke?"

"Why not?"

"Every chance you get, huh?"

"Yeah," Eric laughed. "As long as I don't have to pay for it."

Kate looked up smugly. "Jess buys all of mine. You met Jess?"

"He's one of the main contractors up on the ridge project, isn't he?"

"That's him."

"How do you know him so well?"

"He's my husband."

Now it was Eric's turn to look startled.

"And you're here?"

"Don't worry about it. When it comes to pleasure, I don't draw lines."

"Are you sure?" He asked with baited seriousness and waited.

Kate looked puzzled, but then she saw Eric nodding at the lines of coke she was dressing on the small mirror. They both laughed wildly. Even Randy stirred from his stupor. "Give me some . . . hey!" he managed to groan.

The two each did a line as Randy lay unmoving on the pillow, and soon they were kissing. Eric put a hand under the covers and slowly explored her warm, naked body.

"What about him?" he asked after a particularly long and passionate kiss. "Doesn't look like a problem to me," the girl laughed.

Eric took a big swig of beer, then began taking off his clothes. In a moment, he was in the bed and Randy was soon being rocked so hard that he nearly lost his drink. He woke up only a little to whine and complain, then dizzily cheer before he fell into a final quasi-coma for the night.

After one good spin on the hot burning wheel of euphoria, the lovers joined him in his comatose oblivion, much sooner than either had hoped for when it had all begun. And so they lay in a heap until dawn.

The level of unconsciousness was so complete that none of the three even moved a single muscle when the door came crashing in under the force of a solid bootsole.

Eric was closest to the door, and he was shaken first and hardest. When he finally managed a few sparse flashes of thought, he opened his eyes and saw a scowling stranger at his face. In an instant, he was sure it was Kate's husband and that he was now a dead man.

The deep voice was at him like a lean bulldog. "You Randy Mack?"

"Who's asking?"

"Who's not answering?" the voice snapped back. "We're with the Federal Bureau of Narcotics, and somebody here may be under arrest."

Suddenly, Randy Mack was up and vicious. Hot words shot from his tongue like lava balls. Eric sat up and tried rousing himself more while Kate lay stockstill with wide eyes.

"Get out!" Randy Mack yelled. "You got no right here!"

Eric was totally in shock by the intrusion and lost his temper also. "Yeah, get out, you bastards!" he screamed. "We're not even dressed here!"

The agent was completely unsympathetic. "Well, I don't know who's who here, so I'm taking you both in, dressed or undressed. We'll see how well your big mouths flap off between the bars downtown."

A few days later and several states away, X. Rex Kelby was sequestered deep in his small private laboratory. Long hours passed until it was finally nearing midnight, and at last he grew restless. He knew that Aurora was waiting for him. She hated going to bed without him, but he just could not stop yet. The Vimana was slowly taking shape on paper, and he kept pouring over old designs. Something was still missing. The mechanics of the machine seemed perfect. He had theoretically developed the best fuel and the most efficient engine to process that fuel. It became obvious, based on past working models, that the thruster power would be more than sufficient, topping every design presently developed. But it was the control situation that bothered him. How to make the machine maneuverable to an exactness never before attained. He needed precision in guidance or it would all be only another very expensive, but basically impractical, flying toy. And that was not acceptable.

He sat back and sipped at his juice and pondered quietly. Then he leaned over and looked at some old photos in an army manual. There were pictures of test pilots with the bulky rocket packs on their backs, and it all looked so cumbersome. It just wasn't what he wanted.

When the phone rang he jumped, but it was Aurora, of course. She alone could call him in his work room which was actually a renovated garage at the back of the hill where their house sat. Kelby had made it very comfortable and secure. There were expensive pieces of equipment, including a highly sophisticated computer for testing aerodynamic designs, and Kelby took no chances that anyone might abuse it. The place was never left unlocked nor were others ever permitted in, except Aurora, but she chose to always honor his privacy.

"When are you coming up?" Aurora wanted to know. She was trying not to sound like she was whining, but she was and both knew it.

"I won't be too long . . . " Kelby speculated. "But damn it! I'm so close."

Aurora could tell that he was unusually frustrated. She tried to be funny to break the tension. "Well, if you need to sweat that hard over something, why not make it me?"

Kelby did not laugh for a moment. His mind was elsewhere. But he knew how Aurora could be, and he pulled himself back to play along. He was always mindful of her emotional sensitivity. Finally, Aurora heard a deep chortle and she giggled.

"Where are you?" Kelby asked.

"Watching television in the den," she answered. "And I'm wearing some of your favorite silk lingerie . . . "

"The mint green?"

"No, peach. I'm all alone here on the Persian carpet . . . just waiting for you . . . "

"What do you have in mind?" he asked, feigning innocence.

"Mmm . . . a magic carpet ride would be fine," Aurora whispered sexily. "And you're just the man to do it . . . "

Kelby laughed and leaned forward in his seat. He realized the fatigue was catching up with him and the thought of Aurora waiting for him in erotic splendor was more than exciting. "Well, I do believe that I'm going to have to put all of this other flying stuff aside . . . I mean for the magic carpet ride of course . . . " He was being flippant, but he also meant it. His hand grabbed up a sheaf of blueprints, and he looked closely at the top page then gave the stack a toss across the work table. They spun a half-turn and landed with a faint smacking sound. He felt a flash of anger.

Aurora continued her phone seduction. "I can already feel the wind in my hair," she cooed. "And your soft hands all over me . . . " She waited for Kelby to say something, but there was only silence. "Rex?"

Nothing. Silence.

"Rex!"

But Kelby had taken the phone from his ear. He was sitting with his eyes locked on the top blueprint, with the look of revelation glowing in his smile. "Of course!" he whispered. "Just turn it over . . . "

"Rex!"

"The magic carpet ride!"

7

CALCUTTA hibiscus were sweet with early summer, and the sensual humidity of the morning made Aaron and Oriana feel like tropical wanderers lost in a puzzling port-of-call. They had anticipated the infamous squalor but not the stateliness of the old Victorian architecture. The great silver bridge which crossed high over the Ganges River impressively dwarfed the endless throngs of humanity which lived and died beneath its solid steel girders on the muddy riverbank. And so the holy waters poured down into the Bay of Bengal with more than the memories of Varanasi and Shiva's faithfully departed; there were also the traces of the Himalayan highlands where all began in purity and power and flowed away with a promise of rebirth. The Calcutta rickshaw runners, pounding bare feet on the hot asphalt, knew of that promise. And the old ragged women, bent to another day of collecting cow dung from the burning streets with bare hands to make their patties for cooking fires, knew of that promise. And the mothers with starving babies knew.

But Sanjay Partel also knew of a different promise, and it had to do with rich Westerners who had come to his city from the faraway lands of infinite wealth. When he first saw Aaron and Oriana, he could not believe his luck. He had been quietly sitting on a concrete wall just idling away the time when they had approached *him*! The two were puzzling over a map, and they had finally decided to give up and simply ask directions. Sanjay was taken by surprise, but he quickly rallied to their aid. He leapt off the wall and hurried to the curb. At first he did try to explain, but it did not seem to help. "I take you on the bus!" he told them. But as bus after bus went by so completely filled with riders that people were actually hanging from open windows on the outside, that prospect dimmed. The buses looked frightening, as if they might topple over. They were all laden the same with vast masses, especially at the two doors curbside.

So Sanjay quickly flagged a cab. The Americans leapt in happily even though they had understood almost none of his directions. But, they figured, Sanjay would certainly explain their destination to the driver. He did. From inside. He had simply climbed right in with them, and the turbanned driver nodded once and was off into the heavy traffic. When they arrived at the bank they had needed to visit, they suddenly found themselves paying three fares, and once inside, they noticed through the window that Sanjay did not go away. He waited and waited. So they waited, too, but soon they realized that he had virtually no place else to go.

At last it was a joke, watching him on the street, squinting and waiting. They knew that it was useless to linger longer. With their money business done, they went perturbed back out to the street. Sanjay was at their side in seconds, and his eyes had a worried, nervous look.

"Where you go now?" he wanted to know.

"To the bazaar," Oriana answered.

"But look," Aaron said, "we can't be paying to have you ride all over town with us."

Sanjay mumbled something about walking and he began pointing. "I take you."

Aaron decided to be brutally frank. "Listen, Sanjay, we really cannot afford to pay you to guide us around. You might think that we're rich Americans, but believe me we're not rich!" He felt funny saying that to a poor Calcutta man, but there was a relative truth to it, and he just wanted to be sure that it was understood.

"Oh no, no," Sanjay assured them. "You Americans are very special!" But he did not smile when he said that. Aaron felt slightly irritated. He knew that Sanjay would want money at some point and that might have been alright except that he seemed to be so utterly dull. He obviously had too many worries or perhaps was simply bereft of charm. His presence was not enjoyable and both Oriana and Aaron felt it.

Finally, Oriana decided to be frank, too, so that he might get discouraged and leave. "You don't expect any money at all for showing us around?" she asked as if to fully clarify.

"No, no . . ."

For a moment, Oriana thought to be rude, but then she decided not to fight it. She took a deep breath. "All right . . ." she cautiously told him, "show us to the bazaar then . . ." She was not happy saying that.

They began walking. After a long distance, Aaron had to object. "How much further?" The hot, noonday sun was scorching down.

Sanjay frowned and shook his head. "Long way . . . better cab."

Aaron groaned, but he knew that there was no choice. Soon they were hailing a cab and they all climbed in. When they arrived at the bazaar, Aaron resignedly paid the three fares and they all went on in. It quickly proved to be a virtual circus as merchant after merchant hounded them to come to their tiny stalls to buy. When Aaron tried on a silk shirt from Kashmir, there were eight men attending him, including Sanjay. Then Oriana tried on a pair of sandals and Sanjay led the pack, all hovering over her feet. Sanjay frowned. "Yes, you buy!" And he meant it. He was actually commanding her to purchase the shoes.

After a time, it became too much. "Yes, yes, you buy! Buy! Now! Here! Over here!" Sanjay continued commanding every move. He had become a peasant Raj, and he scowled derisively if he were ignored. Finally, the Americans had had enough and raced for an exit and charged out onto the street for breath and freedom.

"Look, we're hungry and tired, so we're going to go back to our hotel," Oriana told Sanjay. "Thanks so much for helping us out." She managed a smile, but it was not a happy face.

"No, no . . ." Sanjay insisted. "Eat over here! Yes, here!" And he pointed.

"No," Aaron said, "we're leaving. Thanks though . . ."

He grabbed up Sanjay's limp, sweaty hand and shook it.

"Okay, okay," he scowled pulling his hand away, "but now you pay me."

"Pay! You said that you wanted no money! We made that very clear."

"Yes, but I no work!" Sanjay yelled.

"Well, you can't lie to us and expect us to give you money!"

"I must have money!" he demanded. "I guide you everywhere! I have eight kids!" He was very angry.

Then another Indian moved in closer, listening. "What?" he wanted to know.

"They no pay me!"

"You don't deserve it! You lied!"

When a cab came by, both Aaron and Oriana waved to the driver and ran out into the street with Sanjay yelling in Indian to two or three others who were now all a part of the scene. They quickly got in and Aaron slammed the door on Sanjay. But the window was open and Sanjay leaned in screaming. "You pay me! I got eight children! No work! You rich! You owe me!"

"Driver, go!" Aaron commanded. "We don't owe him anything! Get us out of here!"

Finally, in sheer desperation Sanjay leapt onto the car's side and lodged his arm inside the open window. "You pay!" he screamed, and he ran as best he could with the accelerating car. But at last it was lost and he gave up. Aaron and Oriana watched him recede in the heavy traffic amid all the fumes and dust. He was utterly dejected and that hurt was shared by all.

It never did get much better for them in Calcutta, so they caught an early train out and headed north. As they rumbled along, they were both quiet. Calcutta had somewhat unnerved them. Aaron kept seeing the face of a sad, sad mother with her small, wrinkled hand, palm up, and a starving baby under one arm. The child could barely hold his head up and it bobbed limply on the thin neck. He had again given no money to the pleading woman, and he grew despondent and finally just gave up thinking about it altogether, but the ghost image did not go away.

In a cooler new day, high in the quaint mountain village of Darjeeling, Aaron and Oriana found themselves facing a tough decision. A long discussion had led to a simple truth which could not be denied or worked out by tough talk.

"We're running out of money," Oriana said matter of factly. "It's going too fast. We'll never be able to last out a year like we planned."

Aaron looked down at his feet as they walked slowly along a small street at the edge of the village, then up again at the almost unfathomable grandeur of Kanchenjunga, the third highest mountain in the world. The great Himalayan peak was out across a deep valley and ever so slightly veiled by a thin mist. All down the near hillside, waist-high tea plants grew with fine jade green leaves. Workers were carefully tending the plants.

"It's that bad?" Aaron asked, only mildly incredulous. He knew how fast the money was going.

"We're going to have to cut our stay in every country. And probably give up all of Indonesia." Oriana was on the verge of being depressed. For three years they had saved and planned for the trip and none of it seemed to be going perfectly now. The real wild card was the emotional tension which neither had dreamed would occur.

"What do you absolutely have to see?" Aaron asked. "Maybe we can just streamline our plans."

Oriana had no hesitation in her top choice. "No matter what happens, I've got to stand on the Great Wall. Unfortunately, that trip alone, costs us nearly a quarter of our whole trip." She looked off at the mountain and frowned for a split second. "What about you?" she asked suddenly, "What do you absolutely have to see?"

"The Great Pyramid," he replied.

"You would . . . " she remarked. "Here we are in the Orient, and you have to want something in Egypt. This is so much more inaccessible from the States. Europe is like almost a neighboring country now with those low air fares."

"I can't go home without going to Giza," Aaron said determinedly.

"Okay, but I have no idea how we can do it. We're here, we should take advantage of it."

Both felt a flush of the now ever-recurring tension well up behind their eyes. It would leap out like a mauler from the shadows at the first sign of any genuine disagreement. A long silence passed as they wended their way along the curvy mountain-edge road.

Then Aaron's eyes flashed subtly with the glimmer of an idea.

"I think I've got it . . . " he said slowly, not sure that he really wanted to say it at all. The two stopped and faced each other. He took Oriana's hands and held them tenderly.

"Yes . . . " Oriana said with a puzzled smile.

"You know I love you," he said. "And I want you to be happy, completely. It really hurts me to think you can't have everything you deserve and have planned for. I know how much this trip means to you. You've worked toward it for virtually five years, ever since we met."

"Where's this leading?" Oriana asked with a slight laugh. "Don't tell me you've had a secret cache of money somewhere all these years and never told me."

Aaron kissed her gently on the lips, then pulled back seriously. He looked her square in the eye, then said it. "I'll give up China," he offered softly. "I'll cash in my ticket and you can have all the money."

Oriana was fully incredulous at this. She wanted to shout *No!*, but her sharp mind raced over all the implications of the offer. She realized in a flash it was a workable solution. But the real price of that choice was dangerous.

"You give up China . . . " she said finally, "and do what?" She was not happy.

"Just see the places I really need to see. Japan, Egypt, Greece. I'll go back early and stay at my parents' for free. You wander around the Orient, stand on the Great Wall, and then wander some more. Make it last as long as you can. I'll get work and start getting things in order for where we want to live in the States."

Oriana's eyes began to tear up at the corners. She felt an incredible surge of love wash over her as she looked at Aaron's gentle features: his light brown hair, his lively blue-green eyes. For a moment, she was unable to say anything. Finally, she spoke. "Boy," she almost giggled, "and my brothers used to call me magnanimous! You'd really give up all of this?" Despite the laugh, she was very worried.

Aaron was sincere. "If it means you'll get to live your dream, damn right."

Then Oriana's mind locked on Shastri and all he had said. *Travel separately for a while,* he had advised. *Wait until you get back to the States to make a final decision about your future together.* Suddenly, the words were more prophecy than mere advice. She couldn't believe it had really come to this. The best solution was to split up. Her thought wavered off into feelings of near revulsion. No matter how she looked at it, her plans had run amok.

Aaron felt good about his offer, but also struck by the full import of its meaning and that meant pangs of regret and a form of guilt. As the cumulative toll of problem after problem settled in on their relationship, he had become acutely aware of the resistance he had subconsciously built up against Oriana's usual dominance. It had all really begun way back at the very first stop after they had left Australia. They had landed in Singapore and were awaiting the arrival of transfer passengers. Perhaps Oriana had not meant her comment to sound as commandeering as Aaron had taken it, but her words had been explicitly direct. "One of us has to be the boss," she had said, "and I'm it." She had the based the statement on a simple fact. She was a far more seasoned traveler than Aaron, and now they were headed into deep exotica. Quick decisions would have to be made amid all the clamor of indecipherable foreign words, and there would only be more chaos if all ideas had to be batted back and forth between the two. Aaron was actually perfectly happy to let Oriana make those decisions. Still, the tone had grated on his nerves, and his usual instincts toward preservation of his independence had reared up with little heads like Medusa's snakehair.

Aaron had thought about that statement a lot lately. Perhaps more than any other exchange of words between them, that simple declarative statement had caught the gist of the downside of their relationship. It was definitely not that Oriana was like a boss, but she was dominant, and her hyperlucid mind and much vaster experience had put her naturally in charge. She did have a seven-year advantage and had traveled extensively. But also, having been reared in a wealthy suburb of Los Angeles, the only daughter of successful business parents, she had social advantages which Aaron could not begin to match. He had grown up in the rural Midwest where his father had made only a small wage as a salesman and his mother had stayed at home raising the children. It had been an absolute fluke, in fact, that the two had ever met. Oriana had bought a housetrailer for her stay near an Ohio university where she was to study for her doctorate. Aaron had temporarily dropped out of his undergraduate program in frustration and restlessness. He had packed up a van and drove west with his college friend, Justin DeWitt, and they had ended up in Los Angeles, where Justin had relatives. But then his partner had been forced to fly back home to help in a family emergency. Still, Aaron had gotten on well with Justin's relatives and they had gone all out to help. Soon, he had a job working construction at a hotel. He had met a big, long-haired stranger at the union hall, by chance. His name was Jack Katz, and they had quickly become inseparable. Four months later, both quit their jobs and they headed for the mountains. But roughing it out amid the mountains could not last forever. Aaron had grown up with the idea of American success ingrained in his psyche. An exciting year passed, but then he began thinking about college again. His restlessness had been temporarily allayed, so finally he drove back to Ohio and managed to get a factory job and a loan from a bank. He bought a housetrailer and prepared to move in. But his very first day there he discovered that a water pipe had broken and water was still pouring out onto the carpet when he walked in on it. He immediately realized that he had no idea how to turn it off, so he raced next door to the trailer on the neighboring lot and knocked rapidly. When the door opened, he beheld a beautiful, black-haired woman in a bright yellow top. She smiled broadly when he introduced himself and thrust out a firm hand. "Hi," she said boldly. "I'm Oriana Zevallos." He smiled back, pleasantly surprised. "I'm Aaron Harrison," he said, "and right now my house has a river gushing through the bedroom. How do I shut it off?" Oriana was instantly in action. She ran to where the outside spigot controlled all the water in the house and shut it off. Then she went in and together they grabbed up every towel in sight and began mopping up the mess. Aaron would never forget that sight of Oriana on the bed, which had been no more than a mattress on the floor, mopping like a dedicated rescue worker and wringing her towels in a bucket. He would steal little looks at her as he hurried about emptying buckets in the tub. Later, he would refer to that flood as an "omen of love to come."

Now they were on the wrong end of a love affair. Shastri's words had swept over them both like a torrent from hell. This flood was the opposite of cool and manageable. This flood was a lava flow of disintegration and even threatened death. When the best dream shatters, what is left to live for?

Aaron thought again about that day on the plane in Singapore. While he had sat calmly reading and keeping to himself, Oriana had wandered off and engaged people in conversation. Her appetite to learn was insatiable. But men always took her forwardness too personally. She was overly friendly and bold, and they were not used to it. She came across as refreshing, so they would always want more. This time, when Oriana had returned to her seat, she had been followed . . .

His name had been Frank, and he had short, graying hair. He was very young looking and well built and extremely interested in Oriana. He came on with bold arrogance. Aaron had never witnessed a man flaunt his assets in quite the same way. He claimed that he had been a chemist for a top chemical engineering firm in the U.S. and that he had a doctorate and was making "loads of money." Then in the 60s he had joined the counter-culture movement and taken up yoga. He had been aggressively direct about his degree of attainment. He had even pulled out a manuscript he had written on the subject. Now he was headed for the high Himalayas. He said that he would hire up some ponies and Sherpas and literally force his way into some remote mystic monastery. "They'll probably kick me out," he had suddenly giggled like a little boy in a near fit of humbleness which was totally out of character. Then he had grown solemn again and held up his manuscript. "But when they read this . . . " he had boasted, "they'll change their minds. I've created a totally new and higher form of yoga."

Aaron had found him to be completely nauseating, and Oriana saw him as an arrogant boor. But somehow he had set the stage for the new ugly Westerner in the Orient. There they were on a mere first stopover and already they had encountered the absolute wrong model of how to enter the humble lands of the Orient. Both learned from it. But later, when Oriana had declared herself to be "the boss," Aaron had been disturbed and had wondered how well the assertive Oriana would get along amid the notoriously modest Orientals.

Now Oriana was looking long at Kanchenjunga and pondering the awful decision of splitting with Aaron. She did not know what to say. Then Aaron cinched it without even meaning to. He had changed his mind in a moment of guilt. "I can't leave you all alone out here," he said. "This is crazy. A woman traveling alone . . . "

Something in Oriana snapped. "No, no . . . " she said determinedly. "This is it. I want my freedom." She knew that it was over. It was foolish to fight it.

Aaron was stunned. Before, he had been the one expressing misgivings about going on together. This resolute statement from Oriana was like a cannonball from out of nowhere. But all events had pushed it to this and now there was no turning back. The split was imminent.

Now it was Aaron who felt a tear for the finality of the situation.

"So, I give up China," he said quietly.

"Probably more than that, Aaron. There really isn't that much money left. I mean, you'll have enough for Japan and Egypt and Greece, but after that . . . "

"No Bali?"

"I can't see how. We'll travel on together through Burma and get back to Bangkok. We can cash in the ticket there and get a new one for you. I'm sure that you'll get a stopover in Hong Kong."

They walked on together, then came to a path which led down the mountain to a Tibetan refugee camp. Both trekked silently and ponderously, while high above them the great snowy Kanchenjunga loomed upward through the haze, completely impossibly unfathomable.

Part 2

8

AARON Harrison was in a hurry. He had been working late at the office every day for weeks, and he finally had a chance to get off early. He quickly locked the office door and dashed down the hall and out onto the street in downtown San Francisco.

When he saw the mist, he zipped up his suede leather jacket and paced into the cool air with hands deep in his pockets. A moment later, he had rounded the corner onto Columbus Avenue and was pushing for the eight-block stretch to his apartment in North Beach.

Suddenly, he was puzzled. The young woman walking toward him bore an air of familiarity about her. Aaron studied her face and wondered. Then he quickly dismissed the idea. The woman he had in mind had long blond hair, while this woman had short light brown curls. It was too unlikely, he decided. After all, he was only a month new to the city. Still, he watched her as she walked. He thought it odd how her head would sweep from side to side, looking first in a shop window then out at the street, then back again, over and over. But in a flash she was past and Aaron hurried on down the street. At last, he rounded the corner onto Greenwich Avenue and one-half block later he stepped into the small foyer of the building where he lived. He slipped a key into the mailbox and opened it. Inside was a tiny yellow paper from the post office notifying him of an attempted package delivery. He quickly looked at his watch and knew that he had just enough time to get to the post office before it closed. He hurried back to the street again and went on further up the block. Suddenly, a voice was right at his neck. "Aaron? Excuse me . . . Aaron?"

Before he even began turning he knew who it was. For a second, he was unnerved. She had followed him for eight blocks, and if he had gone straight into his apartment building, they would have had no contact at all.

"Vanessa! I can't believe it!"

"I thought it was you . . . " she flushed, "But I wasn't really sure until I got a good view of your profile."

"This is uncanny," he laughed. "How can this be?"

"Well, when I last spoke to Richard, he said that you had moved here. I just always wondered if we would run into each other. He told you I was here, didn't he?"

Aaron thought a moment and tried to remember. He hadn't really given it much thought since he and Vanessa had never been really close, and the chances of a coincidental meeting like this were exceedingly remote.

"I think he did," Aaron nodded. "But I never dreamed . . . "

"Believe it or not this is the second time this has happened to me here! I actually met a guy from my hometown on a bus! Isn't that amazing! Twice! But anyway, how are you?"

"Couldn't be better," Aaron laughed. "Can you walk with me to the post office?" he asked, holding up his yellow slip.

As they walked along, each launched into a simple retrospective of their lives during the past four years. They had last seen each other at college where they had met through one of Aaron's closest of friends, Richard Getz. Strangely enough, that first meeting was nearly as odd as this one. They had both been in an art class for some weeks before it became known to each who the other was. Vanessa was a fine artist who had incredibly high standards. Often during class, the professor would have the students vote on the quality of each other's projects. Aaron would always make positive remarks about the project under scrutiny and give it a fairly high score. He knew how hard everyone was trying. But Vanessa would invariably critique with the worst marks in the class. She could easily see how imperfect all the projects were and even berated her own. Finally, the professor reached the point where he would kiddingly call her "The Dragon Lady," and everyone would laugh and wait for her scathing review. After a time, Aaron and Vanessa would almost automatically go into battle over any project, and they would quickly establish the highest and lowest boundaries of critique for the entire class.

Meanwhile, Richard Getz had a new girlfriend and was freshly in love. The name, of course, had been mentioned, but Aaron hadn't remembered. Then one day Richard listened as Aaron told him about "The Dragon Lady," and his smile grew and grew until it was a huge lopsided grin. All he said at the end was, "I think it's time for you to meet my new girlfriend."

Now they were on the streets of San Francisco, and four years had changed everything. Richard Getz was in Washington, D.C. with his new wife Debbie, a brilliant young lobbyist.

"Where's Oriana?" Vanessa asked. "Richard told me that you two had split. Do you mind me asking?"

"No," Aaron smiled. "We're like you and Richard, still friends, but pretty finished as lovers. She's down in L.A. at her parents' now."

"And why did you come here?"

"I'll tell you that after I get this package," he said. They went into the post office and soon he had it. Back on the street, he suggested they go to a small cafe nearby and have a drink. Vanessa agreed, and shortly they were seated inside.

"So, why did you come here?" Vanessa asked again. She seemed genuinely excited to learn his motives.

"That's easy and not so easy to answer," Aaron explained after he drank from the Irish coffee the waitress had just placed before him. "When I got back to the States, I didn't know where to go. I stayed at my parents' awhile, but I definitely didn't want to live in the old hometown again. I thought about going out to where my brother Eric is in Colorado, but I didn't like what I was hearing about that situation."

"What do you mean?"

Aaron looked away. "Let's just say he got mixed up with the wrong people."

"Drugs?"

Aaron nodded. "Not that he's really a user, but those friends of his . . . Anyway, then there was L.A. with Oriana's family, but I knew I couldn't stay there once Oriana came home. I've got to make my own way."

"Do you still love her?"

Aaron paused before he quietly said yes.

"But . . ."

"But, I need to be free from her for now to be sure about what I want to do."

Vanessa nodded and drank her soda. "So tell me all the countries you went to," she said, suddenly changing the subject.

Aaron looked deep into her hazel eyes and thought again how strange it was he was sitting with her after all the years and distances.

"What about you?" he asked, changing the subject just as abruptly. "Why did you move here?"

"Oh, that's easy," she laughed. "My mother moved out here after the divorce, and I came with her."

"You and Richard were finished anyway . . . "

"Oh, yes. Months." Then her eyes lit up wide. "Hey!" she said. "Didn't you dream about our break-up before it happened? Richard was telling me something about a letter."

Aaron laughed hard. "Not before your break-up," he said, shaking his head. "But I did try some long distance dream interpretation."

"What happened?"

"Well, about six months after Oriana and I moved to Australia, I happened to have two dreams about you and Richard, like just a few days apart. They were both incredibly filled with sadness, and after the second one, I began to worry. I mean, I hadn't heard from Rich in all that time. I had written him, but I never got anything back. Meanwhile, I was reading all these books on dream interpretation and how you should believe and act on your dreams. So, I decided to try a little experiment. I wrote to Richard about the dreams and said if I'm interpreting these dreams correctly, you and Vanessa have broken up and you're feeling like dying. And I gave all the details.

"Less than two weeks later, I had a return letter in my hand. Richard couldn't believe it. Half a world away and six months down the line and my dreams had caught his agony to perfection. And remember, when we left, you and Richard were still on the upswing. I had had no indication whatsoever that you two would have any troubles. I was really amazed."

Vanessa's mouth and eyes were both wide. Richard had not relayed the story with such precision. She was clearly impressed.

"Can I read the dreams?" she suddenly asked. "I mean if you don't mind...."

Aaron raised his eyebrows and half grinned. "Why not? My place is just down the block. Let's finish here and we'll go."

A half-hour later, they were in the apartment. Vanessa busied herself looking at all the statues and wall hangings that Aaron had brought back from his travels. At one point, she picked up a strange Tibetan statue covered in pure gold leaf. It was of a two-headed god, with each head bearing the same bird face. He was engaged in ritual coitus with a holy consort. The woman's face was vicious, while the bird-god had skulls all around both of his heads. The consort looked as if she were clawing her way up his massive body like a demon.

"What is this?" she asked with a near repulsion in her voice.

"I'm not really sure, to tell you the truth," Aaron laughed. "Probably just a symbolic version of a Tantric ritual. Have you heard of Tantra?"

"This is weird . . . " She had never seen anything like it. "Are they . . . "

"Yes," Aaron laughed. "Turn it over . . . you can see him in her."

Vanessa's face was nearly blushing. "Why do they look so fierce?"

"They're performing a ritual *yab-yum* ceremony. It's a purification ritual. They're seeking an enlightenment, a transcendence over death. That's why he has the faces of a bird. A bird is always a spiritual, transcendent figure."

"And normal people do this, too?"

Aaron laughed hard. "When you make love, do you ever feel like you're almost rising up out of yourself? I mean right at that moment . . . "

Vanessa's face grew rigid. For a moment, she could only look into Aaron's eyes and say nothing. Then, impulsively, she set the gold piece down and turned away to a large Greek plate which depicted Apollo, the sun-god, flying on his chariot.

"You know, you never did really tell me why you moved to San Francisco," she said abruptly. "I mean . . . why here?"

Aaron laughed quietly to himself then went to a chair and sat down.

"Two days before Oriana came back from the Orient, I was staying in L.A. with her brother. I had no job yet and no prospects. Worst of all, I couldn't decide whether I wanted to get together again with Oriana or not. Then she called and we talked. When I told her that I still didn't have a job, she made some remark . . . I can't remember. Anyway, I felt the old tension shoot up in a flash and I decided right then and there to do something drastic about my situation. I mean, I was living at her brother's and I was living on borrowed money and everything was just up in the air. I had to act, and I had to act fast."

"What did you do?"

"Called Jack Katz, a friend of mine who lives down in Almaden Valley. We're old travel buddies, and he always told me that I could come and work for him. He's in the moving business. Not what I wanted to do, but he offered me better money than anybody else."

"How come you didn't try to do something with your degree?"

"In philosophy? Who cares? Nobody looked twice at me. And with all my traveling around, I don't seem stable. I mean, I couldn't even get a gas station job!"

"So you moved to Almaden . . . "

"Right after I saw Oriana. It was tense. She knew that my calling Jack, and arranging that, was a vote for continuing the separation. She lost all patience with me. I just left. We parted friendly, but we both realized that it was really final between us."

They both sat quietly for a moment.

"What about you, Vanessa? All we've done is talk about me. What's happening in your life? Still free?" Aaron leaned forward in his seat.

"Well . . . " she said slowly. "I am seeing someone, but I'm not sure . . . He's the one I met by coincidence on the bus here. I actually went to high school with him. I couldn't believe it when I saw him."

"So, you're in love?"

Vanessa laughed. "Now you sound like me!"

Aaron grinned back at her.

"Well, actually, I'm not sure. I had this strange dream the other night, and now I'm all the more confused. You know about dreams. Maybe you can help me."

"Shoot."

"Okay. There was this house, and I went inside and Keith was there. That's my boyfriend, of course. Anyway, he was looking at my butterfly collection, and I asked him how he had gotten it. I told him that he should have left it at my house where it belonged. He told me that he just wanted to help. He picked up one of the butterflies and held it up. Suddenly, it came back to life and started flying away. I chased it like crazy and just as I was about to grab it, a cat leapt up out of nowhere and snatched it and ate it! I was so angry. I turned to Keith and told him how mad I was that he had ruined my collection and he just laughed! When I woke up, I didn't know what to think. But it really made me doubt . . . "

Aaron remained quiet awhile, thinking about possible interpretations. He proceeded cautiously, trying to draw Vanessa's own ideas out. As she hit on various tensions between herself and Keith, he found himself reinforcing the possibilities. Then it dawned on him that he might be exploiting a situation where he shouldn't be. Vanessa was a pretty woman, and she had just become his only female acquaintance in the city. His interest was decidedly there, but he wasn't sure how far he really should go with it.

"The butterfly probably represents your spiritual side, and the cat, your animal passions," he found himself saying. "Maybe because of Keith, your sexual side is surfacing strongly . . . "

Vanessa found herself wincing at that. Aaron's directness was uncomfortable for her. She thought about how she really didn't know him that well.

Suddenly, she shrugged. "Read me those dreams! The ones about Richard and me," she said excitedly, changing the subject again.

Aaron smiled and excused himself. As he came back from the bedroom, he laughed. "I haven't read these in years," he said. He thumbed through the book and then remembered that his dreams had been near the end of the diary for that year. He soon found them.

"Let's see . . ." he began. "I was at . . . Richard's house, and I happened to be alone with his girlfriend. You, of course," he said looking up. "My friend was elsewhere in the house." He paused a moment, surprised. He saw the next paragraph and quickly skipped over it and began to worry about reading the dream aloud before he had a chance to review it again. It was more intimate than he had remembered.

"Then my friend came down the hall and we acted like nothing was happening. But his girlfriend began dropping hints that she wanted to end their affair." Aaron could tell that Vanessa knew that he had left a part out. He grew nervous but pushed on. "Then the three of us were in some jungle, and a war was still raging. It felt strange to find myself walking amid fields of bamboo and through jungle growth, wondering where the enemy was hiding. Suddenly, two bombs exploded on the horizon, and I very vividly watched their bright lights in the air.

"Meanwhile, my friends had disappeared. When I located Richard, he was in a trailer in the middle of the jungle. He told me that his girlfriend had left him. He felt enormously depressed. He opened the oven and turned on the gas without lighting it, then kneeled down and put his head in. He was committing suicide.

"His grief was so great that I could feel my entire body convulsing with the intense pain."

Aaron looked up at Vanessa and she nodded at the obvious symbolism. "Pretty straightforward," she remarked.

"Yes, that's why I took it as real. It was no abstract parable like a lot of dreams. And the grief was so . . . " Aaron shook his head and looked sad.

"What about the other one?" Vanessa asked.

Aaron looked and began quickly reading it to himself. He began paraphrasing while he scanned. "A friend . . . Richard, of course, asked me to go to his girlfriend's house and bring her back for him. When I got there, she was sitting with a small cross in her hand. We talked a moment then took off out the door.

"Suddenly, we both rose up into the air, flying side by side, and then . . ." He stopped abruptly and nervously swallowed. Vanessa leaned forward, her hazel eyes wide.

"It just says that you told me that you had no intention of going back to Richard, that you were free now . . . "

Vanessa frowned, puzzled at Aaron's reluctance to read. Aaron felt momentarily speechless. He had completely forgotten the content of the dream, and reading it aloud was definitely not appropriate. He had always been absolutely faithful in reporting a dream, no matter the level of explicitness. And now it was he, not Vanessa, who thought about how little the two of them actually really knew of each other. His mind flashed on an obscure memory of Richard saying that Vanessa had joined a religious group when they had broken up. Now he was reading a dream which he had no way of knowing might offend her or not. Beyond that, it was just too intimate. His face reddened further. He could not tell her how they had flown together through a brilliant sky, caressing each other's bare skin and making long and sensuous love. He could not bring himself to tell the stranger before him that they had been free and wild flying lovers long ago in his dreaming.

9

SAN FRANCISCO International Airport was athunder with booming jetcraft on the runways. Elegant movers and shakers hurried up and down ramps, strolled back and forth through the crowded wide aisles of the long terminal, and pushed into waiting areas at the gates.

Aaron moved easily through the people and luggage. He was there for a pick up and so had nothing more than a small notebook in his hand. He stepped onto the long level people-mover and kept walking. He wanted to be sure that he was on time, and on the mover he was able to clip along at twice his walking speed. Then he entered the boarding wing and hurried to a flight data screen, searching for his brother's flight number. He quickly saw it: Flight 23 from Salt Lake City . . . delayed 30 minutes.

He went on to the gate and took a seat right at the large window there. He was actually pleased that there had been a delay. It was early in the morning, and he had had a strange dream which he was hoping to get recorded before Eric arrived and all the excitement of years apart came pouring out of both of them.

He sat quietly for a moment watching the jets. He could feel that old yearning to streak off to distant foreign cities, even though he had just moved to a city that was one of America's most beautiful. Still, he just could not shake that heartfelt infatuation he had with exotica. Whether

Rangoon or Rome, Kyoto or Cairo. He could feel memories stirring, and it was all part of the same exotic, foreign retrospective which could flash up in an instant. Ginza . . . Giza . . . Gobi. . . . He had high hopes that San Francisco could be a little of all those places for him. It certainly was a melting pot of cultures, and he was anxious to get to know the city better. He felt glad that Eric was coming so that they could explore together.

He looked at his watch and suddenly decided that he had better write down his dream before his time ran out. He opened his pocket notebook and slowly began with the pen.

I was at a university, he wrote, in a classroom where we were studying the origins of man. I heard a lot of different, exciting ideas but cannot now remember them as I write here.

But after class, I went walking across the campus and soon happened on an old girlfriend of mine. She was attractive as usual with her bright blond hair and cute face. We began talking and soon the urges were there between us again. We hurried to her room and began seducing each other. I was in ecstasy. We lay down on the bed and kissed passionately. In a matter of seconds, we were making love.

Then we finished, and we just laid together naked on the bed. I began slowly stroking her beautiful body. It was so sensual . . . We talked. But as I gazed on her, I was suddenly struck by a realization: she was both woman and man now! It was clearly evident! She was an hermaphrodite! The shock sent ripples all through my body. Then a voice from nowhere exclaimed loudly, "She's from outer space!"

I became very confused and leapt up and hurried out of there. Down the street a ways, I came upon a crowd and pushed my way in to see what was happening. When I got to the middle, I saw a strange circus-like act going on. A huge muscular man, wearing only a loincloth, was holding up two other men as easily as a couple of feathers. He was revolving on his heel as the crowd cheered his strength. Then I recognized him. The big man was actually a friend of mine who had died in a drunken car game years ago. I felt puzzled at his appearance there.

Then I went to a bus stop and when the bus came, I got on. As we drove along, I found out that we were going on our way to the home of an assassinated president. His daughter was with us as well as other family members. Then a large, handsome man stepped forward from the rear of the bus. It was a famous actor who had played Superman in the movies. He was wearing a suit and stood there reciting a very simple rhyme. "We will set them free," he said poetically, "as easily as being in the tree's breeze." I felt an elation at the idea.

But I got off the bus and went to a friend's house. All was fine there until the man showed me a secret cache of high grade hashish he was hiding. I became afraid that I would be caught with him and forced to go to jail. I wanted no part of it, so I quickly left.

I hurried away down the street and soon came to a mansion. I went inside to get a room. The place was incredibly ornate. A great chandelier hung down from way on high, and a long curving staircase wound up the wall to the second floor. As I went up the stairs, I met a woman and she told me that the house was full of visiting communists.

I didn't know what to do, so I just decided to leave. But then I ran into a high-ranking minister of the U.S.S.R. He was extremely friendly and invited me to his room for tea. I went with him and he showed me his art pieces, which included a fantastic painting by Van Gogh.

When I saw the swirling colors of the incredible painting, something in me clicked, and I just had to fly. I flew right out the door and up into the sky. As I flew along, I thought about Superman and how he would use his body to control his speed. I put my arms out straight ahead of me and arched my body. Instantly, my speed increased dramatically. The exhilaration was absolutely fantastic. I flew and flew for what seemed like hours. When I woke up, my head was still swirling with all the speed and ecstasy.

Aaron felt almost dizzy with excitement when he had finished writing the dream. He looked out through the bright California sunshine and watched a jet land and temper its speed with a loud burst of reverse propulsion. He followed the gleaming body as it taxied down the runway, passing other planes that were there, readying for take off. He felt like the pilot of a huge craft of his own. The dream was like an enormous separate environ of people and bustle at the back of the eyes, all in a long cylinder floating slowly over the ground. But the edges were fuzzy, as if he and the whole show were really gliding through another dimension entirely. He sensed that at any moment he might just slip over and never return.

He was still pulsing with mental frenzy when the first passengers began bursting through the door. He watched for Eric, but sat tight. He was wondering about the hermaphrodite he had made love to in the dream. And those haunting words: "She's from outer space!"

Meaning what? Then Eric was there in his dark shades. He had a bag slung over his shoulder, and Aaron leapt up to chase him. There were no bear hugs, just a firm handshake and full grin each. One look and they both knew that they were off on an adventure different from any they had had together in the past. The future was wide open with possibilities, and they were both free as they had never quite been before.

The ride back to the city was lighthearted and casual. It was instantly as if they had not been apart for years. They were the kind of brothers who always knew what the other was thinking as they made their way into any situation. And each always reinforced the sense of the absurd in the other. People they met were often immediately perceived as being characters in a drama that was all their own. Their own actions were always minutely attuned to how the other would see them through the eyes of satire. As far as they knew, it had always been that way. Even as children, they had had the same comic sense of the world. It had been especially evident in any, even remotely formal setting, especially dinners. The two would look each other in the eye, look away at any unsuspecting serious-faced anybody, then lock eyes again and begin convulsing with unbridled fits of laughter over some no account gesture that would have meant absolutely nothing to anyone else. The way someone chewed his food or blew a nose... Suddenly, Eric would arch a brow and all hysteria would break loose while everyone else sat looking on in a state of nettled confusion. They had gotten their father's belt more than once over it. Even many a close friend had become seriously annoyed at times.

Aaron was usually the straight man to Eric's hip buffoonery, but they were never like a comedy team. Aaron and Eric had both railed against all things formal and would never be as actors telling a joke or otherwise. The world was the joke, and no social institution could convince them to see things any other way. For Eric, that meant no classes when high school finished, no more church services, no clubs, no cocktail parties, no formal dates. He would work his job and party with the boys afterwards or in the evenings. If he could pick up a girl somewhere, perfect. For Aaron, it meant struggling through formalities. College classes were always a strain, but he would doggedly attend. He gave up his family's Roman Catholicism to pursue his own freewheeling, eclectic spiritual inclinations. But when it came to dating, it was usually very little different than how his brother did it. At the back of it all, there was a shyness they shared and so they were always struggling to overcome that fear of being caught with all eyes upon them. Yet, that is precisely where they had always felt they belonged: at the center of the action.

But for now there was nothing. They were both strangers to a huge city, and they knew that they would have to be content to just look around until they had both settled in and met people. They thought that would be easy enough, but they learned that it was otherwise in time.

As soon as the two got back to the apartment, they were all adrenalin and stories. Eric was puffing cigarette after cigarette and talking non-stop.

"Do you really have to have another smoke every five minutes?" Aaron finally complained. His breathing was already difficult. He had not been around a smoker for a long time and had forgotten how torturous it could be.

Eric waved him off. "Just open the damn window more," he ordered. Aaron sighed and went to the bay window and pushed it out further. He decided to stay there and made himself comfortable on a cushion. Plants hung down all around him. He sipped slowly from a beer and was again listening eagerly to Eric's recent escapades in Colorado as he looked out at the endless parade of people passing just one floor beneath the overhanging window on the sidewalk.

"They hauled us in in handcuffs," Eric laughed, as he told the story of his brief incarceration with Randy Mack. "I couldn't believe it. I mean, they had nothing on me and they knew it, but they wanted to make me as miserable as they could. I didn't even bother getting a lawyer. Some girl we knew, Kate something, got us out. They're going to try to make a case against Randy, but I doubt if it'll stick. He's not really the one they're after."

Aaron nodded slowly. "I'm just glad you got out."

"Yeah . . ." Eric drawled, flicking ashes at an ashtray, "I really got sick of all that crap real fast."

"You must have had some wild times, though."

"We did!" Eric said with quick emphasis and cocked his head at Aaron to be sure the point was fully acknowledged. "But it sure got out of hand fast. Randy never let up. Even after we were arrested, we were right back at the partying. It was nuts. And I know exactly when it was that I knew I had to get the hell out."

"When was that?"

"We were at an outdoor concert. I was so smashed, I don't even remember who played. All I know is that at some point, I came out of my fog and a highway patrolman had a gun at my head. I don't even know what for. The girl I was with said I got smart with him. But I can't remember any of it!"

"Jesus!" Aaron shouted. "Guns and cops! What kind of life is that?"

"Tell me about it!" Eric laughed. "You know I'm not like that."

Aaron shook his head and shuddered at the thought of his brother with a gun against his head. It was too bizarre, too out of step with his own life. He gazed out the window and followed a beautiful Chinese girl with his eyes as she came forward toward the building. He thought about how happy he was to be in a place where such women were always passing under his window.

"Come here and look at this!" he told Eric. Eric jumped up to see. "Is she not beautiful?"

"Seems strange to me," Eric said, drawing on his cigarette. "It's going to take me awhile to get used to this. It's really kind of scary."

"Don't worry," Aaron laughed. "These Oriental women grow on you. You'll go mad for 'em in days, I guarantee it."

They both fidgeted nervously as the Chinese girl looked up and saw them both staring down at here. Still, her face betrayed no surprise or emotion of any kind. She was as unconcerned as a lean, long-haired cat sashaying down the usual city streets, indifferent to all but her own secret cares. In a moment, she was directly under the window. Both turned to see her as she came out the other side. Eric began grinning broadly as he gazed at her petite bottom.

"Never mind about falling in love with them in a few days," he cracked. "I'm ready now!"

Aaron laughed hard and nodded eagerly for a moment. Then, he was suddenly straight faced. "Oh my god . . . " he said with genuine surprise.

"What?"

"Oh my god . . . " he said again.

"What?" Eric demanded, frowning.

"Here comes Vanessa . . . "

"Vanessa who? You mean someone's coming here?"

"Eric, you won't believe it. This girl is the straightest girl you've ever met. She's Richard Getz' old girlfriend."

"Living here?! Richard Getz . . . " Eric became nearly hysterical with laughter. "I can't believe it," he said.

They both watched as the tall, slim girl came slowly down the street.

"Quick, get back!" Aaron ordered. "She'll see us."

"What? Are we going to hide?"

"No, but I'd like to. You two will have nothing in common. Nothing at all."

"If she's a woman, we can work something out," Eric cracked. Aaron was not so sure.

Then the doorbell rang. Aaron hurried nervously to the hallway and pressed the door release. He listened as steps thumped faintly along the lobby floor, then up the stairs to his apartment.

When she was in, introductions were quickly, if nervously, made.

"We're just having some beers here," Eric explained. "Care to have one?"

Vanessa looked at Aaron with her large, hazel-colored eyes and smiled. "No thanks," she said turning quickly back to Eric. "I don't drink."

"Anything?" Eric laughed.

Vanessa was surprised by Eric's continued interest in the matter, but played along politely. "Oh, I do like some liqueurs and a few mixed drinks."

"Well, let's get you something!" Eric said excitedly.

Aaron shook his head fervently at Eric to get him to lay off, but Eric just pushed on ahead. "What did we get at the store, Aaron? Bourbon?"

"I really don't want anything," Vanessa insisted, looking hard at Aaron. "I just stopped by for a moment. I'm in the middle of a project."

"What kind of project?" Aaron asked, hoping to settle the situation quickly. In his mind, he just wanted to get Vanessa out as soon as possible. For some reason, he was completely ill at ease with the idea of Eric and Vanessa having a conversation.

"I'm in a writing class at the university," Vanessa explained, "and we have to do something we've never done before, then write about it. So . . . I figured why not try some totally different cuisine and write about that. I figured you could recommend something since you've done so much traveling, Aaron."

Aaron smiled and threw back his head a little. "Sure . . . I could recommend something . . . "

"What? You mean food?" Eric asked.

Vanessa smiled and looked sideways at Eric. She thought he was amusing.

"How about Javanese . . . " Aaron offered. "There's a great little restaurant near here . . . "

"Perfect!" Vanessa laughed. Then her voice was pleading. "Come with me!"

Aaron was mildly stunned.

"Come on you guys!"

"Why not?" Eric remarked quickly. "We haven't eaten yet." He lit up another cigarette and drew in deeply. Aaron watched Vanessa turn her nose away and frown. He laughed quietly to himself.

Soon Aaron gave in, and the three made their way down the busy street. At the restaurant, they managed to get a table right against the front window. Eric looked around wild-eyed at the strange bright red Oriental woodwork and the large fantastic statues of human animal creatures. He had never seen a place like it. He was not sure that he liked it.

"What should we order?" Vanessa asked excitedly, almost like a young girl.

Aaron smiled. Vanessa was really different from what she had been like when he had last known her. Their first meeting in San Francisco had been friendly and strained at the same time. Now she was sitting there grinning like a true old friend. He was having trouble adjusting to it.

"How about going with this special here," Aaron suggested. "Ten courses for only . . . "

"Ten courses!" Eric blurted out in surprise.

"Sure," Aaron laughed. "So we try a little of everything." Eric just shrugged.

"Sounds great," Vanessa agreed.

After they had ordered, Vanessa politely probed into how Eric had come to be in San Francisco. Eric was more than willing to talk about his recent experiences. He felt expansive in a way he had never felt before. This was nearing the end of his first year ever outside of the hometown of his first thirty-one years. He was glad to be out and glad to tell anyone about it.

"So what are you going to do here?" Vanessa asked. "I mean, do you have work?"

"No," Eric shrugged. "But I'm sure my brother here can help." He slapped Aaron on the arm and raised an eyebrow until he got a laugh.

The waiter put down a dish of small ribs in satay sauce and a large bowl of rice. A waitress followed immediately with several vegetable dishes.

"Work will be no problem at all," Aaron said as he began filling his plate. "That's my job, putting people to work."

"Where was it you said you worked?" Vanessa asked. "I guess in all the excitement of seeing you the other day, I missed it."

"Paragon Personnel. We send out people who will do virtually anything for you. You name it. Just so it's legal and moral! Everything from private secretaries to domestics and chauffeurs."

"And you're the manager?"

"Yes," Aaron explained. "I got hired down in San Jose to drive for some Silicon Valley computer whiz after my buddy Jack Katz ran out of work for me. Fortunately, his girlfriend's cousin was assistant manager at Paragon there. She got me in and told me that the manager was pregnant and that as soon as the woman left to have her baby, she would move up to manager, then hire me on as assistant. And that's just how it happened. I was assistant there for nine months, then the owner asked me to be manager of his San Francisco branch."

"So, presto, you move to San Francisco."

"That simple."

"And you like the work?"

"Well, yes and no. It's a hard job really. You wouldn't believe all the screwy things that go on in people's lives. There's enough material in just one of these branches to write twenty soap operas. And I have to mediate all of this madness. Old women bitching at me. Workers disappearing . . ."

"So what's good about it?"

Aaron laughed. "To tell the truth . . . I like being boss. I've had literally hundreds of people work for me already, and I've just been with the company about two years. It's not like I'm some tyrannical maniac, it's more like I get to have all those people look up to me and answer to me. It's all on a one-to-one basis, and I just know how to handle people well. I enjoy being the ringleader."

"So you think you'll stay with it?"

"I'd rather be a Jungian analyst! A writer, a musician! A painter . . . I mean . . . given the choice."

"Given the choice I'd be a professional comedian," Eric said laconically through a mouthful of sweet and sour pork. "But who gets the damn choice?"

"Well, I used to think we made all of our own choices. Now I'm not so sure."

Vanessa agreed, her enthusiasm suddenly dampened. "I've been going to college for so long," she laughed, "I've got enough credits in three fields to graduate. But I keep changing my major. I just don't know what I want to do."

The three pushed on through the meal with renewed gusto as more exotic dishes were served. Finally, they were so satiated they felt as if they had overdosed on meat and sauces. But they had had such a pleasurable time, none of the three wanted it to end.

"Let's get some drinks," Eric suggested.

"Fine with me," Aaron said, looking over at Vanessa.

"Sure," was all she said.

They paid their bill and left, then strolled down the street to a nearby bar. They each had a drink and talked quietly. Then Eric got restless.

"Let's try another place," he said excitedly. "There's nothing happening here." He was ready for some action.

Off they went to a second bar for drinks all around again. Vanessa sipped as the men drank down a beer and a whiskey each. Then a shot of tequila.

"Let's go where they've got a live band for Chrissakes!" Eric roared. "Let's move it!" The alcohol was taking effect quickly.

Vanessa frowned and tried to excuse herself so she could go home and study. But Eric wouldn't hear of it. He virtually demanded that she go with them to the next bar. At last she relented and they took off again.

They found a place where the drinks were cheap and the music loud. Eric took total control, buying round after round of kamikazes. Vanessa only sipped, but she could feel the effects, too. The three danced together and it became more and more wild. Aaron became especially drunk, since he was not as used to drinking as Eric. Eric loved it and bought more kamikazes. Meanwhile, Vanessa began withdrawing and frowning as she danced. Aaron was all over the floor like a crazy man. He was dancing with complete abandon and laughing wildly. Eric grinned from ear to ear.

Then she could stand it no longer. "I've got to go!" she screamed through the wailing guitar crescendos and loud drum rolls. "That's it!"

She ran out the door. The brothers both shrugged and ran up to the front of the bandstand. Although Aaron would later regret his total abandon and feel sorry for what Vanessa must have suffered through, he had only one drunken thought at that moment, something on the order of *I know this is happening, but who cares?* like every drunk.

"Let's do it!" he screamed at the top of his lungs. "Burn . . . ! ! ! "

10

PARAGON PERSONNEL had been founded subconsciously on two role models: Pavlov and Sisyphus. Or so Aaron imagined it as he sat in his office barking out a short sales blurb every time the phone rang, which was every two to five minutes. He would hang up and turn to note something on a schedule and the phone would ring. He would say a few words to a co-worker and the phone would ring. He would try to wolf down a few bites from a sandwich at lunch time and the phone would ring. Finally, he felt as if he were salivating like one of Pavlov's famous dogs each time that irritating tinkle rattled in its plastic box on his desk. He had never experienced anything like it before. Only he and one other office mate were responsible for selling every client who called on the pleasures and necessities of the service. By the end of the day, Aaron had talked so much that his throat would start to seize up.

Every week was the same. Push, push, push to get those client hours up. Every hour scheduled meant an hour's payment to the agency. Every week the owner of Paragon would call and rant and cajole and inspire and sometimes scream for his managers to get the hours up. He was a shrewd and brilliant businessman, and he knew how to succeed. He knew how to squeeze every drop of adrenalin out of his managers to benefit the growth of his company. And that was tricky, since every week his managers did virtually the same thing: push for sales, push for new applicants and push the hired personnel to give all they were capable of giving to a paying client. Aaron determined that it was no different than living with the curse of Sisyphus. In that ancient myth, Sisyphus had been condemned by Zeus to the task of rolling a huge boulder up a mountain slope, and just as he was about to succeed by reaching the top, the boulder would roll back down the mountain. Sisyphus could only cry out in severe frustration, hang his head and return to the base of the mountain where he would start it all over again. So it was with client hours. No matter how good a week they might have, the next week was a totally separate entity and every hour had to be booked or re-booked, and the whole process started all over again.

Perhaps the worst part of the job, though, was trying to control what could never really be controlled: people's lives. Aaron and his assistant manager, Peter Varden, were both the kind of men who took their responsibilities seriously. They would never be late, never call in sick, work through lunch, work late, work until the job was done. They had to. Thousands of clients counted on them and a hundred workers. But the workers themselves were often be just the opposite. They were constantly late to the client's home or business, called in sick all of the time and left the job early no matter if the job were done or not. This was actually only true of a minority of the workers, but everyday, several of the people would create these problems and it was Aaron and Peter who had to answer to the client for it. Enter stress with a shotgun in the nerve centers of the brain and body. It was not a fun job, but it did pay well and it had gotten Aaron to San Francisco. If it meant listening to a rude, frenetic dissatisfied shrieking client sometimes, so be it. Such is business as Aaron learned.

But now, it was Peter who looked whipped.

Aaron scowled. "What is it this time?"

"Shirley hasn't called in for her assignment yet, I can't reach Dr. Conrad, and Mrs. McEntire expects me to call her back by noon to tell her why Canuto was lying on her bed when she came home early yesterday afternoon. I've got Maria who doesn't want to work for Valerie Everetts anymore and old Mrs. Brown who doesn't want Cindy in her house ever again. I've got Ross who went out to do yard work for Beverly Nichols and pulled out all her flowers along with the weeds. And now Carlos is on his way up."

"You saw him?"

"Yeah, he'll be here any minute."

Aaron rolled his eyes and looked down at his paperwork. "I'm too busy to bullshit with him for an hour!"

"Can't we ever have a normal day?" Peter whined. "I can't believe this place."

Suddenly the office door cracked open and Aaron looked up to see a grinning Mexican man in dark sunglasses. He strutted with a bounce into the office, his hand clutching a sack with a beer in it. "*Jeah!*" he intoned, his head bobbing like a hipster. "Rock 'n' roll!" His black chauffeurs coat was thrown open and he laughed in a high tittering volley of hyena cackles, his mouth open to an almost repulsive width. "*Yentlemen,* Carlos has arrived!"

Aaron looked over at Eric who had been joining him in the office, working on various promotional mailings. At a glance, they read each other's thoughts with absolute clarity.

"Carlos, we don't have time . . . "

"Oh, the big boss is too busy for Carlos."

Aaron snorted and chuckled quietly. He looked through the other door into the adjoining office where Peter was staring sullenly at several client cards, pretending not to know that Carlos was in the office. Meanwhile, Eric sat back to watch the show. He had been forewarned about Carlos. Previous management had hired Carlos, and now he was a chauffeur for one of Paragon's best customers. Carlos' job was extremely secure. When Aaron had taken over, there had been a clash of personalities. Still, he had had to keep Carlos on. Carlos had not seen the clash as any big deal. Everyone reacted pretty much the same toward him. He was overly friendly, and people responded to that. But he was pushy, too, and he could get annoying. He always meant well, though, and so in the end he would win friends. He especially liked being chummy with his clients and bosses. He always thought of himself as everyone's equal and so he would go out of his way to prove it. When he learned that both Aaron and Peter were guitar players, he went after them relentlessly. "Come on . . . " he would endlessly insist. "Let's get it together and play, man. What you waiting for?" He could not understand Aaron's reluctance. The more Carlos would push, the more Aaron would resist. For Aaron's taste, the man was just too aggressive. Whenever he came to the office, all wheels were forced to a grinding halt. Carlos not only expected the world to revolve around him, he demanded it. Now he was lighting a cigarette and blowing out huge puffs of smoke and rambling on about his clients.

"Got an extra cigarette?" Eric wanted to know as Carlos was pocketing his pack again.

"Sure, man. No problem." He grinned at Eric and cackled softly. "So, the big boss has got you working now, too, eh?" He strolled across the room and flipped Eric a smoke. "I'm Carlos," he said, offering his hand. When the two shook, Carlos managed a hep finger snap at the same time, on the same hand. He laughed hysterically and bobbed back across the room after Eric had introduced himself. "Oh . . . " he moaned, shaking his head. "You are stuck with this guy as your brother," he laughed, looking back at Eric, then askance at Aaron. "This guy never stop working, never go out and party."

Aaron was on the phone to a customer and frowned comically at Eric. "Yes, we could send a secretary out tomorrow . . . " he was saying as he made faces. He put a hand over the receiver and hissed at Carlos, then grinned.

"So . . . you like to party, man?" Carlos asked Eric. "Drink beer . . . ?" he said, holding up his sack.

Eric grinned widely. "As a matter of fact . . . "

"I show you all of the best clubs in town!" Carlos cut in excitedly.

Aaron was waving his hand back and forth to cut the smoke, still talking to his client. "Ssshh . . . " he snapped, gesturing at the phone and whispering. "Not so loud!"

Carlos clicked his tongue and shook his head. "That guy . . . " he groaned, smiling at Eric. He pulled off his shades and rolled his eyes. "Hey," he said. "Come to my car with me. We go out now and eat and drink a beer. I play you some good rock 'n' roll. I have all the latest music."

Aaron was finally off the phone. "What's this?" he wanted to know.

"It's time for lunch," Carlos argued, "and I am going to steal your brother and show him the limo of X. Rex Kelby." He laughed like a hyena, all out of proportion to his statement.

Eric laughed, too. He was bored with addressing envelopes to clients and a beer sounded good. "I can bring you something back," he told Aaron as he stood up to go. Aaron was slightly disappointed that Eric was doing it, but it was his choice, he figured. He only wished that he had made it clearer to Eric what a pest Carlos would become if you played along with him.

"Don't bother bringing me anything," he told Eric. "Peter and I can order from the Chinese place downstairs."

Carlos waved in at Peter as he passed by the door. Peter was nervously smoking a cigarette and staring at a smattering of client cards on his desk. He grinned at Carlos and waved, then quickly picked up the phone and pressed buttons with lightning speed. "Give me a call later," he yelled out to Carlos. "There's been a time change on tomorrow's assignment."

"Don't worry man, I'll be back." He nodded his head at Eric. Peter's blue eyes went wide and curious.

"*Jeah!*" Carlos laughed, snapping his fingers. "I'll be back!"

"We'll be sitting on the edge of our seats," Aaron called out sarcastically, but grinning.

"Oh . . . " Carlos moaned, his eyes going narrow. "*Yust* you wait!"

The music was loud, the limo sleek and the beers as smooth as the limo's ride. They drove through Golden Gate Park, then out and up through the hills of Twin Peaks. Finally, they pulled up in front of a large rustic home behind thick hedges. Carlos was busily jabbering about the ways of women and the woes and ecstasies of love, when Eric suddenly cut in.

"Why are we stopping here?" he wanted to know, instantly edgy. "Are we at your boss' house? What did you say his name was . . . X. Roy Bean, or something like that?"

Carlos trembled and convulsed with hysterics. "X. Rex Kelby!" he roared like a man out of control. He began hacking and coughing, until there were tears in his eyes.

"Yes!" Eric laughed, hissing on the last letter of the word like a snake and sipping at his beer. "X. Rex Kelby." He uttered each syllable with exaggeration and mockery. "And I sure as hell ain't going in there!"

"Don't worry, man!" Carlos sputtered, still coughing and laughing hard. "This don't belong to my boss! This is my house!"

"Your house!" Eric couldn't believe it. "What did you do, rob the place and shoot the owners?"

Carlos lowered his mildly bloodshot eyes and looked long and serious at his new-found companion. "You watch it, my friend," he said with undertones of warning. "You think I am just poor dumb Mexican, you wrrrong!" As he roared out the last word, he raised a fist at Eric and leaned into him. Eric grabbed his hand and quickly wrestled him down onto the seat. Soon the two were both laughing hysterically as beer spilled onto the plush seats of Kelby's limousine.

"Now cut it out!" Carlos ordered.

"You started it!"

"This is my house! Now get out! Let's go inside and raid the refrigerator!"

"Fine!" Eric bellowed. "But first give me a smoke!"

"Tough guy . . . " Carlos grunted. But he knew that Eric was twice his match. He chortled like a hyena again and pulled out his smokes. They each torched one up with big bursts of fire.

When they got into the house, Eric walked around and marveled at all of the beautiful antiques. He could not believe that Carlos was as wealthy as he appeared. He kept probing and probing until Carlos confessed that the home was not his at all.

"Okay, I tell you," he laughed. "My girlfriend owns this house." He turned on the stereo and cranked up the volume. "She got the place when her parents were killed in a car wreck in Mexico. I met her down there. In Puerto Vallarta. We have been together now six years."

"When did you come up here?"

"Five years ago. Lisa wrote me over and over. She begged for me to come and be with her. She was torn up inside for a long time. But I come. I make things better." He chortled quietly. Then suddenly he was up and racing across the room, back to the stereo. He turned its volume even higher and started jumping up and down and laughing in fits.

Eric popped open a fresh beer and began tapping his foot as he sat on the couch. He was staggered by the awesome view out the front window, which overlooked San Francisco Bay far away downhill. He decided then and there that he had found his new drinking buddy and that everything was going to work out fine in his new adopted city.

When the phone rang, they could barely hear it, but Carlos knew and he quickly killed the volume of the stereo and answered. He listened a moment then hung up.

"What is it?" Eric asked.

"It was Peter. Kelby called. He wants me down at the studio in thirty minutes."

"That's not much time."

"Tell me about it! I won't be able to take you back to the office."

"Well, what am I going to do? Walk?"

"No, take the bus, I guess."

"Bullshit!" Eric roared. "You won't get me on one of those things!" He was clearly distraught. He hated buses.

"Well, come on, man! Let's get going then! Hurry!"

They were both up and out of the house in minutes. Soon they were racing down from Twin Peaks toward U-Star Studios in the heart of San Francisco. Eric decided that he would walk from there to Paragon. Carlos quickly called the studio on the mobile phone. Aurora Kahele took the call and explained the urgency of needing the car.

"We just found out that some professor friend of Dr. Rayburn is arriving at San Francisco International. Rex wants to meet him personally at the airport," she said. "I'm sorry to interrupt your lunch, Carlos."

"Well . . . yes . . . it's okay. But I have a friend with me and he needs a ride back to his office. What am I supposed to do?"

"I don't know, but we've got to hurry, Carlos. Take your friend with you to the airport, I guess. Rex will understand. It's no big deal. What is a big deal is that Rex meet that man when he steps off the plane!"

"Roger *Weelco* . . . Aurora. Over and out." He slammed down the phone and hurried through a yellow light. "Now we see who is the boss man when X. Rex Kelby need Carlos." Eric laughed and fidgeted in his seat. He was always shy about meeting new people, let alone celebrities he had barely heard of before. But everything was happening so fast that it was out of his control. He drew deeply on his cigarette and watched all the crazy traffic with apprehension. But he knew that it would be alright. Something important was happening in his life. He liked it. He decided not to fight it. He finally relaxed the foot he had been mashing down against the floorboard.

X. Rex Kelby slipped out a side door into the waiting limo, which immediately screeched forward with Carlos at the wheel, hurrying toward Geary Boulevard. Carlos apologized for the stranger at his side. He tried to explain.

"It doesn't matter," Kelby said in a quiet voice, cutting him off. "We'll just say you work for me, Eric, if anyone asks. But they won't." He winked at Eric and then pulled out a sheaf of papers from his briefcase. "So, what line of work are you in, Eric?" Kelby began studying over notes he had made in the margins of the scientific transcripts he had with him.

Eric was impressed with the friendly interest and felt instantly at ease. He began explaining how he was new to the City and that he was staying with his brother.

"His brother is manager at Paragon," Carlos interjected. "We are good friends."

Kelby smiled and rubbed the stubble of the beard he was growing. He and Eric looked at each other and laughed quietly.

"So you've got no job yet, Eric?" Kelby asked.

Now it was Eric and Carlos who exchanged glances.

"No," he answered flatly. "Not really."

"Well, you look like a good strong man. I might be able to help."

"What? Do you need a bodyguard now, boss?" Carlos asked, laughing.

"No . . . and hopefully never. But this man I'm going to meet is coming here to consult with me about a special project that I'm working on. If I read between the lines correctly where this man is concerned, I'm going to need an able-bodied assistant immediately. Somebody with some guts."

"What am *I* for, boss?"

"For driving my car, Carlos. You're reckless enough with this, let alone with what I've got in mind for your pal here. I'll pay good money to the right man, Eric, and my instincts tell me that you might be that man." Kelby did not reveal the full import of that statement. He had had a precognitive dream. He did not know who the strong blond man had been in it . . . until now. Kelby felt absolutely positive about it, and he smiled so subtly that not even Carlos could detect it as he snatched glances at Kelby's face in the rearview mirror.

11

THEY WERE LEAPING off the cliffs near Half Moon Bay, streaking down beach, then swiftly out over the surf and back again on cool ocean currents like boomerangs. When Aaron and Eric Harrison left their car, they had no trouble discerning which flier was the man they had come to see. Jack Katz' voice boomed out loud and full. He was a hang glider instructor now, and he was busy working with three new students who wanted to learn the art.

"Stall the airfoil!" Jack called out with a hand at the side of his mouth like a megaphone. "Bring her in slow and steady!" Aaron closely watched the flier's face as he landed. He could see the controlled terror and cautious excitement. Down below, the other two fliers were landing safely in the sand. They had not yet learned sufficient technique to bring the glider back to the launch ramp.

"*Wu-Wei*, hey!" Jack yelled over at the brothers in a sing-song rhyme after the flier had set it down. Jack had an incredible fascination with Oriental philosophies, and he often used its jargon in completely inappropriate ways. Then he would laugh loudly.

The brothers grinned and cast quick glances at each other, then strolled on toward Jack. In a moment, the three were rapidly bringing each other up to date on the latest events in their lives.

"Nicole is here!" Jack said excitedly. He watched Aaron smile coyly, as if not committing. But the two had discussed her before, and Jack and Tamara had both wanted to make the match. "I told her you'd be down . . . "

"There's always a party at Jack's house," Aaron said half derisively. He had never seen Jack but that he was invited to a party. He didn't mind really, but Jack always pushed for an all-nighter and he was less and less up to it as the years went by. His friend, on the other hand, would merely be observing his usual hours.

Jack laughed lightheartedly. He knew that Aaron could not resist meeting Nicole, who had just flown in from the east coast. She was described as having black curly hair, as curly as the black Irish of her ancestry. She had a muscular build and a first-rate mind. Her great cerebral passion was computer programming. Tamara had grown up with her and was still a best friend.

"Did she come alone?" Eric wanted to know.

"Yeah, . . . " Jack answered, "but I know some other ladies in the valley. Just be there!"

Eric was excited. "We'll follow you back," he told Jack immediately. "Nothing else to do."

"Except fly!" Jack laughed. "Now what was that business about urgently needing to learn. I invited you here before!"

"I know," Aaron admitted. "But this is big, and it could mean lots of bucks."

"Well, count me in then!"

"Hopefully we can."

"So, what's the deal?" Jack asked while looking over at his student who was patiently restrapping a harness. The other two were slowly working their way back up the cliff on a path where they could just barely be seen.

"Have you heard the name, X. Rex Kelby?" Eric asked slowly, pronouncing each syllable with pride and respect.

Jack squinted his eyes. "The video . . . " His hand waved frantically as he searched for the right word. "The video guy," he finally said. "Sure! What about him? Do you know him?"

"From Paragon," Aaron boasted. "And Eric has met him. In fact, he's got a special project he wants Eric to do."

Jack's hand was waving again. "Go on!" he ordered.

"This is top secret," Eric informed him with a menacing eye. "We mean it!"

"Go on . . . " Jack said again, glossing over the obvious solidness of their friendship. "I suppose he wants to film you flying one of these things . . . " he said pointing at a hang glider.

"Nope!" Eric shot back, grinning. "He's built a new model rocket pack that he wants me to test fly."

"Oh my god . . . " Jack said, stunned. His mouth was literally open. "Get me in on that!"

"Maybe we can. But first, he just wants me there," Eric explained. "Now . . . I've flown a small plane before. Didn't get my license because it was just too damn expensive. But I know a little about that and now I need to learn a lot about this."

"It'll be pretty different really."

"Yes, but all the same, you're out there flying alone."

"I hope he gives you a reserve parachute," Jack laughed.

"Don't worry," Aaron assured Jack. "X. Rex Kelby is no fool. He's thought about these things."

"Yeah," Eric quipped. "I'll be harnessed to a helicopter, in fact, on the first trial runs. Just in case. The whole thing has been worked out."

"Why did he pick you?"

"Pure accident," Eric said. "I was in the right place at the right time."

Suddenly, Jack's student was there and the three grew quiet. Jack quickly introduced everyone, then shouted at the wind. "Hi-dee-ho!" he yelled. "Let's get to it bros!" He swiftly readied his student first and got him up on the launch platform. Then he hurried to his van and began pulling out his own rig which was like a great golden pterodactyl. "Eric!" he yelled. "Get over here and get this thing! You want to fly then let's fly! Let's get her on the wind!"

Hours later the energies had been well spent, and both Eric and Aaron had gone out with Jack on his two-man glider. Jack suggested that they all come back on the following day, which was a Sunday, to solidify the lessons in their "crash course."

"We'll pass on the crashing part," Eric joked. "But we'll definitely come!"

"If we can walk," Aaron said, again using a sarcastic tone. He knew they would all get drunk.

"Then let's get started!" Jack grinned, without missing a beat. He reached into a chest in the back of his van. "Presto . . . tequila!" he announced like an old mescal god from Mexico. "Let's practice on the cactus!"

Meanwhile, X. Rex Kelby and his entire doctoral project was receiving the full Luebec scrutiny.

"The calibration is more than that percentage of emission, Kelby," Dr.

Luebec was arguing. "Why should my transference module even work in your synthesis feedline?"

"Because . . . " Kelby stated confidently, "I have modified your modification and we first feed the mercury bromide through this chamber here, see?" He pointed on the diagram and then at the open interior of the fly pack demo model. "This allows me to achieve that extra percentage of emission into the main propulsion unit, and the thrust is perfectly streamlined in accordance with the velocity amplitude of the computer-generated model."

Luebec smiled faintly and continued studying the diagram. He felt strange waves of excitement gush up from the base of his spine, but he was not yet ready to offer his approval.

Dr. Rayburn decided that it was time to take Kelby aside. He gestured with a nod toward the door, and Kelby signaled nonchalantly with his eyes. "Well, Dr. Luebec, we've been at this for hours now," he said, rubbing a strained eye. "I need a little air."

"By all means . . . " Luebec responded without looking up.

"I believe I'll join you," Rayburn laughed. "If you'll excuse us, doctor?"

Luebec nodded and turned a diagram sideways under the magnifying lamp. "Go ahead . . . " he said. "I'll be okay."

When Kelby and Rayburn reached the corridor, they both let out a sigh. Luebec had been unrelenting in his devil's advocate role, and both men could feel the toll in fatigue.

"Doesn't he ever let up?" Kelby asked.

"In your case, he'll have to," Rayburn smirked. "We've both put in too many hours in doublechecking that design for him to trip over some flaw we haven't imagined."

Kelby laughed. "But why does he keep coming back to the transference module? Does he resent my tinkering with it that much? I told him he could retain patent status on it."

Rayburn pushed the door open and stepped outside first. He held the door for Kelby and watched as Kelby squinted at the bright light a moment, then sneezed. "Got your glasses?" Rayburn asked, smiling.

Kelby didn't answer. His hand had already groped into his lab coat and brought the dark shades out. "I just can't figure why he's dragging his feet."

"There could be a number of reasons," Dr. Rayburn insisted. "Remember, you're not an ordinary student, Kelby. For God sake, you have more patents than any professor you've studied under. Think how that intimidates people like Luebec."

"I don't think it's that . . . "

"Well, you don't know the man like I do," Rayburn persisted. "Here . . . " he said suddenly, stopping at a bench. "Let's sit a few minutes then get on back in there. It makes me nervous with him eagle-eyeing everything."

"That's why he's here."

"Yes, and he'll see things our way. Don't worry."

"I'm not worried, I'm just impatient. We've been at this for four days straight. I tell you, there's something he's not telling us that he should."

"Yes, but I can't let you jeopardize your own success, Kelby, and keep that smug tone with him. He's a brilliant man, and he has to move at his own speed. He's the last hurdle. That's why I got you out of there. Just cool off and take deep breaths. Once he's given his approval, we're ready for the sky test."

"We were ready four days ago!"

"Look, Kelby," Rayburn snapped. "I don't understand his motives either, but we have to follow procedure!"

Kelby looked down and frowned. "I never could stand waiting on somebody else to give me the okay on anything. That's why I started my doctorate so late. But I won't make waves. We're too close now, I realize that."

Rayburn stood up slowly and sunk his hands into his lab coat. "What about your test flier?" he asked suddenly. "You have somebody lined up?"

Kelby grinned and stood also. "You, Dr. Rayburn. I want you to test it."

Rayburn's smile went lopsided. "I'll be right behind you, Rex! We'll be the new Wright Brothers!"

Kelby laughed hard. "Probably feel like them, too."

"Yes, brittle-boned and ancient."

They continued laughing and walking. In a moment, they were back inside the building and they headed up the corridor.

"Do you have a test flier?" Rayburn asked again. "Somebody who can keep his mouth shut?"

Kelby nodded. "He's not a student here at Berkeley, if that's what you're wondering. He lives in the City. In fact, he just moved here and knows nothing about science. I'd say we're safe."

They went on into the lab. Luebec shot a hard look at the men. "I've got something very serious to show you two," he said sternly.

The traffic to Jack's home in Almaden Valley was heavy as usual, and it was a long hour's drive. As soon as they reached the valley, Jack pulled in to his favorite bar there and the brothers followed. Once inside, Jack let out a loud "Hi-dee-ho!" and about ten cowboys and two cowgirls turned to look from the bar. They each knew who had said it without turning. But whenever the huge long-haired Jack entered a bar, heads were instinctively turned, even without the well-known greeting he hurled out automatically everywhere. He just had that outlaw look, and everyone always felt a little nervous at first. Then they would see that big gaping grin and immediately settle down to party even more relaxed than before they had seen him. He had put an end to more than one barroom brawl, and his reputation was well established. He was almost a guardian presence. Aaron knew that better than anyone.

After they had ordered beers, the bartender gave Jack a fake mean look. "Your old lady has been calling for you, Jack. She told me to tell you to hustle it home as soon as I saw you."

"Terrific," Jack laughed. "So now you've done your duty."

"And when you gonna do yours?"

"As soon as I feel like it."

Aaron and Eric smiled, then looked around apprehensively. They did not feel fully comfortable in a cowboy bar, so they sipped warily and looked around.

"Let's play some pool!" Jack suggested all at once. "Loser buys the next round."

"Easy for you to say!" Aaron objected. "I hardly ever play."

"Eric can take me on then," Jack insisted.

"Bullcrap!" Eric laughed. "I don't have the money to be buying rounds."

"Well, you're gonna do it if you lose," Jack said matter-of-factly, and both Aaron and Eric knew that he meant it.

"What if I don't play?"

"You'll play."

He played.

Hours later again, Tamara called and for the third time Jack interrupted his pool game and argued for more time. But Tamara had reached a point which Jack knew well, and he realized that he had pushed it as far as he could. It was dusk outside when they went to their vehicles. But the drive home was short, and in minutes they were all strolling into Jack's place with imperfect steps.

"Well, finally!" Tamara yelled as the children ran for Jack. "We're all starving around here! Can't you figure that out?"

Jack nodded and quickly introduced Eric to Tamara. Tamara countered with introductions of their friends, Ben and Kay, Johnny, and finally Nicole Cassel. Aaron was immediately more intrigued than he thought he might be. Nicole had a stunning presence with her dark black hair and large blue eyes. Her hair was kinkier than he had expected, but it lent a certain exoticness to her look which he immediately appreciated. Suddenly, he was very sorry that he had let Jack waste so much time at the bar.

Jack meanwhile was hustling out the back door. He went around on the back deck, then up a short flight of stairs to a second deck which was nearly as high as the roof on the low cabin-like house. There, he lit the propane grill and soon had chicken pieces barbecuing over mesquite coals. He had left a fresh bottle of tequila on the kitchen table, and his buddy Ben was pouring rounds and firing up homegrown marijuana. Eric looked a little bewildered as Ben kept pushing drink and smoke at him, but he was already too far gone to resist. Aaron took a few drags then went over to where Nicole was sitting and began talking. He refused more drink from both Ben and Tamara. Nicole was sipping quietly on a weak mixed drink.

When Jack returned to pick up more chicken, Ben grabbed him and the two roared and grunted like a couple of rutting moose, then struggled up against a wall together. They loved pitting their large strong bodies against each other and getting wild for a quick moment. Then they would each down a shot of tequila and roar like mountain men. Finally, Jack went back to the deck and basted the new chicken pieces with barbecue sauce. He was an expert at grilling and had a great love of food. In fact, his pursuit of oral pleasures seemed unending.

A full hour later, the chicken was finished and Jack brought it into the smoky dining room. Tamara barked out orders to the children and drew nervously on a cigarette. A new couple had arrived, and Ben was busy bringing them into the party fun. Eric sat stone quiet in a corner, nearly sleeping. But Aaron and Nicole were talking like old friends. They were both surprised. With all the build up each had received about the other, they had both pretty much decided in advance to dislike each other. Instead, they found that the advance word was based on truth rather than fluff, and the attraction was immediate and satisfying.

When Jack interrupted and insisted that Aaron do a shot of tequila, Nicole jumped up and excused herself abruptly. Aaron was reluctant, but it was always easier to go along with Jack than to resist him. He did his shot, and Jack moved on. Then Aaron found himself looking everywhere through the haze for Nicole, but she was gone. He waited and tried talking to the man they called Johnny. Every sentence seemed to torture him. He could not appreciate small talk with Nicole gone. People were grabbing at plates and spooning potato salad. Children screeched. Aaron kept waiting, but Nicole did not return. At last, he slipped out the back door to look. The suspense was ripping him up.

It was dark on the back deck. When his eyes adjusted, he could see no dim figure in any of the chairs. He decided to try the upper deck. He hurried quietly up the stairs to where all the stars were pulsing out, high above the huge trees. He could feel the awesome cosmos of light swimming down into the altered crystalline mind he was flashing at the sky. The smoke and drink had geared him for a reckless night of searching, if necessary. He could see the barbecue grill still glowing at the far end of the deck, but no one sat near it. He stood puzzled for a time looking out into the dark yard. The creek was rushing loudly near the back of the house and he turned suddenly to look, but the trees were black silhouettes reaching down into total nothingness. He felt completely lost for a moment. Through a closed window, people were laughing and eating with great hardy abandon, but he knew that he could not go back in there. He did not want to be one of the boys. Years of loneliness were after him. Finally, he just looked up at the stars again.

Then he heard a soft voice say "Hi . . . " He turned and looked up to the roof where he could barely see Nicole reclined there like a dark shadowy phantom near the apex. She did not repeat her greeting. Aaron smiled and easily leapt up on the low end of the sloping roof. He could hear his sandpapery shuffle as he made his way to her side, saying nothing. His heart began beating fiercely as he neared her. Nicole appeared to be completely relaxed. She lay unmoving, buried in one of Jack's huge coats, her hands behind her head. She was ready for everything and nothing. Aaron looked reassuring to her. She trusted him as he approached.

"I've been looking for you," Aaron said as he sat down beside her.

"Aren't you hungry?"

Aaron laughed quietly and leaned over her at once. He wanted her lips, and he had already figured that the woman did not play games. She had been very open in their earlier conversation. In a moment, their bodies were rolling awkwardly, but the kiss was graceful, warm and long. The smell of pines permeated the cool evening air.

When Aaron pulled back, he found himself looking into huge round eyes which glinted in the starlight.

"This is right . . . " he said after a silence.

"Why?"

"Because it's right that we meet in high places."

Nicole grinned broadly. Aaron felt very satisfied, as if he'd found a long lost love. Then it scared him. It was uncanny and he knew it. The hair on his neck raised. He had found a long lost love, indeed. That huge smile was familiar. It was the smile he had known for years. For an instant, Nicole had become Oriana in the starlight.

12

IT WAS DAWN before they made love in the guest bedroom as a cinnamon sky streaked out across the hills through the window. Nicole's skin was milky pale, and Aaron watched peacefully as she passed into dream. He felt satisfied in a way he had nearly forgotten. He slowly rubbed her soft skin and thought about how she was the first lover since Oriana who had made him feel as if everything was finally right again. But he knew too that he should not leap to conclusions about Nicole. She had mentioned a boyfriend in passing, but he had not wanted to explore it thoroughly at the time. He did understand that their relationship was an open one, but he had no idea where that would leave him.

As he looked at Nicole's face, he thought about how she did not look like Oriana in the light. The darkness had fooled and unnerved him at a critical moment, and he still was not sure how he fully felt about it. Then he remembered that Oriana had written that she was coming for a visit soon. It made him apprehensive. A lot of time had passed. And it kept passing.

Then he drifted off to sleep again. Hours went by. When he came to, he could only remember a very small dream segment. A black whale had come gushing up and out of the creek behind the house. He couldn't say why, but he associated the whale with Nicole. He wondered if she would have the kind of impact on him that a creature as mighty as a whale might presage.

He kissed her neck several times, and Nicole moaned quietly. He slowly slid down her neck and licked over her skin. When he looked up, he could see Nicole smiling with her eyes closed. He took that as a signal to proceed, and soon they were rocking together gently in the warm bed.

When they finished, they were both smiling as if they had just cut across all fabled time and stolen the motion of both the turtle and the hare in the perfect race against pleasure.

"This is working out better than I ever could have imagined," Nicole said, fluttering her long dark lashes, though not to be purposely seductive.

Aaron grinned and nodded his agreement. "I just wish that we had more time together."

"Well, I don't go back for five days yet. Maybe we can make more time for ourselves."

"Sure," Aaron laughed. "In fact, why not just spend the week with me?"

Nicole smiled and kissed Aaron on the side of the neck. "I'd love to," she answered. "But don't you and Jack have plans today?"

"Yeah, we're going hang gliding again. But you can go along. In fact, you can fly if you want to. Have you ever tried it? It's a lot of fun."

Nicole smiled enthusiastically. "I'd love to try it. Do you think I can handle it?"

Aaron nodded, then laughed. "Just as long as Jack doesn't try to handle *you* on that glider of his?"

They both laughed hard and rolled together playfully.

"Do you really think that I can do it okay?" Nicole asked again.

"Look," Aaron insisted. "If you can climb mountains like you do, I'm sure that you can do just about anything."

Nicole shook her head agreeably. She was proud of her climbing skills. "It's the one thing that Dave and I can get into together," she explained. "And computers, of course. But when we reach the top of a mountain together after that long struggle . . . "

Aaron did not really want to hear about it, but he continued smiling politely.

Nicole had a far away look in her eye. "I just wish that he could express his other side better," she said wistfully.

"What do you mean?" Aaron asked.

"I mean, like after all of that climbing, we'll get right there at the top, ready to go over. I look at Dave and we exchange something special with our eyes. I always expect him to say something romantic then, but he never does. He just lets it pass by every time. If he says anything at all, it'll probably be about the latest computer program he's working on."

"Is he that hung up on his work?"

"Yes," Nicole said, without hesitation. "But he also has another side, it's just that . . . he's so quiet." Then she looked Aaron straight in the eye. "I guess that's why I ate that up last night, kissing under the stars and everything."

Aaron smiled with some combination of humility and arrogance. Nicole could see it plainly.

"You know, I was really set not to like you," she laughed. "You're definitely lovable despite the fact that you think that you're wonderful."

Aaron grinned hard and started to speak, but then said nothing. Instead, he kissed her on the side of the neck and then on her lips. "I guess that I'm arrogant enough to openly admit my spiritual side which is the same as my romantic, artistic side, and yet be somewhat humble about it since I know that I've got a dark side, too, and I definitely admit that."

Nicole's large blue eyes flashed with understanding. "I suppose that I wouldn't be here now with you if I didn't admit my dark side too," she said. "Dave just can't seem to accept it, but it's real and it keeps coming back. That's why I don't marry him. I get hungry for other people."

"That's not necessarily a dark impulse."

"No, but it does throw a relationship into the dark, and that's where I'm at again with Dave."

Suddenly, there was a knock at the door and Jack Katz' voice boomed out loud and clear. "Hey in there!" he said rapping on the wood. "The sun's waiting for you two to get your butts up now! Let's go flying!"

Aurora Kahele was ecstatic again. She sat on the bed with a tray across her lap and watched Kelby place coffee, toast, an omelette and cantaloupe there for her. It always thrilled her to be served in bed, and she loved Kelby's cooking. Kelby smiled and kissed her full on the lips.

"I've got to get mine," he said, pulling back. He hurried off to the kitchen and returned in a moment. Soon they were both eating heartily and sharing the Sunday paper.

"Oh, Rex, look at this!" she showed him the front page of the travel section. "Tahiti, Rex! When can we go again?"

Kelby frowned comically.

"I know!" Aurora laughed. "Wait! But I love that place!"

"So do I! There's no place I'd rather be than walking the beach on

Moorea or Bora Bora. But this is no time for a vacation. We're ready to begin testing on the fly pack."

Aurora looked concerned. "You never did get around to telling me how it went with Luebec yesterday."

Kelby laughed and shook his head. "You wouldn't believe it. After four days of his crabby attitude, and he pulls a total surprise yesterday."

"Luebec? A surprise? What happened?"

"Well, just when it looked like he was never going to approve the next phase, everything changed. We never even saw it coming. I told Rayburn how Luebec was constantly going back to the transference module. I knew something was really bothering him about it. Dr. Rayburn figured that old Luebec was just upset because I had changed something in the design."

"That was his original design, right?"

"Yes. Dr. Rayburn decided that it was a case of professional jealousy. I was ready to believe him, too. But no sooner had we said that than we went back into the lab and Luebec had hit on something. At first he was gruff about it, but then the more he talked the more excited he got. As it turned out, he had a brilliant idea on how to modify my modification! He was like a kid in a candy store!"

Aurora laughed hard. "I would have loved to have seen that. He seems so dry."

"I know," Kelby chuckled. "But now he's all for us. He even explained why he put me through the mill like that. He said that by the end of the first day he began getting an idea on how to improve the design capability and that every night he would sit in his hotel room and work on the model on his portable computer. Apparently, it just suddenly dawned on him and it was that perfect spark. The man had a gleam in his eye!"

"And you don't mind him messing with your design?" Aurora asked, chewing on some omelette.

Kelby laughed. "I messed with his first! That's what scientists do. They all mess with each other's work. That's the only way we ever get anywhere."

"So will you use his modification?"

"Absolutely! It's brilliant and it'll make the pack more powerful, meaning the flier will have better control, especially over landing."

"So what happens next?"

"Luebec is going to stay a few more days and we'll get the new module ready. We should be flying by Wednesday."

"Will Luebec stay for that?"

Kelby nodded. "Aurora, you wouldn't have believed it to see Luebec yesterday. I'm telling you that he is a true scientist. His love of knowledge transcends everything. He wants in all the way on this project now!"

"Do you want him around?"

"Absolutely! With his backing and design recommendations, we'll push this whole project up by months."

"Then we can go to Tahiti!" Aurora joked.

"Yeah, I'll give you Tahiti right now!" And he grabbed Aurora playfully by the hair and began wrestling with her, despite the tray and its clattering contents.

By Wednesday morning, Kelby, Rayburn and Luebec had achieved their goals and the test was given the go ahead. Kelby sent his chauffeur to pick up his flier and meet the scientists at a secret location in the country. But when the men arrived, Kelby was incensed to find that Carlos had brought along an extra couple without his permission, and he nearly leapt out of his car to express his anger over it.

"But boss," Carlos argued. "This is Eric's brother. He is the manager at Paragon. He is no problem!"

Aaron could hear from a distance, and he looked guiltily toward Eric. "I hope we don't blow this for you," he said, shifting nervously on his feet. Nicole had a look of awkwardness as she tried to smile.

"I better go over," Eric said. "Carlos will never persuade him."

"You had no right!" Kelby yelled at Carlos as Eric neared. "I gave you very specific instructions."

Eric stepped forward despite a tremble he felt rising up his throat. "It's my fault, Rex," he said, his face faintly flushed. "I got nervous thinking about being here with you guys. Carlos did his best to talk me out of bringing my brother along. He really did."

"Well, damn!" Kelby turned and looked up at a hill. "I don't usually get mad like this, but you've got to understand the necessity of privacy for us in this project. We're trying to get a patent and first rights and so on. Do you know what it means to protect an investment? Well this is even more than that! Much more."

Eric nodded. "I can understand."

"Okay, so it's done," Kelby muttered and flashed a half-grin at Eric. "Let's just get on with the work. Carlos, you and Eric get the gear from the trunk. Maybe your brother can help, too, Eric. Let's get moving!"

Carlos grinned and rubbed his hands together briskly. "Now we fly like Superman . . ." he said, cackling softly. Then he let out a little hyena chortle and hurried back to the car.

Eric and Kelby exchanged glances and laughed.

"He still thinks that he's going to fly," Kelby said, shaking his head.

"Maybe some day he can if everything goes right here."

"Not if he's going to keep boozing and doing drugs the way he does. I absolutely forbid it."

Eric looked down.

"You've stayed clean right, Eric? I told you how critical that is."

"Oh yes," Eric insisted, cocking his head and turning a steely expression at Kelby. "I had a few beers Saturday, but that was it."

"Good," Kelby answered, not pursuing it further. "And you went hang gliding?"

"Yes, Saturday and Sunday. I was soloing in no time. I'm ready for this."

"Then let's get to it!" Kelby shouted. "See that tower over there," he said, pointing. "Hustle the gear over there. We'll be working on that safety cable."

"What happened to the helicopter?"

"We decided that it would create too much wind interference. Dr. Rayburn secured this air force training field for the day when we decided that this is the kind of test condition we needed. You'll be harnessed to the cable and fly from tower to tower. It's a good long distance. Don't let it fool you.

"So if all fails, I get to hang up there on the line like an old bedspread."

Kelby laughed. "Better than having your face mashed in on rock."

Eric grinned and took off for the car, where Carlos was busy pulling gear out of the large trunk. "I won't end up on the rocks like Carlos and his whiskey," he assured Kelby with a laugh. "You can count on that!" He wanted Kelby to like him.

"I hope so," Kelby muttered quietly to himself. He shook his head again then went on back to Rayburn and Luebec.

"Who are the party crashers?" Rayburn asked when he got there.

"It's Eric's brother and his girl. He says he was too intimidated to come here alone. I guess that he just feels a little insecure. He's no college man. But . . . it'll be alright. Maybe we can even use the brother sometime."

"Maybe soon," Rayburn said. "Dr. Luebec and I have been discussing an accelerated timetable for these tests."

Luebec nodded with a thin smile. "And getting several more models built and finalized soon."

"Words I like to hear," Kelby said with a quiet laugh. "The sooner with everything, the better."

"So let's get on with the tests today!" Rayburn moaned. "She's whizzed through everything in the lab, now for the real thing!"

Soon everyone had gathered at the tower, and Eric began climbing up with the pack strapped over one shoulder. "Why don't I just put it on and fly up?!" he laughed as he made his way slowly.

"Why don't you just climb up then lower a rope and pull everything up that way," Dr. Luebec suggested.

"That's what I thought," Carlos huffed sarcastically. "Gad!"

Eric quickly stepped back down, then unloaded the fly pack on Aaron. Soon he was hustling freely up the tower with just a rope. Once at the top, they began hoisting equipment up piece by piece. Carlos hurried to the top to lend a hand while Aaron and Nicole secured each piece at the bottom.

Another hour passed before Eric and the scientists were finally together on the tower checking equipment. When all measuring devices were operable and double checked, Luebec and Rayburn climbed down. They went to the car and drove to the far tower. Again, they slowly made their way to the top. Aaron and Nicole had been recruited to carry a few measuring devices and accompanied the scientists. When all was ready, Rayburn called Kelby on his walkie-talkie.

"We're finally ready at this end, Kelby. Have you double checked the safety line for the boy?"

"Ten-four, doctor. Eric is suited up and the pack strapped in place. Both safety lines have been checked and are in place."

"Okay, Kelby," Rayburn said. "Fan the delta wing and let's warm up the jets."

"Ten-four, doctor," Kelby answered. He then turned to Eric and nodded. Eric pressed a safety latch and switched on a pre-launch engine. The pack was strapped to his front side, and two wings instantly opened out into a simple fan shape. The wings would provide a solid support for the flier to lie on and aid in the aerodynamics. It was also made of a special heat-resistant material which would deflect all heat from the jets.

"Pre-launch mode operative," Kelby said into his walkie-talkie.

"Ten-four," Rayburn answered. "We're ready when you are, Rex."

Eric pulled his helmet visor over his face. It was a shaded visor, but Kelby could clearly see the smile on Eric's face.

"No need for me to say good luck," Kelby laughed. "This is science. Now burn wind, buddy! Go for it!"

Eric gritted his teeth and switched on the launch mode. He was instantly propelled forward by a powerful thruster burning beneath his chest. The trajectory had been pre-set so he went immediately straight along above the huge safety cable strung between the towers. The exhilaration was stupendous. Far below he could see trees and rocks streaking by. And a waving racing Carlos shrieking with his mouth wide and excited, both arms high in wild triumph.

The Vimana XRK-1 was a screeching, immediate success.

13

AARON STOOD at Gate 23 waiting. He wondered how many times he had gone to an airport to pick up Oriana in his life. When the two had first gotten together, he had barely flown at all. But Oriana had been flying all of her life, and her mother would constantly send checks for her to fly somewhere and meet them for a few days. Soon Aaron was the one rushing Oriana to the airport in Toledo or Cleveland. Then he would be there for her when she returned. Those trips provided his first glimpses into a new world. He became the face at the window, gazing in on something wondrous, but something he was not a part of yet. He yearned for it strongly. Then Oriana made it happen. They began with a trip to Europe while still both students. After graduation, they flew to their new temporary home in far away Australia, where Oriana had secured a position at the University of Melbourne for two years.

Thinking back to those early days, Aaron had to laugh. So much had changed. He remembered a hot spring day back before he and Oriana were more than just neighbors. At that time, Oriana had been dating a man who was an avid pilot and owned his own small plane. He was an instrumentation expert who was always on assignment to different U.S. companies in the field of aviation. He and Oriana were seldom together once she had left L.A. for school in Ohio. But he would fly in on occasion in his plane. It was always dramatic. She would know that he was coming but never a precise time. Suddenly, a roar would be heard in the skies. He would buzz Oriana's roof like an ace fighter pilot, and she would race out the door to wave at him. When he saw her, he would tilt his wings back and forth. Oriana would wave again, then jump into her sports car and screech off to the small university airport to pick him up.

Aaron had been amazed to witness that sight. He never once entertained the idea of competing against such a man. It all seemed so heroic and exciting. He never dreamed that one day he would win Oriana's love and the hero pilot would be left circling in a cold sky, alone and lonely. But he had . . . and now the question was whether he too had lost Oriana forever.

Oriana was always a surprise. Yet Aaron was not at all prepared for the latest surprise she was about to spring on him. All at once the doors were open and passengers were hurrying through. Oriana's long black hair shimmered in the glare of bright lounge lights. At first, Aaron did not even think about looking at anyone next to her. And of course Oriana's smile was as captivating as ever. But then it became obvious that a tall dark man was hovering by her side. At first, Aaron could only look at him blankly.

"Aaron!" the man said holding out a hand. "You do not remember?"

Aaron frowned, then a gleam of recognition slowly crept across his face. It seemed impossible. Finally he said it. "Mauricio!"

Oriana laughed hard and hugged Aaron joyously. She knew what a total surprise she had foisted on her old lover. "Come on," she said, "let's get the luggage and we'll tell you all about it."

Mauricio grinned through his full beard and nodded at Oriana.

"I can't believe this," Aaron laughed.

"Come on," Oriana ordered. "We'll tell it all later."

Soon the three were in the car with their luggage. Aaron drove out of the airport garage and listened quietly as Oriana explained her unexpected companion.

"I keep in touch with all the best people we met on our travels, even Shastri. Mauricio said that he wanted to visit the states sometime, so I invited him to L.A. Then, one day I got a phone call."

"Yes, and I don't have to sleep on street after-all."

When the laughing ended, Aaron could not help but express his surprise again. "God!" he exclaimed. "The last time I saw you, you were as sick as a dog and I figured I'd never see you again."

"You think I die?"

"No. I knew you'd make it. But I still figured I'd never see you again."

"He went back up into the mountains after we last saw him. He actually stayed with some Tibetan yogis in a monastery in the Himalayas," Oriana explained.

"Only place I could afford to stay," Mauricio laughed.

"This I've got to hear! And you don't have to worry about a place to stay in San Francisco," Aaron assured the Brazilian. "I've got room at my apartment."

"You do?" Oriana asked, genuinely pleased. "But what about Eric?"

"Oh, he's got a new girl he can stay with. Her name's Rachel. He met her where he works."

"Where he works?" Oriana said. "I thought he worked with you."

"Not anymore. He's gone on to bigger and better things."

"Such as . . . "

"Oh ho . . ." Aaron laughed. "Now it's my turn to roll out a few surprises."

As the San Francisco skyline came into full view, it was awesome as always. Aaron could see Mauricio's eyes grow wide as he watched him in the rear view mirror.

"Ladies and gentlemen," Aaron announced like a phony pilot. "We are now entering the famous City by the Bay, and your pilot has a most amazing story to tell. Relax and watch the skyscrapers roll by, my friends. One day you may look on these pillars of light from a new and startling angle!"

Oriana and Mauricio had no idea what he was talking about, but they smiled anyway.

Two nights later, Aaron and Oriana went alone to an Italian restaurant. Mauricio was left with Aaron's co-worker, Peter Varden, who had plans to take him out to a few night clubs. At first, it was awkward for Aaron and Oriana to be alone together at the restaurant. But that slowly changed as familiarity set in again. After a while, they were laughing and talking like old times. Oriana, as usual, was very direct.

"Have you met any young ladies, yet?" she asked with a teasing grin.

Aaron looked puzzled for a moment. "You don't really want to hear about it, do you?"

"Sure I do!" Oriana said enthusiastically. "I just want you to be happy, Aaron. That's all I've ever cared about."

Aaron shook his head and smiled as the waiter brought wine and opened it. He offered the cork to Oriana, and she smelled the bouquet approvingly. Glasses were filled, a quiet toast exchanged.

"So tell me about it!" Oriana said again.

Aaron felt nervous. He began skirting the issue, rambling on about his chance encounter with Vanessa, whom they had both known in college. Oriana's eyes lit up wondering if Aaron had actually had an affair with her. She would not have disapproved, though she would have been very surprised. But the story led to no such ending. It was a safe story, and Aaron knew that. Consequently, he told the tale with gusto, including all of the tantalizing possibilities. As he talked on, he felt more and more relaxed with the whole subject. Finally, the ending went up in a puff of smoke and both Aaron and Oriana laughed at the strangeness of the whole encounter.

"All I can remember about her," Oriana said, "was that day Richard brought her over to the trailer and she sat on the floor . . . "

"Oh yeah," Aaron laughed. "When she looked at that porcelain rose your mother had sent and said 'Oh, I like this! No, I don't!' All in a matter of two seconds. She never knew what she liked back then."

"Is she still like that?"

"No, she's much more together now. She grew up and, in fact, she's an incredible artist in her own right."

The two laughed quietly for a moment, then watched eagerly as the waiter placed their meals in front of them. After they began eating, Oriana became curious again. "Who else have you seen?" she asked. "I mean romantically." Her eyes were wide. "I really hope that you've met someone, Aaron."

Aaron smiled and took a small forkful of lasagna, then sipped at his wine. "I've had some interesting relationships," he said at last. "There was a Japanese girl and, believe it or not, a nineteen year old named Alyson. Then there was a young lady I met through Jack's girlfriend. Her name is Nicole. I guess she's had the biggest impact on me."

"Are you still seeing her?"

"Well, that's hard to say. Number one, she lives on the east coast. Number two, she has a boyfriend of sorts. But, yeah, I guess you could say I'll be seeing her again."

Aaron was silent for a moment. "What about you?" he asked suddenly. "Are you and Mauricio getting together?"

Oriana laughed. "No. Not yet anyway. He's certainly made advances, but I'm in no hurry."

"Somebody else?"

"I've met several. One guy offered to pay my way anywhere. He just wanted me to travel with him. Then there was Dr. Holcomb. You remember Ian?"

"Ian from Australia! You're kidding! I never would have guessed."

Oriana laughed. "He even wanted to get married."

"What about Elizabeth?"

"Oh, she found out and was totally upset about it all. But, I don't know . . . I just couldn't get serious about him."

"He's a handsome man."

"Yes, but he's not you, Aaron. I guess that you're just a hard act to follow."

Aaron was flattered. He reached out and gently stroked Oriana's hand. "I feel the same way about you. I seriously doubt that any woman could ever take your place."

Oriana looked sad. "So why can't we get back together? I don't understand it."

"I don't either," Aaron laughed sullenly. "We can't seem to synch our lives. When I'm ready, you're not. When you're ready, I'm not." Then he looked Oriana deep in the eyes. "But we could still have a baby. I'm willing to do that, Oriana. Time is running out."

"I've still got a few years left!" she answered quickly. "I'm only thirty-seven."

"Yes, but . . . the danger of complications gets greater every year you wait. Why don't we just try for it now?"

"Because that would rip you up, Aaron! Knowing that you had a child when you couldn't be around it. Besides, the only way I'd do that is if the child did not know that you were the father. You could be Uncle Aaron. But I couldn't see making him or her live without a father, knowing that the father was out there, but that we weren't together. It just wouldn't be fair."

Aaron could feel his face heating up. "I told you before how I felt about that. If the child doesn't know that I'm the father, then I don't want any part of it. Talk about ripping me up . . . that would do it!"

"You just want to make the mind of the child in your own image. I remember what you said."

"You always twist that! Sure I said I wanted to teach the child how to think for himself. Look at all of the social and religious dogma foisted on us when we're young. I want to teach my child how to cut through that stuff. Why do you always want to make me out to be worse than that? You know me better . . . "

Oriana looked away a moment, then smiled ruefully. They both ate quietly for a time.

"Listen to us," Aaron said finally. "Here we go again. Why do we do this?"

Oriana shrugged. "I don't know . . . probably because we hurt each other so bad, and the fact that we really love each other so much. All of these years have gone by and we still talk about getting back together. Was it really so awful?"

"Of course not," Aaron insisted. "It was wonderful. It only got bad once we left Australia. Travel is hard on a relationship. I think people are at their most vulnerable then and their weaknesses show."

"And yet after we decided to split, we were able to travel on together for four weeks in perfect harmony. How do you explain that? We went into Burma and Thailand. We saw all the sights of Rangoon, Pagan, and Mandalay. And all of the sights of Bangkok. Then, even down to the island of Koh Samui for a beautiful last week together."

"That was so touching," Aaron said wistfully.

"What? When we split?"

"Yeah. I mean we did it perfectly. The last day together was our anniversary, and then poof! Gone. I'll never forget that ride in the back of the truck. You standing there waving under those palm trees. Those bright green waters behind you. A perfect tropical paradise. What lovers dream of all the time! And we gave it up."

"We had to."

"Yeah, I guess. But it's so sad."

"Do you think that we could have done otherwise?"

"Not after that last night. You got so angry. I mean we were just sitting there eating with those other couples and suddenly you were up and leaving."

"Because those other couples didn't interest me! It was our last night together and we're sitting there making stupid conversation about nothing. It wasn't as if we were sitting with some Thai family, learning a way of life. It was typical Western traveler bullcrap, and it meant nothing to me."

"So you just leave."

"Didn't you see me looking at you? I kept wanting you to take the lead. My heart was breaking sitting there."

"So you disappear into the darkness. Don't even tell me where you're going."

"You found me."

"Yeah. Sitting on the beach singing those old Hollywood movie songs. You were sitting there like a rock."

"I like to sing those songs when I'm upset. It makes me feel good."

"It makes you feel like a child, you mean. Like you don't have a care in the world."

Oriana flashed angry eyes. "This is dumb! It's pointless to talk about all of this now. It's over and done. I'm the way I am, and you're the way you are. You're always floating out there on cloud nine, and I have to play the heavy. Well, I'm tired of it. I'm not this awful person who screams all the time!"

Aaron hung his head and took a deep breath. "I know you're not, Oriana. In fact, I've never met anyone as caring and full of life as you are. You're truly an incredible person. If anything, too incredible! The rest of us can't keep up! Nobody has more energy than you. I've never met anyone with a better mind. I guess that's why I can only surmise that the fates blew us apart. It had to be a higher power. Otherwise . . . "

"I know . . . " Oriana said, wiping at a tear and smiling at the same time.

"God, Oriana! I'm so sorry that it's come to this. I never wanted to hurt you. I'd just like to take you in my arms right now and make love. I'd give anything if we could erase all of the problems."

Oriana was deeply touched. "There's nothing I'd like better either . . . "

"So, let's go."

"Go?"

"Back to my place. Let's go back and make love. Right now."

"I'm . . . I'm not sure that we should."

"I am," Aaron said confidently.

Oriana felt more tears coming on. She pulled some tissue from her purse and began dabbing at her eyes. Finally she had stopped. She took a small sip of wine, then smiled lovingly at Aaron. "Okay," she said nodding. "Let's go. I know we shouldn't, but I also know that there's nothing I'd rather do."

They hurried back to the apartment and undressed by the bed, then lay together quietly for a long while, each just feeling their warm skin against the other for the first time in painful years.

They both had tears in their eyes and on their lips and up and down each other's necks before it was finished.

14

IT HAD been over two months since Aaron had driven Oriana alone to San Francisco International. Mauricio had chosen to stay in the City for a time and pursue his jewelry-making on the streets of North Beach. Peter Varden had agreed to let him sleep on the floor in his apartment for free, so everyone knew that he would be all right for a time.

Meanwhile, Kelby had become Dr. X. Rex Kelby, and he and his associates were already hard at work on eight new models of the Vimana XRK-2. All timetables were accelerated, and patents had been secured as planned. There were now four test fliers. Eric Harrison and Jack Katz were full time, and Aaron and Peter Varden part time. There seemed to be endless excitement in the Sierra hills where the testing was being pursued. Men on Vimana were screeching back and forth through the sky without safety cables. Kelby was in ecstasy.

"These new landing sensors are perfect!" Jack Katz roared as he set down gently near Kelby. He was referring to a laser sensor which would instantly retract the small delta wings when a flier was ready to land. The wings reached down to just below the knees, and the flier was not able to walk or run with the wings out. But with the retractor beam automatically folding in the three-piece wing on each side just as the flier set down, the legs were freed for landing upright. It was the main new feature of the XRK-2.

Kelby smiled radiantly at Jack. He was especially proud that his Vimana could support a large man with as much ease as it did the smaller fliers. "Bring her around another couple of times, Jack! We need to be sure that the sensor mechanism is failsafe."

"Hi-dee-ho, doctor! I'm burning wind!" He ran four large steps while switching on the thruster. In a second, he was airborne again, and the delta wing moved smoothly into place beneath his body. He rode at a sharp angle up into the sky, then looped back onto a parallel course with Eric, who was monitoring a device which measured effects of wind currents and air temperatures of his flypack. Jack waved slyly as he raced ahead of Eric and laughed hard to himself. He couldn't believe that he was now being paid for doing something that was so much fun. The only hard part was dealing with Kelby's insistence that he cut out all stimulants. He thought about how much fun it would be to smoke some herb and fly around the countryside. But Kelby was an absolute tyrant in the matter. Each day he checked his men before they flew, and if there was any suspicion at all, he would ground the man for the day. It had only taken Jack one grounding to understand how serious Kelby was about it. There would be no adverse publicity or the injuring of a flier as long as Kelby had control. He would see to that.

After Kelby stood watching for a time, he was summoned to the phone in his limo. Carlos told him that Aurora was on the line and he had quietly walked off to watch the fliers and give Kelby his privacy. In a moment, Kelby had the phone at his ear.

"Hi!" Aurora giggled. "How's it going out there?"

"Very nice, darling. I'm very pleased."

"Good!" Aurora shouted. "Then you will finish on time today?"

"I suppose so . . . " Kelby answered noncommittally. "I'll try."

"We miss you here in the studio these days," she whined. "But nobody misses you like me." Her voice was almost childish.

"Just wait until I get you alone tonight," Kelby laughed. "I won't miss."

"Oh, I can't wait . . . " Aurora bubbled in that Oriental voice which Kelby found irresistible. "I will finger you all over with special ancient massage treatment. How does that sound?"

"Too perfect," Kelby laughed. "I bet these flying boys could use a treatment like that after everything we put them through today!"

"Not by me, Doctor Rex! I'm only for you!"

Kelby laughed uproariously. "You know, Aurora, it's hard to believe that a woman who sounds as cute as you do can be the executive president of a national company and get away with it!"

"That's because the dollar talks louder than me. I have no trouble there."

"So business is good today?"

"Business is fantastic! You should come in sometime again," she kidded. "You'd be amazed how fast we're growing."

"Well, you'd be amazed how fast we're flying! We've got eight new models going, and we sure won't be stopping there."

"Maybe we should merge," Aurora laughed. "We could have flying cameramen and incredible dream flying scenes! It would be even better than what the holographic simulator makes. It would be the real thing!"

"You're beginning to sound like Aaron, now!"

"Aaron! He's one of your fliers, right?"

"Yes. He's Eric's brother."

"What did he say?"

"Oh, you should have heard him. He's worse than me! He spent all morning telling me how we should corner the market fast on flypacks and offer the world's first personal recreational flying club."

"That would be dangerous, exposing the general public to this kind of flying. People need to be trained."

"Which was precisely his point. If we offer our devices through a controlled outlet, we could see to it that only trained people ever fly them. In fact, we wouldn't sell any at all. Why should some spoiled rich kid get one of these things and go out and smash up on the side of some building?"

"So . . . there would be a club?"

"Exactly. We rent the flypacks to responsible people only. We keep control. It is essential that we make this form of flying safe! One death and our name is mud."

"You sound rather convinced about the whole thing."

"I'm not positive yet, but I am intrigued by the idea. My biggest fear is the way young people drink and do drugs these days. It's way out of control, and I'm scared to death that one of them is going to go for the ultimate high on one of my fly packs. What could be more exciting? He thinks he's on a flying motorcycle! Hell's Angels with real wings! Then, smack! He slams head first into a mountain. Not that drugs don't do what we all know they do . . . but there is a time and a place for everything."

"So, maybe a club is the only answer."

"Yes, and screening all members."

"You need to educate your fliers, too. Expand their minds and show them other ways to ecstasy. Just make them more secure in themselves so that they can be strong . . . "

There was a long pause. Suddenly, Kelby laughed. "Aurora? Are you thinking what I'm thinking?"

Aurora giggled. "Yes, of course, the answer is obvious, isn't it?"

"It is now," Kelby said. "It is now. Looks like we're going to merge after all!"

There was another long pause. "Maybe this Aaron fellow might be the right person to set up the whole operation," Aurora suggested. "What do you know about him?"

"He's the manager at Paragon."

"Oh! He's the same one! I've spoken with him many times."

"Of course."

"So, he has management experience, and he's very stable."

"Well . . . " Kelby said, drawing out the word. "At least he has been stable."

"What do you mean?"

"Maybe it's nothing, but he did say something strange this morning."

"What's that?"

"He said that his ex-wife had called him this morning. She lives in L.A. And now, apparently, she's pregnant."

"By him?"

"That's the story."

Part 3

15

HE STREAKED over Kong Chow Temple then playfully looped a pagoda back on Grant. He could see hundreds of Chinese characters on hundreds of signs, pagoda-style lamplights with writhing dragons, vegetable, flower and trinket vendors on the sidewalks and soaring archways leading into endless Oriental emporiums. Chinatown was humming as usual. But in those early morning hours, it was Aaron Harrison who both surprised and delighted the residents and tourists with the genuine sound of humming that day. He felt imperious and impervious and light-heartedly impish. He imagined himself as some alien here, mounted on a purring gentle dragon, cutting through a warm sheath of air over a cheering crowd of well-wishers. People pointed and children clapped their hands. He only wished that he had a great long dragon kite tail trailing behind him to make the spectacle even better, even more exciting. But he knew that his metallic gold flysuit was glittering wildly in the sunlight and that the matching Vimana XRK-4 and its shimmering delta wings made spectacle enough. His heart beat a reveler's beat. Adrenalin rushed supreme through his veins. He was on top of the world, both literally and figuratively, and he cut a perfect dashing form as he pushed on, screeching joyfully over San Francisco.

The flier wended his way past sleek skyscrapers and old Victorian mansions. He marveled at witch's hat turrets and Gothic balustrades. A cable car clattered along in the distance.

Finally, he was over Haight-Ashbury. Colorful houses and pedestrians were everywhere. A small street fair appeared like a miniature jamboree as sunlight poured down over it all and hundreds looked up happily in dark sunglasses, many waving.

Then he saw it up on the hill. It had domes and spires and an incredible stained glass window. The shape of the window was circular and bore three wings revolving around an axis. It was the now famous triskelion symbol of the Order of Vimana, and it nearly rivaled the greatest rose windows in the finest cathedrals in the world. It had been X. Rex Kelby's special pet project, and he had spent huge sums to have it designed and installed in place of a pre-existing circular stained glass window. Now it represented the Order to millions. Kelby knew it would, which is why he spared no expense on perfecting it. Within the wings were a thousand and one tiny dream scenes. The axis itself was a small round window of deep purple glass, and it represented the void out of which all life flows.

Aaron flew on. He zeroed in on the special landing platform set up high near the roof of the Vimana Cathedral. In a moment he was cruising in toward it, slowly descending with an arrested velocity.

Suddenly, the jeers went up. Loud voices booed, and picket signs stabbed at the air. Fists flashed high and menacing as Aaron's heart pounded nervously. He looked down on the restless protesters and immediately felt upset and resentful that the crowd's hostility should threaten to drive out the joy and upbeat excitement of his flight in. But they were there and they could not be ignored. Fortunately for the flier, the crowd had no wings of their own. They could only yell and make loud noises. Police kept them out of the building, and where Aaron landed no one had yet succeeded in climbing up to actually pose a serious challenge. Then, too, the Order of Vimana had its own guards at the landing platform, though none had guns. But it was safe, and Aaron felt glad about that. His delta wings began slowly retracting. By the time he set down, his legs were unencumbered and he ran a few quick paces as the folding wing became a narrow and semi-forward pointing aeroflap. He immediately notified the tower through the radio transmitter in his helmet that he had touched down successfully. When he removed the helmet, he looked up and waved at the young lady behind glass in the control spire. She had guided him in perfectly and she waved back with a grin.

The crowd was still jeering. Aaron could only make out one chant as he strode on into the club. "Out of God's house!" they shouted over and over. "Out of God's house, now!"

Aaron shrugged and went on into the storeroom on the balcony level. When he closed the door, he could hear no more angry cries, only upbeat rock on a P.A. system. He moved with the bouncy rhythm and went quickly to his large locker to stow his gear. He unzipped the gold flysuit, stepped out of it, then adjusted his dark blue jumpsuit. In a moment, he was headed out another door and down the flight of stairs leading to the foyer. As he passed the huge wooden front door, he heard something thud against it and he cringed inside for a second. But then he pushed open the interior doors and entered the nave. Beautiful rainbows of sunlight poured down onto the pillars and floor of the grand central chamber. His heart was instantly aflutter again with excitement. The sight always sent his mind reeling. He looked ahead forward to where an altar had once been and marveled at the Titan gold-plated sculpture which dominated the entire wall. There his eyes beheld a fantastic rendering of a naked man and woman flying in a great arched orbit, both in tasteful repose and each appearing to chase the other in an eternal circle. From their backs fluttered huge wings as if they were angels. It was a masterful Blakean work, and Aaron felt proud of its sheer majesty. The awesome interplay of color and light shimmering over it made it seem even more grand in the fabulous morning rays of the new day. He quickly forgot all about the disturbing scene outside the walls of the cathedral-cum-fortress.

"Should have known it was you causing all the ruckus out there, Aaron!" The voice was friendly and mischievous. It was Rachel Rarick, Eric's long time lover.

"Hi, Rachel," Aaron laughed. "Why are you here so early?"

"Probably the same reason you are. I wanted to record a dream and run it through the computer to see about motif parallels. It was most interesting!"

"Great . . . I'll have to hear all about it. By the way, how's my brother doing these days? I haven't seen him for awhile."

"He's crazy as ever. You know Eric . . . always the clown."

Aaron laughed quietly then nodded for Rachel to accompany him. "How about giving me a hand on the analyzer? I always mess it up, and I've got a dream to record."

"Oh yes . . . it's so difficult," Rachel teased.

"Okay!" Aaron snickered. "So I just want your company."

Rachel had every intention of joining him, but she pretended uncertainty. "I don't know . . . "

"Oh, come on!" Aaron hissed, grabbing the girl by her neck playfully. They both laughed and walked on toward the far door to the right of the nave where the computer room was located. "Now tell me . . . " Aaron joked. "When is that trapeze weasel going to get here? I assume that he's coming to the Rite of Passage, isn't he?"

Rachel nodded. "He'll be here. When? Who knows." They both knew how he loved to sleep in.

Inside the computer room, Aaron sat at a keyboard and typed in his special code letters and the date. "Hey!" he suddenly laughed. "That's right!"

"What's right?" Rachel asked, looking perplexed. Her thick brown hair had been thrown over one shoulder, and she sat forward on her chair.

"It was four years ago today that I first flew a Vimana. I forgot all about it until now!"

"I guess that it's becoming old news," the girl said dryly. "I've only been flying a little over a year and a half, and it already seems like I've been doing it forever."

"That's because you started so young. It's hardly any different for you than getting your driver's license."

"Oh yeah, you're an old man at thirty-three."

"About to be thirty-four," Aaron said as if correcting her.

"Well Eric's thirty-five!"

Aaron laughed and threw a switch on the console.

"Are you going to voice-type?" Rachel asked.

Aaron nodded. "Wait until you hear this dream. It's funny and mystical all at the same time."

"Are your dreams ever not mystical?" Rachel teased. "Mr. Cosmic strikes again."

"Rachel!"

"Okay, I'll be quiet. I'll be quiet."

"Thank you. Now . . . "

"Push that code index button first."

Aaron looked sideways at the girl as she giggled. "Thank you again," he said smartly, but with a grin. It was all friendly banter.

"Beginning body of dream," he said into the microphone after he had switched on the code indexer. "Aaron Harrison, dreamer: I was with a young lady at a long table like in some medieval banquet room. I do not know who she was and therefore conclude that she was the anima. I cannot describe her looks at all except that she did have long hair. Anyway, we were alone at this long wooden table, and I was asking her everything about herself. I wanted to know her ancestry, where she came from and where she now lived. Her likes and dislikes, everything. I wanted to hear about each day she had lived since she was born. I went on and on . . .

"Finally, it was too much! She pulled out a scroll of her life and rolled it down the long table. It was so long that it went clear off the end and onto the floor. We both began laughing madly.

"Then I acted like a dog! I leapt up on the table, right on the scroll, and went speed-reading over it. I even sniffed and yipped playfully like a dog as I crawled along. We were both laughing hysterically! We couldn't stop! It was too hilarious." Aaron made faces to accompany the dialogue, which brought gales of laughter from Rachel.

"After a while though, we quit laughing and I laid on the table and kissed her. It was very warm and loving . . . "

Rachel smiled broadly as Aaron looked over at her. She had tears in her eyes from trying to refrain from laughing aloud when Aaron had recounted the first part of the dream. She shook her head and turned away from his gaze.

"Then, after a time," Aaron continued, "she suddenly sat back and had a startled look on her face. 'See that spirit over there!' she said with a serious tone to her voice. I looked but I couldn't see anything at first. But then I saw a faint white glow begin to grow over by the wall.

"All at once it spiralled toward us, then flew in circles around the girl's head. It spooked her, and she began flailing her arms. I jumped up and began shouting the Tibetan exorcist chant. 'Phat!' I yelled over and over 'Phat! Get out!' At last, I succeeded in chasing the demon away, if it was a demon.

"After that I was outside at a Tibetan festival. I could see huge snow-covered mountains all around and Tibetan people in dark woolen clothes. Several men were dancing, and they all flung glasses against a stone wall at the end of the dance. I was shocked but intrigued. Glass shattered and flew everywhere.

"Then I looked up at the fabulous Himalayas again, and in the distance I could see a strange flying vehicle coming toward us. It descended as it neared the festival, and as it passed over I could see that it was a sleek convertible car without wheels. I really marveled.

"Meanwhile, a special magic act began nearby, and I saw a magician create bizarre pieces of fruit out of nothing. They were fruits I have never seen before, and I just looked on with my mouth wide. I was totally in awe."

After a moment's pause, he finalized the text. "End of dream," he said in a straight tone. "A.H. 284, out."

It was Rachel who reached over and flicked the voice decode button. "Wait until Mauricio hears about this one," she laughed. "He'll love it."

Aaron smiled and began pushing other buttons. "The motif parallels should be intriguing."

Rachel jumped up. "Mauricio's here already. I'll go get him while you run that through. He'll want to see the results."

"Well don't interrupt him if he's in the middle of teaching a yoga class."

"I won't," Rachel called back, then disappeared out the door. Two seconds later the door opened again.

"That was fast," Aaron laughed, without looking up. There was only silence. Then he lifted his eyes from the console. Peter Varden stood there grinning beside his girlfriend, Rebekka, a small black girl who always wore bright red lipstick. Peter presented a stark contrast beside her with his pale white skin. He had astoundingly large blue eyes and a receding hairline. But his sidelocks were long and he had a full beard, which gave him the look of a gentle monk.

"Nice crowd out there today," Peter cracked, but his voice bore no real malice.

Aaron rolled his eyes. "Yeah . . . it's just too bad that I didn't persuade a flock of pigeons to follow me when I flew in today."

Rebekka pretended to be shocked. "Aaron!" she roared. "How could you?"

"Well it wouldn't be easy."

Peter began chuckling quietly.

"Maybe I could become friends with the leader of the pack . . . "

"Stop it!"

"Or better yet! How about if we jump in our gear and we'll fill up lots of balloons with dye and water and we'll make a little bombing run."

"I don't believe this guy," Rebekka moaned, shaking her head.

"What's wrong?" Aaron laughed. "When we were in Nepal, people threw balloon bombs at us! And they called it Holi Festival!"

Rebekka looked off at a far corner and grinned in silence, shaking her head. Peter was quietly amused.

"Don't worry, Rebekka," Aaron finally said. "I understand why they're out there. But that doesn't mean I have to like it. Anyway . . . so, did you two have a nice flight in?"

"We didn't fly."

"You didn't!"

"No, we drove," Peter explained. "My leg's been bothering me. I twisted it on a landing the other day."

"But I'll be flying today at the Rite!" Rebekka cheered, holding up her arms in triumph.

Aaron grinned. "Congratulations," he said, his head bobbing approvingly.

"Guess who else is being initiated today!" Peter laughed.

Aaron leaned back and shook his head. "Who?" He had no idea.

Peter's face began twitching with suppressed amusement. "Carlos!" he laughed finally.

"Again!" Aaron roared. "How does he manage to get initiated once a year?"

"He falls off the wagon," Rebekka sneered affectionately. "And he gets grounded. I don't know why Kelby puts up with him sometimes."

"He's really a good guy," Peter laughed. "Kelby knows that. It wouldn't be the same around here without him."

Aaron snickered, but was nodding his agreement at the same time.

Then Rachel was back and Mauricio was with her. Greetings were exchanged all around.

"Where's Eric?" Peter asked.

"He'll be here."

"Good, I need to talk to him about demonstrating techniques to some of my students while my ankle's laid up."

Mauricio sat with a print-out and began studying it. "This is an interesting dream, Aaron . . ." he said quietly. The women went to another console, and Rachel began showing Rebekka how to operate it.

"Will you be able to use this in your study?" Aaron asked.

"I can't remember one quite like it, though the motifs have a lot of parallels. Here, look at these." He handed the print-out to Aaron, and he and Peter hunched over it and began reading.

"What are these codes?" Peter asked, pointing at some numbers on the right hand side of the page.

"Those are codes in my study," Mauricio explained. "I'm compiling an anthology of Tibetan influences on modern society."

"The magic and the mystery . . . " Aaron laughed.

"Do you think all of those stories are for real?" Peter asked.

"When I was staying in Tibet, I once saw some yogins being initiated in *tummo*." Mauricio explained.

"What's that?"

"That's where they sit in the snow in the mountains, stark naked, and the older men put wet sheets over their bodies. They have to make fire within. I mean, the inner heat has to come and they have to dry the sheets in freezing weather to show that they've mastered that yoga. They make so much heat that all the snow around them melts!"

"And they do fire-walking, too," Aaron explained. "Not at the same time though!" There was laughter.

"I've heard about that stuff," Peter said, nodding with a serious look on his face. "But what about levitation? And do some of those guys really walk from mountain-top to mountain-top without going down into the valley?"

Mauricio's eyes went wide. He and Peter looked hard at each other, and Aaron thought about how the light blue of each man's eyes seemed to mirror the other. There was a mounting excitement in Mauricio's face. But just as he began to speak, Rebekka and Rachel cut in.

"It's about that time," Rachel said.

"Yeah!" Rebekka laughed. "Honey, we are gonna fly like angels! Let's get to it!"

16

THE GOLD organ pipes were already breathing out vast drafts of polyphonic melody when Aaron made his way to his seat in the nave. Almost everyone was in place, and Aaron looked out on the crowd with solemn pride, although he did have to laugh when he saw Eric rushing to his seat out of breath. The great nave had thick padded, black theater chairs all in a ring around the huge room in twenty-three rows. Each chair could tilt back fully, so that optimum viewing comfort could be had by all when the Rite began.

Then the organ song ended, and there was a restless pause as voices filled the hall. The silence signaled that the ceremony would begin. A special introduction had become the opening theme of the Vimana Rite of Passage. Everyone recognized it and fell quiet. A synthesizer began skittering short bursts of echoic counterpoint harmony against the flowing melody of the organ. Aaron could feel his body quavering as the deep resonant bass notes shook the hall. The smell of aloeswood incense filled his nose, and he mused on the curling jets of smoke which floated lazily up into the colored beams of light which were there drenching the room in warm sun rays. Stained glass rainbows were prismed high and low over all the walls and faces of the assembly. Aaron felt almost as if he were floating.

For a time, the tune persisted with deft syncopation, then all at once it broke into a fast-paced rhapsody which soared on chromatic splendor. A choir of voices joined in when the melody swelled into mournful minor chords. And so it went through the prelude until the voices began to rise on a quickened rhythm, as the organ and synthesizer both built for a heart-rending crescendo.

Then the fliers began their first ceremonious foray into the bright rainbow light of the high-ceilinged nave. They flew out from a special balcony, one by one, at a rapid clip until there were twenty-four thrusters hissing out in windy unison from the chests of the exuberant initiates. It was here that they would demonstrate the control they had long sought under the rigorous Vimana training program. And it was here that they would attain to a privileged status in the hierarchy of the club, though this was only the beginning. But it was the important first step so necessary to continuing on in the exciting world of Vimana flying. So they soared round and round as they had rehearsed it, hissing through the ethereal wispy luminescence high above the assembly in a great moving ellipse.

Then suddenly, two fliers broke rank and darted gracefully into the center space and began a contrapuntal air ballet, chasing and mimicking each other's movements. It went on through twelve pairs, each couple creating their own flying dance as the music rippled with crescendo after crescendo. It was a masterly show, and the crowd responded with rounds of applause for each pair. At last, they all made their way back onto the balcony and quickly lined up at the front of it with their helmets off. Sustained applause welcomed them into the Order of Vimana as their names were read and insignias were given to each. The initiates smiled and waved with sincere appreciation. The ceremony had proceeded flawlessly, and hopeful future initiates sat in their section drawing in deep breaths of air, each imagining what it would be like when their day finally came.

Afterwards, Eric found himself confronted by one such worried hopeful and he thought it humorous. "Are you kidding?" he joked. "These packs have enough power to send a fat old witch screeching from here halfway to Salem in one blast!"

The girl had not yet had her first flying lesson, but she had witnessed the Rite. Now she had Eric cornered and was pumping him for information. The Rite had frightened her into thinking that she could never achieve such adeptness. Eric's remark had made her laugh, but not before her lip went limp and a startled look had flashed across her face.

"Slight exaggeration," Aaron said in his deepest voice as he approached.

Eric turned and laughed. "Well, well . . . if it isn't Sky King himself."

"What's this guy telling you?" Aaron asked the girl. She giggled and quickly introduced herself.

"I'm Sara Tynes," she said. "I already know who you are."

Aaron bowed slightly, then raised his eyebrows. "So what's this about screeching witches? Is my brother trying to scare you?"

"Just a little lesson in power," Eric laughed. "She's afraid she might fall down out of the sky."

"I don't think so . . . " Aaron chuckled.

"So it's powerful enough . . . "

" . . . that it would set your fanny up in the clouds with power to spare!" Eric wisecracked. "Don't worry about it!"

The girl smiled coyly.

"You'll see, Sara," Aaron said seriously. "We've got classes to teach you everything that you'll need to know."

"But it's not guaranteed that I'll fly, right?"

"True. We do have preliminary tests that you'll have to take. You'll probably get a crack at some flying, but it's up to your own abilities if you ever reach an initiation."

"Yeah," Eric snickered. "It depends on how crazy you are."

"Crazy?"

"I think he really means how daring you are. This is not a club for the fainthearted. We screen our applicants as well as we can, and when they get to this point like you, then . . . well, it's up to you."

"I can understand that," Sara said. "But I really don't understand why you make people report their dreams. And why is this club in a church, anyway?"

"Eric looked away and began slowly tapping his foot. Aaron tried to field the questions in as simple terms as possible. He was anxious to talk to Eric alone.

"Dreams offer a way of staying closely in tune with your deeper thoughts. If you know your mind, then you know your Self. The deeper Self. We feel that dreams are directly linked to the forces which exist outside of time. It's the eternal in all of us. By tuning into that, we connect with our spiritual side. That means a balance of our dual natures, because we're both physical beings and spiritual beings. So we're looking to complete ourselves, to be a whole being."

"So that's why you took over a church. You've made this thing into something spiritual."

"Well, yes and no. What I'm telling you is that there is that side to it because we don't want our people to be a bunch of shallow hedonists who abuse these incredibly expensive flying machines, get in wrecks and think that it's all television lunacy. We want responsible people who can offer society something. Kind of a new order within the old. We feel that we're forerunners of a new age."

Sara was frowning when Aaron finished his explanation. "So you didn't really have to have this in a church?"

"No, not really. It was purely for spectacle. And . . . the fact that both Kelby and I had dreams of flying in a cathedral. We decided to make it for real."

"X. Rex Kelby?"

"Yes. Of course."

"Where is he, anyhow?" Eric wanted to know. "I didn't see him here this morning."

"He and Aurora are setting up the San Diego chapter."

"Why there?"

Aaron shrugged. "Well, for one thing, he got a lead on a huge church which was going under there. The congregation just couldn't support the high costs anymore. Then when Kelby found out through some contact down there, I think it was an assistant at U-Star, he and Aurora began making calls. Looks like it's a go now."

"Where at, exactly?"

"I'm not sure, Sara. I understand that it was a Lutheran church, though."

The girl seemed suddenly impatient. "Well, I've got to get going now. It was nice talking to you two. I really look forward to getting to know you better." She was polite but abrupt.

"Okay, so good luck," Aaron said.

She began walking away. "See you, Eric!" she called out, glancing over her shoulder.

Eric smiled and nodded. He quickly looked at Aaron with a raised brow and shook his head when the girl had disappeared through a doorway. "Don't say it," he told Aaron in a serious voice.

"Well, she's different anyway," Aaron commented. "She has potential."

Several people walked by and both Aaron and Eric gave greetings, then turned back to each other.

"So how goes it?" Eric asked. "I haven't seen you for awhile. How's the baby?"

"She's great!" Aaron laughed. "I've been having more fun with her . . . !" He became lost for words and finally just shook his head.

"We'll have to get over there and see her again. Did you talk to Rachel today? Maybe we can get together for dinner or something."

"Yeah, I saw her. She was here really early. What did she do, leave you to sleep in again?"

Eric laughed. "Every chance I get . . . "

"Let's go see if she's back there with the initiates." He gestured with his chin.

Eric turned and the two slowly began walking.

"I've been needing to talk to you about something, Eric."

"What's that?"

"You know that new student in your class, Brad Neiman? I believe that's the name."

"Yeah, what about him?"

"Have you noticed anything strange about him? Anything at all?"

"I'm not sure. I guess nothing stands out in my mind. Why?"

"It may be nothing, but just keep an eye on him, okay? He worries me for some reason."

"Well, what am I looking for?"

"Not this!" Aaron shouted suddenly as he saw the huge shadow of a man come at them, poised to attack.

"What?" Eric barked, turning in total confusion. But then, all at once, he was in the air, hoisted up by powerful arms. He began writhing to free himself until he saw who it was who had him. He quit struggling at once.

"Awww . . . !" came the booming voice. "You'll never escape the grip of the dragon!"

"More like an ape!" Eric yelped. "Put me down!"

It was Jack Katz, and he was grinning like a card shark on a roll. He set Eric down, then adjusted his flysuit with a flourish. "Well . . . how do you like it?"

Aaron looked stunned. Jack's suit was a glittery black with a large yin-yang symbol on the left side over his chest. The right side bore the Vimana triskelion of wings in the exact same size. When he turned around, a huge bright dragon with fiery tongue shimmered there on his back below his long, blond hair.

"You've outdone yourself this time, Jack!" Aaron laughed.

"More like *overdone* yourself, I'd say!" Eric wisecracked. He began laughing hard as he studied the costume.

Jack was unfazed. He pulled a small object out of his pocket and pushed his finger through a loop of string. "And . . . to top it off . . . " He flashed the side of the object. It was a hand-sized yin-yang. On the other side was the triskelion. He suddenly flipped the object out of his palm. It was a yo-yo. "That's right . . . my friends," he laughed loudly, "a yin-yang yo-yo! And one for my bros." He reached into a pocket and pulled another out and gave it to Eric. "All the secrets of the universe right at your fingertips!" He gave his a toss and let it spin just above the floor.

"I see you've finally marketed it," Aaron laughed. "I never thought you were really serious."

"I'm not really serious. That's why I marketed it!"

"I begin to understand," Aaron said, rolling his eyes as Jack handed him one. He was genuinely amused.

"So what's doing today? You're coming with us, aren't you?"

"Sure, as soon as I find Rachel," Eric answered, flipping his yo-yo and chuckling.

"I'll go," Aaron added, "but then it's straight home for me." He gestured with his hand, pointing.

The three began walking on toward the locker room to get their equipment.

"There you are . . . " Eric said when he saw Rachel. She was standing in the hall talking to Katerina Markovich and Damon Burke. She gave Eric a quick hug then whispered something in his ear. He grinned and let out a sly laugh.

"So Rachel is flying lead this morning!" Katerina said exuberantly to Aaron and Jack. "I can't wait to see where she takes us!"

Rachel turned and grinned. "Don't worry, I've got it all planned."

"So let's get suited up!" Damon laughed. "We've got a couple of dozen anxious virgins back there waiting in the wings. They want to fly, so let's not disappoint."

"Is Tamara flying?" Katerina asked Jack as they all hurried off to the gear room.

"You bet. She's waiting with Peter and Rebekka now. It's time to burn wind!"

Rachel Rarick stood poised like a goddess on the launch platform, or so Eric thought as he watched her take her position at the front of the contingent. Her metallic purple flysuit gleamed in the sun, and she had to tuck her thick brown hair under her collar before she could put her helmet on. Her gold earrings flashed as she turned her head from side to side. She turned, and Eric looked deep into her brown eyes. He was ready to follow her anywhere forever.

In a moment, the helmet was on. She held up her hand and signaled the pack to prep. Eric quickly donned his helmet and moved up nearer to Rachel. Then she signaled again, and her jet began purring. She checked the delta wing, and it moved easily, ready for the final unfolding. A last signal and she was running; four quick steps and the thruster thundered with a muffled roar. Then she was over the edge as a crowd of protesters screamed far below in the shadows of the great Vimana Cathedral. But flypack after flypack screeched out in rapid succession, each flier literally hot on the heels of the preceding flier. In seconds, Rachel was beyond the hostile crowd, streaking high over old Victorian houses, then over Golden Gate Park and on against the ocean breeze. The fliers moved into formation and followed with precise navigation. Soon they were passing over the old park windmill, then on out over Ocean Beach. Rachel leaned into a semi-roll and curved off to the right as great white ocean breakers rose up and curled powerfully beneath them. Surfers and sunbathers waved excitedly, many jumping up and down on the hot summer sands.

In mere minutes, they were all passing over Seal Rocks and the Cliff House and moving on out straight to the mouth of San Francisco Bay. They screeched on until curving right again. Huge tankers and small sailboats were cutting over mildly choppy waters. Then they began the inland push, streaking exuberantly forward toward the soaring pillars of the Golden Gate Bridge. Fourty-four fliers at the top of their form. Forty-four agile colorful fliers riding the downwind breeze. They looped the great bridge. They roared over Alcatraz and flashed by Coit. They rolled into a huge glittering ring as they soared round and round the sharp tip of the monolithic Transamerica Pyramid, creating the most fabulous carousel of all time high over the cool gray city of San Francisco.

17

WHEN AARON landed on the roof of his apartment building in North Beach, he was met by a pair of cool gray eyes. The man was tall and thin with gray hair. He wore a blue navy coat and walked slowly with a limp. Aaron did not know his full name, but the man called himself R.B. He was often standing alone up on the roof. A few times he and Aaron had talked. But the man said very little. Yet he would always listen attentively as Aaron talked about his own life. The few times Aaron had asked directly personal questions the man had just looked at him in stony, but friendly silence. He would not reveal his past, his present work situation or even his last name. He had at one point revealed one piece of information about his mysterious past: he had been a heroin junkie for sixteen years. But he was clean now, and he had found God in his own way, and he was very grateful to be alive. His eyes showed a very subtle spark of inner joy, and Aaron always found him to be warm and kind. He nodded slowly when Aaron took off his helmet and began talking to him.

"How's it going today, R.B.?"

The man nodded.

Aaron walked slowly to his side and they stood quietly together a moment, looking out over the houses and hills of North Beach.

"How's the garden?" Aaron asked, referring to the small plot the man had in the tiny back yard of the apartment building.

"It's fine," he answered. Aaron waited for him to say more, but he didn't. Finally when he did speak, it was not about gardening. "How's Ariel?" he wanted to know?

"She's doing great! I'll have to bring her up sometime. She's so beautiful and getting so big!"

R.B. smiled. "I haven't seen her for awhile. How long's it been?"

"The fourth of July, I think. Remember that? When the zeppelin flew over and we could see the fireworks exploding everywhere. That was great! And all the firecrackers. Those stupid rockets that sounded like some Martian getting his throat slit . . . "

R.B. began laughing hard. He remembered well, and it had struck him as hilarious. He began convulsing and rocking on his feet before slowly limping toward the edge of the rooftop to catch his breath. Aaron looked on chuckling, but more amused that he had gotten such a big laugh at all. It made him feel really good.

After a time, the two were both quiet again. R.B. had limped back toward Aaron then abruptly headed for the rooftop door. He was unpredictable.

"Got to go in . . . " he said, nearly straight-faced again. "I just hope those damn bikers are finished working out front. The fumes are awful." He shook his head.

Aaron fell in behind him, holding his helmet and watching as the big man limped down each stair carefully. "See you later," he told him as R.B. went to his door. R.B. nodded and smiled, saying nothing. Then he was gone. Aaron hurried down another flight of stairs and was soon opening his own door.

"There's my baby!" he laughed as he stepped in and saw Ariel. She gurgled and flung her arms helter skelter with sudden excitement, a huge toothless grin spreading across her face as she sat in her infant seat. Aaron went to her and rubbed his hand over her head of tossled brown hair. She squeaked with delight, then gurgled again, rolling her huge blue eyes.

"Hi! When did you get in?" a voice called out from the kitchen.

"Just now. What's new?"

"What could be new here? I feed her, I change her, I watch her spit up on me. We have fun."

Aaron stood up and went quietly to the kitchen as if sneaking. Suddenly, his hands grabbed the woman's waist, and she screamed as if she had not been expecting the pretend attack. She quickly responded by shaking out a little salt at Aaron over her shoulder.

"There's an assault for you!" she teased and they rolled into a laughing kiss. Then, just as quickly, she was back to her salad, chopping up green peppers and mushrooms. "How did it go today?"

Aaron leaned back against the counter and shook his head. "Great! We did the Grand Prix flyrun! Right up the bay and curved on in to circle the pyramid."

"Who led?"

"Cleopatra."

"Rachel, again?"

"What can I say? She's good."

"How would you know?"

"Hey! You're supposed to say 'Lucky for Eric.' "

"I never say what I'm supposed to say, that's why I always get myself in trouble."

Her name was Phoebe Faneros, and she and Aaron had been living together for just under two years. Her hair was short and spiky and colored blond. Her eyes a pale green but etched at the edges in a powder blue. She bore the look of the streetwise and flashed her radiant grin only when she was truly amused. Though very pretty, she did not smile to be pretty. She had been toughened way beyond her years by the two long relationships she had had prior to meeting Aaron. Now finally the pain of all that was nearly gone. And with the birth of Ariel, she had at last found the real meaning of love. After all the years of angst, she could at last relax and be happy, though there were times she was still sure that it would all go away. But that vulnerability had given her a purity of vision such as Aaron had never before encountered. It often stunned him. What she thought was immediately made vocal and that had changed Aaron's way of thinking.

It had all begun as a lark. Both Aaron and Phoebe had neither wanted to be serious with the other. They had both needed good times again, lightness of being, raw physicality. Phoebe was well known at the rock clubs, and Aaron was happy to be a part of that scene. When it got serious, they both fought it, but it was meant to be, they decided. Ariel was proof of that.

Now Aaron had his arms around her as she worked at finishing the salad. He was hugging her gently. Her gold chain, which was loaded with charms and pendants, rattled as she moved.

But, just as she finished, the phone rang and Phoebe scurried from Aaron's hands to answer it. "Go ahead and start . . . " she called out behind her as she crossed the living room. She flopped down in the big chair and grabbed the receiver. "Freddy's Fish Market!" she said in a loud exaggerated voice, ready to laugh.

Aaron turned to look and could see Phoebe's reflection in the mirror. She was turning pale and serious. She spoke in a low voice for a moment, then shuffled back to the kitchen.

"I don't believe it!" she whispered, looking embarrassed. "I was expecting Phil to call. I just made a fool out of myself."

"Why? Who is it?"

"Oriana . . . "

"Really? I haven't heard from her since the birth!" He smiled and looked teasingly at Phoebe. "What did you say when you answered? Freddy's Fish Market? My god!"

"Well . . . you know how Phil loves fish!"

Aaron laughed as he crossed the room. Then he had the phone at his ear, still grinning at Phoebe.

"Hi!"

"Hello! I see that you're not lacking for humor these days. Funny . . . "

"Yeah, she's funny alright." He winked at Phoebe, then sat back in the chair.

"How's the baby? How are you?"

Aaron laughed. "Oh, we're fine." He went on to bring Oriana up to date on Ariel's progress, which was remarkably precocious by any standard.

"And how's Vimana?" she asked next. She always led a conversation with rapid questions and would never tell about herself until the other party forced their way in to get a quick question, too. Aaron knew this better than anyone, so he was surprised when she began telling about something which had happened to her.

"I had a flying dream last night!" she said excitedly. "I've got to tell you about it!"

Aaron waited a moment, then suddenly responded enthusiastically. "Well . . . go on! This is great!"

"You won't believe this."

"Sounds cryptic."

"No. I can't even remember much about it, really. But . . . well, all I know is that I flew, see, and then I had to land and I didn't know how."

"Ooo . . . I hope you didn't belly up on a crash landing!"

"As a matter of fact, that's exactly what I did! I had my arms out like an airplane, and I flew in over some trees then came in low over a field. And then splat!"

"Oh no!" Aaron made a funny, painful face. "Your first flying dream and you crash land! What happened next? You didn't die or anything did you?"

Oriana laughed.

"Well!"

"No. But something remarkable did happen . . . " There was a long pause.

"Go on . . . "

"Well, I landed kind of on my side." Her inflection went up on the last word, a habit she had picked up from living in Australia. "And when I woke up . . . there was a bump on my hip. A small swollen area! I'm serious!"

Aaron was fully intrigued. He began rapidly asking questions. He wanted Oriana to take a picture of the bump, but she told him that the swelling had already gone down.

"I've got to put this through the computer and see if this has happened before! I know I've heard of similar kinds of events, but I don't remember any occurring due to a dream."

"Yes, but remember that story I told you about when I was an undergraduate here at U.C.L.A.?"

"The boy?" Aaron could barely recall the story.

"Yeah! He was coming in because he had a speech problem, and we kept working with him, trying every conceivable way of getting to the root of the problem. Then one of the therapists said something about his father. I can't remember exactly what she said, but it really triggered something in the boy. He started to cry, and one side of his face began turning red. Then, all at once, we could see it: a perfect hand print across his cheek. We were stunned!"

"It's really true isn't it? The psyche never forgets."

"And neither does the body. It's all there in the nervous system."

"Just like your dream. The mind sent a message and the body responded. But this is incredible. Did you show it to anybody?"

"My brother saw it."

"What did he think?"

"You know Jim. He tried to tell me that it was a bug bite. He never believes anything I tell him."

Aaron laughed. "Well, I'm glad that you called to tell me!"

They chatted for awhile about other things. The tension of the years was at long last gone from when Oriana had lost the baby. In the torturous months that followed, it just had not worked out between them. Finally, Aaron hung up and started for the kitchen when all at once the phone rang again.

Phoebe jumped up. "That's got to be Phil. Wait until I tell him what happened."

It was Phil. Aaron handed her the phone and Phoebe giggled as she told about her gaffe. Before long, she was roaring and making all kinds of throaty noises. She loved talking to Phil. He was easily her best friend. They had gone to high school together in the valley and had kept loyally in touch, even during Phoebe's most rebellious years when she had first moved to San Francisco. She had gotten in with friends who were part of the rock scene, and it had been fairly crazy for a few years. But Phoebe herself was a guitar player, and she had never risked her own self-esteem to appear as a mere groupie. Instead, she had spent long nights talking riffs and licks with the local talent backstage and even longer nights practicing on her guitar, lost in her own private determined musical reveries. It had paid off. Just before her pregnancy had forced her to break temporarily, she and her band had hit it big in the Bay Area clubs. Their name was Ptero Boa, and it had been Phoebe who had been their creator. When she had first joined Vimana, she had indulged in a lot of reading and at one point she had studied a book on birds. Below a picture of an ancient pterodactyl, a flying creature which had become extinct near the end of the Mesozoic era, she had noted that the word "ptero" meant "winged" or "feathered" and that had stuck in her mind. Then, later, when she happened to notice in a book on myths about the Aztec god Quetzalcoatl, that he was usually symbolized by a feathered serpent, it just connected and Ptero Boa was born. She had recruited Marc Decker, the synthesizer/piano player at Vimana rites to join her. That led to other recruitments of talent picked carefully from the Vimana ranks. And when it all got tight enough, Kelby stepped in to provide money for equipment and a record demo.

Meanwhile, Aaron and Phoebe had grown closer and closer. Aaron had been more than charmed from the beginning, and it had gone quickly into a full-blown infatuation. But Phoebe tried keeping her distance for a long time, not wanting to jeopardize any devotion to her new band which was about to achieve its first successes. Still, the more they saw of each other, the more the distance receded. It was inevitable. It happened.

When Ptero Boa met with limited local success, Kelby decided that it was time for a video and as the premier song the band chose one of Phoebe Faneros' compositions. A song called *Black Jet*. The tune began with a bouncy piano lead-in comprised of a catchy bass line, followed by lead singer Stu Reuben's breathy vocal overlay:

> Red flashing lights in the far
> dying sky above a silhouette . . .
> Black Jet!
> Midflight, at midnight, and you
> lose the bet . . .
> Black Jet!
> Yeah, down from the sky
> like the crack of a whip
> lashing out a cry . . .
> Black Jet! Black Jet's in sight!
> And there at the side of the suns
> in the sky try to forget . . .
> Black Jet! Black Jet's red light!

So it went with its menacing bass notes and soaring synthesizer melody rising up into dance fantasia. The song was still big in the Bay Area when Phoebe had necessarily dropped from the scene. But manager Phil Black, with Kelby's support had begun a cross-country tour of top radio stations and important regional video programming centers. Six months had passed and *Black Jet* was finally beginning to climb on the national charts. Phoebe Faneros was more than a little nervous about all of the attention. Between following the record's progress, working out madly to get back into shape and taking care of Ariel, she was indeed anxious and often mentally and physically exhausted.

"Yes, I'm taking my vitamins," she assured manager Phil, kicking her long, slim legs over the arm of the chair. "I know! Can you imagine how tiring it is to feed a baby all day long!"

They talked on for a long while, then finished, and at last Phoebe returned to the kitchen to eat with Aaron.

"Where's Phil?" Aaron wanted to know.

"He's in New York again. He loves it there! I think that he'd really prefer to live there." She shook her head. "Maybe he's got a new boyfriend . . ." She had said it with mock condescension. "Phoebe!"

"Well . . . he makes tacky jokes about me being a mother, so I can make tacky jokes about his being gay."

"I don't know . . ."

"It's okay, Aaron. That's the way we play it. Nobody is more accepting of Phil than me."

"Anyhow . . . what about the record?"

"Good news! Oh, but I'm nervous!"

Aaron laughed. "Yeah, but this is great! Do you realize what this record could do for Vimana?"

"Always thinking of Vimana!"

"Well, I'm not worried about you. I know what that record is going to do for you!"

Phoebe leaned forward and pouted her lips erotically. "What's that?"

"Make all of the teenage boys want you as much as I do . . . "

"Well, they are really more my age." She was teasing.

"Yes. So I've noticed."

"That's what you get for hitting on a broad ten years younger."

"A broad? Is that you talking?"

She leaned further forward and nibbled at Aaron's ear. "Mmmm . . . "

"Not now, Phoebe . . . " he complained through a smile. "We've got to eat and run, remember?"

Phoebe thought a moment. "My god . . . that's tonight?!"

"Yes. Tonight. I promised certain people that we'd be there."

Suddenly, Ariel began making baby whimpers, and Phoebe looked hard at Aaron. "My god . . . I feed her and then *it* happens?"

Aaron nodded slowly. "It worried me, too, but yes, *it* happens tonight!"

18

"THAT'S IT!" the Reverend Donovan Reaves barked, throwing down his newspaper.

The others in the office looked up startled.

"What is it, Don?" Jenny Reaves asked. She feared the worst. She knew her husband's tone of voice in all of its variations. This time he was truly angry.

"They're coming to Chicago."

"Who?"

"Those California kooks, that's who. The flying people. It's right here on page one. A man named Justin DeWitt is leading it, and local people are putting up money."

"I don't understand," an elderly lady said, twisting slowly in her seat. "Who are they, Reverend?"

"Mrs. Greer, do you remember a front page picture a few months ago showing a bunch of people flying over the Golden Gate Bridge in San Francisco?"

"Flying?"

"In those new flying machines!" The Reverend was becoming more and more irritated. "Remember? They tried to make it look like a Superman joke. It's a bird, it's a plane . . . "

"No! It's Vimana!" Jenny Reaves chimed in, hoping to lighten her husband's seriousness. She laughed quietly.

"It's not funny, Jenny. They buy up old churches and convert them for their own anti-Christian ends. It's sacrilege! They desecrate the House of God!"

Mrs. Greer cringed and looked around the room. She had a look of despair on her face. The Reverend's anger had struck her at a visceral level, and she wondered if she might get sick.

"I made a vow!" the Reverend went on. "In California it's one thing. But here, it's quite another. I could care less if they want to fly around like a flock of vultures, but you know what vultures do. They prey on the helpless. In this case, they target some poor congregation that's losing its mortgage and swoop down out of the sky with big fat rolls of money. Then they take over. They've started in New York, in Boston. They're talking Atlanta, New Orleans and now Chicago. This thing is spreading like a cancer. A fast, terminal cancer. And I'm going to put an end to it!"

There was a long silence. Finally, only old Mrs. Greer dared to provoke another outburst from the Reverend with a question. "Well . . . how are you going to do it?" she asked in a quavering voice. Jenny Reaves frowned.

"Politically," the Reverend answered, somewhat more calmly. "Now, I'm a man of God, but I'm also a great believer in our political system. I've done lobbying before, and I can do it again."

"Lobby against them buying churches, Don? I'm not sure that you can."

"No, of course I can't stop them from buying churches, Jenny! This is America. They can buy anything they darn well please. But I've been following this thing. There is a lot of new legislation pending concerning where and how these Vimana things can be flown. So far these people don't even have pilot's licenses. They've flaunted state laws completely, and they're a real hazard flying around in heavily populated metropolitan areas. The whole mess has gotten tangled up in the House and Senate. But that's going to change. Nobody has been pushing hard enough against them! I will be that man who makes the difference!"

"Does that mean that you'll be going to Washington again?" Jenny Reaves wanted to know. She felt tense all over. She did not like being left alone.

"Of course!" Reverend Reaves bellowed. He was still in the throes of anger. "I have to Jenny! I don't want to." He looked mournfully at his wife. "I have to," he repeated.

"And what do I do? Sit here? What will the church do?"

Reaves thought a moment. "I'll call Jim Pate," he said. "I know that I can get him to fill in for a time."

Mrs. Greer was worried. "How long do you have to leave to do this?" she asked.

The Reverend looked at Mrs. Greer's daughter. She had been sitting quietly, saying nothing, but it upset her to see the Reverend perturbed by her mother's questions. She leaned forward and began whispering in her ear.

"I don't know, Mrs. Greer," he said suddenly. "Jenny, I don't know." He was apologetic. Mrs. Reaves stood up and walked over to her husband's desk. She picked up the paper and scanned for the article. She felt very uncomfortable about the whole issue. Their own children were great fans of science and science fiction. They had been raised to appreciate the marvels of the new technology, just as both she and her husband had been. There seemed to be an inevitableness connected to the Vimanians which she found to be worrisome, especially when she thought about her husband going up against them. She did not want to see him hurt.

The Reverend Donovan Reaves did not share his wife's idea of inevitableness where the Vimanians were concerned. The technology was acceptable to him, but not the arrogant expropriation of Christian property and the disrespectful alteration of Christian iconography. Reaves had found his life and passion in the service of his religion, and his calling had arisen out of the unexplainable void of personal tragedy, an event which had shattered the man for years and could not be fathomed except in terms of God's fate. It had occurred when he was yet a teenager and he had gone with his parents to the Caribbean for a vacation. Days went by in the bliss of an island paradise, and Reaves had found himself lost in the simple pleasures of wading in sapphire waters and romping energetically on the wide beaches. He had even met a young lady from Dallas who was vacationing with her parents there and who permitted Reaves a very exciting innocent romance. But one morning his father had gotten up early to go for a walk at dawn. He had found a remote path back through the tropical jungle which intrigued him, and he followed it. There had been a sign set out, warning against trespassing, but he simply ignored it. It had been easy for him to do, he had no intention of bothering anyone. Besides, the sign had not been there the day before when he had first discovered and followed part of the trail. And so he met his tragic end. It was swift and probably painless. He was just strolling joyfully alone when he heard the sound of a machete hacking at wood high up in a palm tree. He did not realize soon enough that his path took him directly beneath the tree that the young boy was working in, cutting down coconuts for a local hotel restaurant. Suddenly, a huge cluster fell, all connected to a sharp heavy branch. The end struck him right on the top of his head, and it easily fractured his skull. He was killed instantly.

Reaves had been a very slow phoenix to rise from the ashes of that cremation, very slow to rebuild from the ashes of his own inner death. His father had been by far the greater influence in his life. But he and his mother grew very close after the tragedy, and together they sought solace in the haven of a Baptist nave, looking up at a Savior who dominated the huge altar with his sad countenance as he forgave his malevolent torturers while he hung dying on the cross. And so one day his heart was awakened to a personal Savior who promised eternal life, life beyond this fleeting world with its unending pain and cruelties and evil unexplainable voids of tragedy. From that day forward, Donovan Reaves humbled himself and stepped into the light of the service of his Lord. He became an ordained minister years later, after a long struggle to provide income for himself and his new wife and still meet his study requirements. But he was successful and after more years of perseverance, the Reverend Reaves was given one of the largest Chicago area congregations. He became well-loved and, at times, even controversial as he fought to champion the causes of his faith.

Now he had a new mission, and his mind was racing over lists of names he had encountered in the past. Many were people who owed him favors, and many more were simply very altruistic associates and friends who would rally to his cause if he sent out the word. Some were even political contacts, and these few were especially important to him now.

But first, he thought, the battle must be taken to the nation as a whole, and he knew just the man who would offer the choicest pulpit available to the widest audience. This would be his preliminary move, to drum up instant support. "I've got to call Reverend Hennessy about this," he said aloud.

Mrs. Greer's mouth dropped. Hennessy was an enormously popular television evangelist. Mrs. Greer was awestruck. She turned and looked at her daughter, then back again at Reaves.

"You'd better do some research before you rush off and go on national television!" Jenny Reaves cautioned.

"Oh, for heaven sake!"

"Something about all of this bothers me," she said quietly.

"It bothers me too!" Reaves argued. "Jenny, do I need to repeat myself? We're talking about a consecrated House of God, here. This is not a complex issue. Unauthorized people are buying churches and turning them into pleasure houses. Would Jesus Christ approve? That's the only question. It's very simple. What would Jesus say?"

◦ ◻ ◦

Jeremy Atkins had finally made it to his goal. It had been a very long day, and the sight of Cheops, the Great Pyramid, rising up massive and sharp in the twilight was a sight he knew that he would never forget. The bus was rickety and old, and Jeremy rushed for the door when the battered vehicle finally stopped. He hurried out onto the ancient sands of the Sahara and stood dead in his tracks staring at the great mysterious structure. But he could bear to wait only a moment. In an instant he was running for the tiny opening he saw at the center of the pyramid near the bottom stone blocks. Men on camels shouted at him, but he did not look at them. He was a man possessed. He had to get inside.

And soon he was. Standing alone, looking deep into a dark corridor. Suddenly he felt nervous. Old movie mummies rose up stiffly in his mind's eye, and he stopped to summon his courage. He quickly looked back out the door, almost in reflex, but as if he expected to see something important there. Then an entourage of black limousines pulled up near the door as goats hurried out of the way along with men in jalabehs and frantic children. It was not what Jeremy had expected to see.

Guards leapt out of doors and ran to open other doors. Jeremy strained to see who would step out at the center of such a bustling scene of power. The answer came quickly. Jeremy found himself looking on the face of the President of the United States.

When Jeremy saw the entourage heading for the doorway where he stood watching, he felt panic. He turned and hurried in deeper down the dark corridor where he entered a small chamber. He wondered if he would be safe there. He sighed, momentarily at ease.

Then he saw it. It was within a semi-open crypt, and it's face was uncovered. He began to scream but suppressed it. The mummy was familiar in a strange way. Then it dawned on him. It was his grandmother he saw lying there, lying as crippled and arthritic as she had been in life. Jeremy hurried to her and bent down. He took her shriveled hand in his own and felt overcome with emotion. "I love these old bones," was all he could say, though he had no idea why he said it.

"Then get beyond here," the old woman said quietly, but in a very serious tone. "Beyond the bones."

Jeremy nodded. He turned and ran as quickly as he could toward the door. He raced down the dark corridor. Suddenly, the presidential entourage was there in the way. He struggled to get past. He fought with everything he had in him. And he made it. He flew through the door and right on out into the dim evening sky. He flew as he had never flown. He flew right up into the red glowing clouds.

Then it was over. X. Rex Kelby turned a few knobs and pondered silently a moment. He thought about reworking a section on the simulator, then turned to a computer keyboard to log a note to himself about it. He also added a notation about color enhancement. He figured that he could sharpen the colors featured with a bit of rework before he showed the final product to his client.

When Aurora entered, Kelby looked back casually over his shoulder. Her expression was dour. "They're here, Rex."

Kelby swung around in his chair and raised an unconcerned eyebrow. "It's okay Aurora," he assured her. "Send them in."

They were just outside the door. Aurora led them in, then excused herself. Kelby stood up and nodded. "I've been expecting you boys," he said.

The Air Force captain extended a hand. "I assure you we haven't forgotten you, Dr. Kelby. We were just waiting until the time was ripe."

"Let me spend all the research bucks, eh Captain?" Kelby laughed and shook the extended hand.

"This is Captain Barton," the man said by way of introducing his companion.

"Riding with equal rank today, huh? Nice to meet you," Kelby said, shaking the other man's hand. "Well, Captain Mackey," he continued, turning back. "Shall we be seated?"

The men all sat down, and Kelby was promptly prodded for explanations of his wondrous equipment. Neither of the men had ever sought the services of U-Star Videos in the past, but like most Americans, they had read numerous magazine articles and had seen some of the nightly news coverage which had made Kelby a very famous man. They were clearly awed to be in his company and to actually see the behind-the-scenes technology which had catapulted Kelby into the public eye. Now they were ready to discuss Kelby's latest brainchild and its possible use as a military tool. Kelby was not pleased, but it was inevitable that the Pentagon would knock on his door one day. Government representatives had been involved in each step of the patenting procedure, and necessary reports had to be filed. Besides, it was Kelby who had made the original contact with the Air Force. He had sought blueprints of existing rocket packs when he first began his research on making an improved version of a single-person propulsion unit. Of course, they did not make prints available without a certain understanding pending a successful outcome.

Now they were ready to talk. But first Kelby decided to indulge the men's fascination with his programmer.

"Here, watch this," Kelby laughed. He turned a dial and the screen lit up. He typed in a code and pressed a retriever switch. Suddenly, a landscape appeared. The two captains found themselves viewing a very cool white snowy set of hills with dark pines waving beneath a starry sky. A young lady was walking, swishing along through the snow. There was a closeup of her face as she stopped and scanned the bright sky. Then she turned and looked over her shoulder as six or seven shooting stars plunged in unison. Fiery streaks of light trailed behind them. When the girl looked back, she found herself watching two moons slowly rise over the pines. They were a brilliant yellow-green color and rose higher and higher in the sky until they dominated everything. The snowscape was drenched in the light of the two moons. Then the screen was again upon the face of the girl, and she bore the unmistakable expression of startled realization. When the moons were viewed again, they had changed ever so subtly, but the answer to her awe was evident. They had become the yellow-green crystalline eyes of a cosmic cat, and they stared down with an unsettling gaze.

The girl began to run. She ran and ran until she came to a bridge over a small creek. As she began her walk across it, she was suddenly startled to see dead snakes lying across the wooden planks. But she pulled out a bag and gathered up the creatures, then went on across the bridge. After a time, she came to a house and went inside where she met with a stranger who wasted no time in taking the girl as his lover.

Kelby and the captains laughed modestly at the ending. "Well, what do you think?" Kelby asked, turning around on his chair. "Do you think my client will like it?"

Captain Mackey thought about his daughter and nodded approvingly. "That's pretty way out, doctor, and it's a perfect little fable even if I don't know what it means." Captain Barton laughed really loudly and shook his head agreeably. He had no idea what it meant either, nor did he try to decipher it. "Maybe those big cat eyes mean something, eh, Dr. Kelby?" Captain Mackey winked.

Kelby arched a brow and grinned deviously. "You should know about that, Captain, otherwise you wouldn't be here. Of course, that's not to say that that is what it meant in the dream sequence."

Captain Mackey shook his head. "I'm not sure I follow."

Kelby smiled and looked away. When he turned back, his face bore a very grave expression. "I think that it's time for us to get down to the business at hand," he said somewhat coarsely. He was ready to go head to head on negotiations. "Let me see what kind of contracts your superiors sent you here with. I'm not really in favor of any of this, gentlemen, but I know when to stand my ground and when to roll with the punches." He was ready for serious dialogue.

19

PHOEBE FANEROS was near frantic about leaving her three-month-old daughter Ariel with a babysitter for the first time, but Aaron tried to reassure her that it was safe.

"You can't trust people today!" she complained. "There are such awful stories in the newspapers!" she shuddered to think about it.

"Now, now . . ." Aaron said softly. Paragon would not send their old manager just anybody. I made sure her references were fully checked."

"Turn here!" Phoebe suddenly insisted. Aaron quickly slowed the car and whipped it across the opposite lane just ahead of oncoming traffic.

"I usually go up a few blocks before I turn."

"Yes, but this way you can go straight through the park without having to turn every which way. Take my word for it."

"Well, you should know. You're the one who hot rods all over the city all the time."

"I love my new sportscar! We should have driven it tonight!"

Aaron laughed. "Look . . . tonight's going to be crazy enough as it is! I don't need my heart tossed around like an old leather ball as you Grand Prix the streets of San Francisco!"

Phoebe began to laugh. Then she noticed something out the window and giggled even harder. "Oh look! Look! How funny!" She was watching an old bum trying to set up a tattered hammock someone must have left

171

behind in the park. He was back by some trees in a wild area, and she could see him struggling to get on and stay on. A bottle of cheap wine was sticking out of his coat pocket. "That's probably how I'll end up," she chuckled. "An old bag lady with some shabby old tomcat to keep me company."

Aaron snorted quietly. "Why do you say things like that?"

"Because . . . all my life everything has been taken away from me. Why should it stop now?"

Aaron smiled and put a hand on her knee and rubbed gently. Phoebe had come of age during an especially bitter divorce, and her father had moved out of state and never returned. From that time on, it had been rough. Money was tight, and her mother had to put in twelve-hour workdays to make it. Phoebe had been left to care for her younger brother and household chores. But the hardest part of it all had been her mother's increasing irritability and aloofness. Phoebe had often resorted to drastic actions to get her mother to notice her and appreciate her hard work. The most hurtful part had been that her creative efforts were all but ignored. But that did serve to make her try harder. Now she was well on her way to being a recognized talent, but old insecurities would still often creep back up into her mind when she felt nervous or on edge. In the beginning with Aaron, there had been a number of very tense situations between them, and Aaron had tried hard to understand. But his background had been very much different. His father and mother had always kept the family tight in spite of the tension created by lack of money. For a number of years, his father had grown distant like Phoebe's mother due to the burdens of work, but he had finally quit his sales job, which had so repeatedly depressed him, and gone into the peaceful business of antique furniture restoration and collecting. Meanwhile, his mother had started her own door-to-door sales business and loved it. Later, she put Aaron through college on her own earnings. So it went, a very average uneventful childhood and adolescence, and he had never had to face insecurity in any form. But Phoebe was strong enough to rise above her doubts, and Aaron had been especially impressed by her drive.

If not her driving . . . which was actually quite good but made him nervous. Now they were nearing Vimana. They turned and descended into a security lot underground. After they parked, they made their way to an elevator and were soon up to the main corridor. The place was bustling with people and activity and resembled nothing so much as a Mardi Gras! People were everywhere in their most outrageous clothes, and many were dressed outright in carnival garb. Some wore clothes from other cultures; some, clothes from other times. Many of the faces were painted a pure white, many were a rainbow of color. And interspersed amid it all were a wide variety of fantastic masks.

Aaron and Phoebe were amused. They had worn much more subtle streetwear, because they had no roles as performers this night. The most outlandishly dressed people were obviously the actors and actresses who would participate in the evening's dream dramas, although some were dressed crazily just for the fun of it. The Vimanians had found their weekly fiesta, and they were all reveling in it as rock music blared out over large speakers in pulsing upbeat rhythms.

Eventually, the two happened across Peter Varden and Rebekka. Peter's face had been painted white, and he wore a brown robe, tied at the waist with a cord of rope. He had the look of a monk, but was completely recognizable. Rebekka, on the other hand, was only recognizable due to being at Peter's side. She wore a very sexy dazzling glittery costume and a great plumed hat-mask.

"Don't you two make a startling sight!" Aaron laughed. "What's going on?"

Peter chortled shyly and kept pointing his finger at Rebekka. "It's her dream," he explained.

"I'm a Parisian showgirl," Rebekka declared, spinning around exotically and laughing. "And this guy here is the one I met when I was walking down a dark street in New Orleans."

"Seems appropriate," Aaron cracked.

"Do you dream alot about your childhood?" Rebekka suddenly wanted to know. "I grew up in New Orleans, and I'm always dreaming about it, even though I've been here over ten years. Does that make sense?"

"Believe me," Aaron laughed, "I dream about my childhood all of the time, too. It doesn't matter where you go. Those images are locked solidly into the subconscious forever. I still get surprised by how often I dream of home and events taking place outside my parents' home." Then he looked at Peter. "You're going on tonight, I presume?"

Peter shook his head no. When Rebekka looked over and saw him, she slapped him gently on the arm and squealed. "You are too!" she yelled, grinning hugely. "I can't do my dream without you!"

"Do you really see Peter as a monk?" Phoebe asked. "I always do, but it's probably just his hair."

"The night I had this dream was right after we had been talking about reincarnation one time, and he showed me a birthmark he has over his ribs, see? It's shaped like how a sword cut would look if somebody stabbed you."

"Ah, so Peter may have been a warrior crusader . . . " Aaron speculated.

"Well . . . maybe," Peter cut in. "Or the other way around. I get the impression that maybe I was in a monastery in Europe somewhere and we were attacked by outsiders. I think that I might have been killed then. Of course, I don't know how much I really believe in reincarnation anyway. I guess I do, but how do you decipher who you were in a past life really? It's alot of guessing."

Aaron looked agreeably baffled then turned to Rebekka again. "So you had a dream, and he was a monk?"

"He sure was!" she cracked, drawing out the *was* part with a funky whine. "And he saved my life, but I ain't telling you more, honey, because you got to come in and see my dream drama! We'll be on third tonight."

"Oh, we'll be there!" Phoebe assured her.

Aaron smiled a wily grin. "So the sacred and the profane ride in the same saddle again . . . "

"What! Say what?"

"Never mind, Rebekka," Phoebe said. "Half the time, even I can't tell what he's talking about . . . "

It was an hour before the dramas actually began. Peter and Rebekka had disappeared into the dressing quarters, and Aaron and Phoebe had gone in to find seats.

At last the deep resonant voice of Damon Burke sounded the welcoming call. "For those of you who are here for the first time, let me explain a few things now. We do not introduce the actual names of the participants until after the show when programs are made available to all of you. No actor or actress is announced in advance for a simple reason: we try to keep ego out of these dramatizations as much as possible. We want to continue to be absolutely true to our dreams. If we give ego free reign, we might distort that truth to satisfy our desire to be admired by our friends and the public. That's not why we're here. We're here to share our deepest visions, and our collective vision as a whole. If you need glory for your portrayals, then go be a movie star, we say! We're here to have fun and learn. We want to penetrate the mind of man and woman and see what's there and then reveal it. All actors and actresses, therefore, become anonymous participants in this mysterious extravaganza. And those of you who are shy, you can join in, too. Paint your face and go beyond your ego. Put on a mask and become anyone or everyone. We become the collective unconscious, just as in ancient times the earliest rituals mimicked the gods. Or like in olden days when the passion plays put the fables and folklore of the ages in distinct form and dramatized man's incredible heritage.

"The dreams we share here go beyond the personal realms we all revel in daily. We strive to touch something untouchable and ultimately unknowable, something that reveals itself in a flash and then is gone. Something that riddles us with its subtle spark as it sends fiery waves of form hurling out across this universe and then disappears. Ladies and gentlemen, we strive here to touch the eternal.

"But let's not be dull about it! Enough! We can have fun and still gain in wisdom. So enough said. Are you with me?"

The crowd roared its excitement.

"Can we have a good time? All right then! Let's begin with a dream drama which has been titled, simply: Gravity Fable. Our dream presenter tells us that this dream drama is a composition drawn from three dreams he had. He testifies that each and every event which you will witness now is from an absolutely authentic dream experience and has not been altered except in as much as storyline continuity required. We will, of course, have the usual discussion groups following the show, and you are welcome to join in. And now . . . let's dream!"

A keyboard rolled out waves of full chords and so the show began, centerstage, in the darkened nave with a wide spotlight on two men. They were both in flysuits, and one man was obviously a Vimana instructor and the other a student trying to learn how to fly with a rocket pack. Pockets of laughter and clapping broke out instantly as the two launched into a very identifiable situation for most in the crowd. It was like a slapstick routine with the instructor getting progressively more irritated as the student continued flubbing even the simplest directions. Finally the instructor was howling mad. "Just take off running and snap on the thruster power!" he screamed. The student stepped forward boldly and tried racing into the wind, but then lost his courage and began hopping like a kangaroo. The crowd was roaring with laughter. At last the instructor, acting completely exasperated, went off into the wings and then came back leading a mechanical kangaroo! The animal was actually a hologram projection, and the crowd laughed and applauded as the student was taken off into the wings like a child with the kangaroo.

Then the darkened stage began to glow with a luminescent landscape.

The crowd grew silent but broke into fits of laughter as the kangaroo and its rider reappeared suddenly, both being light projections but looking very life-like. The kangaroo made huge bouncing flights as the computer-generated landscape rolled quickly by, giving the impression of great speed and distance being traversed. It was an hilarious and silly sojourn which continued to bring gales of laughter from the audience. So it leapt over hill and dale, ever onward in a perfect three-dimensional frolic.

Then an old stone palace came into view, and the kangaroo came to rest just outside the palace door. The young man dismounted and went on in through the door as suspenseful music played.

The stage went instantly black for a moment. Then, slowly, a luminescent glow began subtly taking shape. An interior became evident, and it included many tables and people seated on chairs, as if a banquet were in progress. They were real tables and people, and the hologram projector merely provided an illusion of walls and fabulous old tapestries of a medieval culture. As the lighting came up on the seated figures, the crowd again began tittering gleefully, for many of the figures wore the mask of an animal or reptile. It was a most bizarre spectacle and very humorous. People laughed, then applauded and hooted as the kangaroo rider suddenly came in a door and found himself in such strange company. He walked around and talked to various people. It was like a great huge party, and everybody seemed to be celebrating. Then he met a beautiful young lady who was walking through the crowded room. She was dressed in very sexy, modern clothes and had long, flowing red hair. The Rider was totally captivated and began trying to charm her. Soon they were embracing and kissing as the audience oohed and razzed them like a pack of school kids. The couple began strolling together through the crowd and chatted amicably with everyone.

But then the Rider came up behind a seated man with the head of a lizard. He pulled out a long knife and stood there staring at the creature. Now the audience was ambivalent about its laughter. The Rider looked menacing with his shiny blade at the back of the neck of the lizard. Then he made his move. He drove the knife up the lower end of the lizard mask and sliced it open like a thin rubber hose. When he ripped the mask off, he was surprised to see his own face there!

All at once a commotion began stirring on the far side of the room, and a bearded, black-haired man came rolling through the crowd on a motorized wheelchair. He had a laser gun, and it shot a thin bright red beam. People began scattering wildly as the killer beam burned a hole through whatever it hit. Things were catching on fire everywhere as he wheeled around like a madman shooting his gun.

The Rider saw him coming and threw down the knife and lizard mask. He began backing away in mortal fear and looked around for a way to defend himself from the killer beam. He saw a book on the table and grabbed it up. He held the book in front of him just as the madman came at him shooting his laser. The beam struck the book cover, and it began burning. After the cover had burned away, the Rider stood looking at the bold title print on the white page. It read: *Faust* by Goethe.

Meanwhile, the others had run away and even the madman had gone out some door. The Rider looked around for his new girlfriend, but she was not to be seen. Then suddenly she was there again. Ten exact clones of the girl appeared, and the Rider was totally baffled by the strange unsettling sight. He did not know what to do. He could not tell which of the figures was the real woman. He became so vexed by the situation that he finally just ran out the door.

The stage went dark.

When the lights again came slowly on, the Rider was in another room filled with bizarre objects, as if at some exotic bazaar in the old world. He began looking around at all of the mysterious statues and vases and furniture. Then one piece caught his eye and he went to it. It began to glow brightly. It was the statue of a half true-to-life size elephant. It bore all of the royal trimmings of an Indian Raj, including the canopied chair on the great beast's back. To his further surprise, at the back of the chair was a large airplane propellor. At first, he thought to spin it and maybe even climb up into the chair and fly away! But then he noticed something very disturbing. The propellor was not just a propellor. It was, in fact, a crucifix, and Jesus Christ was there upon it in full crucified agony.

The Rider raced out the palace door, and the stage went black. Momentarily, the luminescent landscape appeared. The mechanical kangaroo was still sitting where he had left it. People strolled by in old tattered clothes. As the Rider went to his animal-vehicle, he passed by three very sad-looking young men. He stopped and asked them why they were so melancholy.

One answered, "It's because of the poverty."

Another said, "We had always heard about it, but to actually see it is shattering"

The Rider was touched by their sensitivity to the poverty of the people. But something about one of the young men puzzled him, and he could not figure out what it was. Then it dawned on him, and he pulled off the dark wool hat covering the man's hair. Suddenly, the long red locks spilled down onto the narrow shoulders hidden under a bulky coat. It was the young woman he had met in the feast hall, the one who had been cloned!

He led her away to his waiting mechanical beast as the lights of the landscape faded away into blackness. It was over and the audience cheered frenziedly. It had truly left its viewers breathless. Each scene had been drawn out for maximum effect, and the preprogrammed computer-generated images had been spellbinding. The audience sustained its applause as laser lights flashed over the cheering throng in a rainbow of colors. It was a dazzling display, and the synthesizer poured buoyant melody down through it all.

Outside, a quiet restless crowd watched as stained glass windows erupted in flashes of brilliant light. It was as if roman candles were exploding under colored glass and creating a kaleidoscope of delirium. People on the sidewalks would stop and marvel and wonder about what was really going on in the controversial Vimana Cathedral. The crowd at the front doors had already decided that whatever it was, it was not good. "Out of God's House!" they chanted. "Out of God's House, now!" Even as the show went on for another two full hours.

Rachel Rarick sat at the head of a discussion group after the dream dramas and deftly guided the students into reviewing their own private thoughts on the symbolism presented. "We're not going to sit here and tell you what each particular symbol means. That's not how it works," she explained. "There is no dream sourcebook that we just look up the answer in. Each person has had a unique upbringing and experiences that are not shared with any other people. Therefore, what a symbol means to you may not be the same as what that same symbol means to me, even though the symbol itself may be universal. To pick an obvious example, in the first dream drama, the lead man used a book as a shield against the man in the wheelchair firing his laser beam. The book turned out to be *Faust* by Goethe, which is the story of a man who sells his soul to the devil. But what does that story mean to you personally? Do you think that is really a possible event? Is there a devil? Does a man have a soul? What about those people that read the entire story as an alchemical treatise in disguise?

"My point is, of course, that meaning strikes all of us on different levels. Also, what if you've never read *Faust*? Then the story means nothing to you at all. Or what if someone once told you that Faust was a Roman emperor who conquered half of Europe, and you never bothered to find out that that wasn't true? The book would still give meaning. Perhaps you would figure that either man in the dream drama might be nurturing a desire to conquer others. It could lead anywhere. That's why we encourage you to study myth and history, fables and religion. The more you know, the better equipped you are to interpret dreams at level after level."

"I suppose the same would be true about the propellor with the crucifix," one of the students volunteered. "I mean, what the cross means to me may not be at all what it means to someone else. Some people take it as literal fact and others as fiction, as if it never really happened at all."

"That's exactly right," Rachel answered. "That's why we have you keep dream diaries. You need to work with interpreting your own dreams to yourself first. Look up a reference and follow up. Eventually, you see patterns emerge. Look at groups of dreams, find the common motifs. Learn how to recognize an archetype when it appears. They are the most basic patterns of the psyche, and they have no form of their own. But we see them in the form of someone, a wise old man perhaps, or a beautiful goddess, or a scary, dark figure lurking in the shadows. They are our own most basic urges personified. This is how the psyche talks to us and how we learn. It is the inner dialogue that expands us as people, and we find meaning and, therefore, a reason to live beyond mere animal survival."

Eric was sitting at the back of the class. "I'm not sure I need a reason to live beyond mere animal survival," he joked. "It's always been the most fun!"

The class laughed, but Rachel was only mildly amused. She took her teaching position seriously. But finally she could not resist and laughed hard also.

"Eric, get out of here!" she yelled, grinning. "I'll talk to you about animal survival later!"

"And I'll talk to you about animal fun!" he shot back. But he knew that she preferred he leave, and he jumped up and went out the door, still laughing. He grabbed a chair near the door and sat down to wait.

Soon, he had unexpected company. It was Sara Tynes, and she pulled up a chair beside him. Eric immediately became restless and began twitching around in his seat. "Got out early, huh?" he asked, as if unaffected.

"Yes," she answered, smiling demurely. "And I see that you did, too."

"So how do you like it so far?"

"It's fascinating and disturbing all at once. I'm not sure yet."

"Well, you haven't really gotten to the fun part yet. You'll see what I mean."

Sara shook her heavy brown curls and smiled. Eric was not sure if she was being charming or phony. He wasn't comfortable, but she did intrigue him with her attractive features.

"What's the fun stuff?" she wanted to know.

Eric was surprised that she was following up. "You mean besides flying?" He was perturbed suddenly.

"Yes. Like when you start getting to higher levels in the Order."

"Well . . . I can't really talk about that . . . "

Sara pressed on. "I heard that there are dream rooms . . . " She smiled almost seductively, and Eric shifted anxiously in his seat.

"Oh! The orgy rooms . . . " he cracked nervously. "You mean where everybody sleeps over and we get real wild!"

The girl's face registered genuine shock. "Really?" she wanted to know. She was blushing.

Eric was glad that the discomfort was shifted to her. "Sure," he laughed. "We all sleep together in the experimental dream chamber. It's unbelievable! Wait until you get asked in." He wanted to see her squirm.

"I'm not sure I want to be!"

Eric laughed hard. "Oh come on! I'm just kidding."

"Are there really dream rooms?" she asked again.

"Yeah, there are dream rooms," he answered, still laughing to himself. "We have experimental equipment which is able to register brain waves, and we sleep in groups to see if collective dreaming is possible. Also, the equipment can send subtle electrical messages to the brain and stimulate nerve centers. It's all experimental! The results have been really interesting."

"So, you sleep together here?"

Eric nodded. "In the basement there are soundproof rooms, we go in there and, yeah, there's a bunch of us who sometimes sleep in there together."

"And do what?" she winked. "Tell me the truth."

"And have orgies, I told you!" Eric laughed hard again.

"Come on!"

Eric raised an eyebrow. "You'll just have to wait and see . . . " He was being playful.

Suddenly, Sara was up. "I've got to get going," she said, looking at her watch. "It's getting late, and my parents will worry." She seemed bothered by something.

"Well, don't let the big bad wolf get you."

"No chance," Sara smiled. "I'll see you later."

"Not if I see you first," he thought, laughing to himself at the old line. But his eyes followed her as she walked away, and he liked what he saw. He began smiling and shifting restlessly in his seat again.

20

IT WAS A LONG, rolling kiss full of exploratory sensuality. She was over him, then he was over her, then they rolled again, riding the sweet breath of passion through angles, circles, the point of no return . . .

And finally flipping on the continuum, over into peace after the fervor and long aerial euphoria. Skin quivering in waves, heartbeats slowing. Winding down and winded. Giving final tender kisses. Throwing off the top sheet. Breathing easy, satisfied.

"Well that finally proves it for sure!" Phoebe exulted in a sultry voice, rolling back for a quick kiss on Aaron's neck. "I was beginning to wonder if it would ever feel like that again."

"Just takes time."

"Yeah, easy for you to say! This childbirth business . . . makes you wonder if your body will ever be the same. But who cares now? That was fantastic!"

"I can't believe how quickly you got in shape! The sexy Phoebe Faneros is back! Back . . . " He grinned and reached out his hands. " . . . and hot as ever!"

Phoebe laughed, then suddenly rolled away. She quickly twisted the volume control on the stereo at the side of the bed. "I love this song!" she warbled, rocking and writhing to the loud beat. "And to think that I actually know these guys!"

"What?"

"Phoebe turned the volume down slightly and rolled back over to Aaron. "I remember all these guys before they were famous. We used to hang out at parties together, and sometimes I'd dance on stage with them. We had so much fun!"

"I could just see you up there."

"I was so skinny. And my hair was pure white. I dressed outrageous! I wish you could have seen me."

"Just too bad you had that crazy drummer on your hands. It would have been perfect."

"Yeah, I know." Her voice was wistful and sad. "But . . . that's the breaks." Then she smiled. "Anyway, it's all better now, right?"

Aaron laughed. "Sure. You have me and you're a star! Too bad that I'm just no good on stage. I'd be up there with you!"

"Oh, that would be perfect! Then we could go away on tour together. Come on! You're good enough!" she insisted.

"Not really," Aaron confessed. "When I was last in a band, I was just a teenager still learning how to play a guitar. We got pretty good, but then we didn't have enough money to buy better equipment, so we gave it up. We had a great time though, while it lasted!"

"Well, that wouldn't be a problem now! Obviously! Listen . . . that would be so great. We could pack up Ariel and all be together traveling around America."

"Probably the world!"

"Yeah!"

Aaron shrugged. "I know . . . " he laughed. "But I've got my work here now." Suddenly his mind flashed to a TV show he knew he had better watch. He began frowning.

"What is it? We were having so much fun . . . "

"That show . . . "

Phoebe grimaced. "Is it time already?" She was disappointed, but knew how important the show would be to Aaron and all Vimanians.

Aaron had grabbed the television control. "Turn the radio off," he ordered.

"Are you sure that it's time already?"

"Yeah, past time. The show should have started ten minutes ago." Aaron was very serious-faced in the bright television light. "I wonder what those preacher men are gonna say about us . . . " He was being flippant. He knew that some serious opposition was being hurled in the press at the

Vimanians. Now a special was being aired on a religious channel which had advertised itself as "A Christian View of the Order of Vimana: The Crisis in our Churches." Its host was the Reverend Robert Hennessy. His guest: the Reverend Donovan Reaves. They were in the studio in Los Angeles, and their images instantly flicked into view on Aaron's television.

"That must be him," Aaron commented.

"How do you know?"

"He was in the paper once. He's got that coal-black hair with the receding hairline and gaunt face."

"At least he looks better than you describe him."

"Maybe I'm just automatically prejudiced."

The two men sat in plush chairs discussing the Vimanians in soft, but decisive tones. "What they propose to do," the Reverend Reaves was explaining, "is to find a large church or cathedral in each major city in the United States and buy it so that they can establish themselves there. Then, I would guess, they hope to eventually acquire more and more churches in those cities until they are totally entrenched and politically rooted."

The silver-haired Hennessy nodded, then adjusted his glasses. "But why do they want churches? Why not civic buildings, auditoriums and such?"

The camera moved in close on Reaves. "Because they want the controversy, I suspect. Their Mr. Kelby is a financial wizard and a very clever entrepreneur. He knows how to market his products. As you know, he's the man behind U-Star Videos. His success with that is a capitalist's miracle. Now he wants to do the same with this Vimana empire he's building."

"So the more controversy, the more press he gets . . . "

"And the more press, the more business. It's very clever. But I do not approve of his tactics. This is not ethical taking over churches to promote his business enterprises. It shows a complete lack of respect for our Christian values."

"Could there be other motives as well?"

"Well, there is another aspect to this desire of Mr. Kelby's to arouse controversy. There are, at present, a lot of laws and regulations being put through our various legislatures regarding where and how these flying vehicles may operate. I know that this is true certainly in the cities which have these flying clubs, and I have been to Washington and know first hand what is happening at a federal level. These people are outlaws, Reverend Hennessy. Right at this very moment, those people are actually thwarting federal regulations which cover all forms of flying vehicles, from jets to air balloons. They have no licenses with which to legally operate their vehicles, and again they just thumb their noses at our laws. But this, I suspect, will be their downfall."

"How so?"

"Because by continuing to thwart the laws of our land, they will soon invite federal officials to simply shut them down."

"So they are really bringing about their own doom."

"That is correct. Their own immorality will bring them down. God has blessed this nation and sanctified her laws. Those who break the laws of the land are breaking God's laws!"

"So, Reverend Reaves, then you are indeed promoting God's righteousness when you go to Washington and lobby to stop these people."

"Absolutely. Because in the end they are denigrating God's sacred House, and that is the bottom line beyond which God will not tolerate such evilness."

Reverend Hennessy shook his head and looked furious. "How can we help you with your sacred mission?" he asked with a sweeping gesture to all of his audience.

"We should not act with violence. We can win this for God without any physical confrontations, and here is what we must do: write to your city council, write to your state representatives, and write to your senators. Here is a simple list of all the regulations we can fight with our combined efforts. One: they have no licenses to operate their vehicles and no licenses on their vehicles. Two: there are no age requirements at present. That is unsafe for our young people. Three: there are altitude laws which they are completely ignoring, and they have no altitude gauges on their equipment, which means that our skies are now unsafe. There are many, many light aircraft which are now at risk due to these free-flying Vimanas. Four: these vehicles virtually go anywhere and are therefore quite capable of invading the privacy of our citizens. They can fly right over our backyards, they can fly right by our office windows, they can go anywhere they choose. Is this what we want? No privacy in our own homes? Five: there are no restrictions on the carrying of objects by these flyers. What if they drop something through your car window as you're trying to drive your children to school or church? Six: there are no restrictions on where these people can land. Do you want them landing in your school yards?

"Now this is just a brief list that we can work with. Remember, too, that there are a great deal of technical laws which regulate equipment which I have not even gone into here."

"So, we have an abundance of laws to work with against these people?"

"That's correct, Reverend Hennessy. But let me reiterate, we are not really concerned about whether or not these people fly. We all enjoy the use of airplanes and such. This is an ethical problem. They have taken our churches and turned them into something unholy." Reaves was suddenly very angry. "If you don't believe this, you will. We intend to offer you very candid proof!"

Hennessy nodded. "The Bible talks about the worship of false idols. Would you say that that is what we are dealing with here?"

"Absolutely!"

Hennessy looked into the camera. "We have another guest here this evening who will substantiate these claims. He is a former member of the Order of Vimana, and he has knowledge of the inner workings of that organization."

Aaron frowned and looked at Phoebe as they lay together on the bed watching. "Who could that be?" He was immediately tense.

"Ladies and gentlemen, let's welcome Mr. Brad Neiman."

Aaron was stunned and sat forward with a bolt. "Brad Neiman!" he yelled. Then he shook his head. "We knew all along but never took it as a serious threat. He really acted like he loved flying!"

When the studio audience quieted, Brad Neiman waved and sat back in his chair. The Reverend Hennessy shook his hand and he began at once asking questions. "When did you join the Order of Vimana, Brad?"

"About six months ago, Reverend Hennessy."

"And you meant to be a full member."

"Well . . . initially, yes. Mind you, I did have reservations, but my desire to fly got the best of me, and I turned a blind eye to the fact that they were in God's House without His authority. But I assure all of you that I have deeply repented that error in judgment and have asked the Lord to forgive me."

Reverend Hennessy smiled and put his hand on Neiman's shoulder. "God is merciful, Brad. When we go astray, we need only ask forgiveness and it is given. Perhaps God even had a hand in your error of judgment so that you could be here today with us as an instrument of His divine will. You have been inside the heathen temple, and you have seen. Now it is God's will that you reveal to all of us the unholy practices to which you have been a witness."

Neiman looked at Reaves, and they both grimaced subtly. They had talked before the show, and they knew exactly the fury that they were about to unleash on the public.

Neiman began slowly. "The idol of the Order of Vimana is not a physical idol, although I might mention that there are two huge sculptures where an altar ought to be, of a naked man and woman, each with wings."

The audience could be heard suddenly, making quiet noises. Reverend Hennessy bent his head. "Go on . . . " he commanded like a lawyer in a court of law.

"The idol they worship is pleasure. They fly, they live their dreams no matter how evil . . . anything goes! Morality is shoved aside. And that is not the Lord's way. We are to be instruments of God's will, not our own, especially since we do not have the absolute answers of ourselves."

"Not my will, but Thy will be done in me," Reverend Hennessy concluded, quoting scripture.

"Exactly. But they are acting according to their own interpretations and cannot, therefore, be acting in God's interest."

"Has not God spoken to His prophets in dream? There is Jacob and . . . "

"Yes, but they were prophets. Chosen men of the Word."

Reverend Reaves leaned forward. "Remember, Satan speaks to men, too. For example, Adolf Hitler is said to have had a dream which sent him up and out of a bunker in the middle of fighting one night and as soon as he got out he heard a bomb explode. When he hurried back to the bunker, it was completely blown up. Not one of his fellow soldiers lived. Only he. And he interpreted that to mean that God had spared him for a divine purpose!"

"So Satan does speak to men through dream."

"Obviously."

"Well, Brad, what leads you to conclude that there is evil here with the Order of Vimana? Are there any specific things which you can tell us?"

Neiman and Reaves exchanged tense glances again. "There are rooms in the Vimana Cathedral in San Francisco which are there for the higher members of the Order to sleep in. They spend whole nights in there experimenting with dreams, and they have sophisticated machines which they use on each other."

"Now let me get this straight," Hennessy said. "Are we to understand that they are sleeping in the church?" His voice boomed out on the last word of his question.

"Yes," Brad answered. "Definitely."

"Men and women together?"

"Yes."

"Men and women are sleeping together in the church!"

"Yes. In fact, I have it from an inside source that actual indiscretions are occurring in the dream rooms of the church."

The audience stirred with stunned disapproval. Hennessy made no effort to quiet them and they began hissing.

Aaron felt his face growing flush. He was livid with anger. "That liar!" he yelled. "I don't believe this!"

But the audience believed, and Hennessy kept the fires burning.

"Did this source you mentioned actually participate in sexual acts there?"

"No, of course not! She's a Christian. But she was invited to participate by one of the highest placed members of the Order. I'm sorry, I cannot reveal her name due to safety considerations."

"Sure, sure . . . but this is outrageous! This is . . . "

"Sinful!" Reaves roared. "And there's more!" He was furious. "Tell it, Brad."

Neiman frowned and twisted in his seat. "They have machines in there that both receive and send electrical signals to and from the brain."

Reaves jumped in. "They have machines that send signals to the brain! They can alter brainwaves!"

"Are you saying that they can influence the way a person thinks?"

Reaves nodded. His mouth was tight and implosive.

"Are we talking about brainwashing here? Is that possible?"

"Of course it's possible!" Reaves barked. "We've got all of the classical symptoms of cultism here! Can you imagine?"

The audience grew louder and louder.

"We've got to stop it!" Reaves yelled. "We've got to get money to fight this thing. We've got to get volunteers to help us save the innocent among them. We've got to educate our children before it is too late! We've got to drive a wedge right through their ranks! With people like Brad here, we can create the schism that will destroy them. It is God's will!"

Within minutes, Kelby was on the line. He was furious. "How did it come to this?" he wanted to know.

Aaron was just as angry. "Because it's all just unsubstantiated speculation. It's lies on lies, and we can prove it!"

"But look at the damage they've done tonight. This is going to get wicked."

"So what do we do, Rex? Do you want me to call a press conference or should you? Given a choice, I'd much rather have you do it."

"Sure, I'll do it!" Kelby shouted into the phone. "And we'll take camera crews down into the dream rooms. We'll bring scientists in to check our equipment! Brainwashing! What crap!"

"Who do you think the snitch is, besides our dear Mr. Neiman?"

"I should ask you that!" Kelby barked.

"I have no idea! But I'll find out, and she'll be out on her butt!"

"Well, be careful. We don't want her crying rape for God's sake."

"Bah . . . " Aaron blew out a long breath and swallowed hard.

"There has never been sex in the dream rooms, has there?" Kelby's tone was confidential and gruff, but then all at once he laughed.

"Rex . . . to my knowledge, I swear that I know of no cases at all."

"At all?"

"At all! None!"

There was a pause. "Okay," Kelby said. "I'm calling the press now, and I'll set up a conference for ten-thirty. Then I'll phone Dr. Rayburn and ask him to contact a couple of neutral unaffiliated scientists to accompany the camera team tomorrow. Meanwhile, you follow up on the snitch and find out who she talked to and what was really said or if she made the whole thing up. Our best defense is to answer each and every one of their charges as straight as possible. And let's be fair," Kelby argued. "If I were in their shoes and I heard stories like that, I'd be outraged too! Remember, we're not anti-Christian by any means. Not at all."

"Yes, but how do we convince them of that?"

"By not battling with them in the press. Put out the word that everyone says nothing ill-willed about them. In fact, let's offer positive comments. Let's never resort to denigrating comments at all."

"And let the rage pass?"

"Absolutely."

"What about all the political stuff? All the laws and regulations that they're threatening us with?"

"Don't worry, I can deal with that single-handedly, and I know just what to do."

"What do you mean?"

"I'm not exactly unknown in Washington these days!" Kelby laughed. "Perhaps it's time for me to play one of my aces. I'd say that it's time to pay a visit to the Attorney General of the United States."

Aaron gasped quietly and started to comment, but Kelby continued on as if just thinking out loud. "Yes," he went on, "I believe it's time for me to give our law enforcement officers the privilege of using the most sophisticated, most maneuverable flying craft in the world today . . . "

"You mean . . . "

"I mean they've been hounding me ever since I gave the Pentagon their contract! Now the police want Vimanas for obvious reasons. It won't be hard for us to keep the law on our side, Aaron. We'll win this fight hands down!"

"And wings up!"

"Why not? You wouldn't believe what's really going on behind the scenes at the absolute highest levels of government, my friend. It's amazing how even the most bizarre of events can be twisted right into the wider game plan. And this game has truly just begun!"

Aaron didn't know quite what to make of that. "There ... seems ... to be a whole lot you haven't told me, Rex ... "

Kelby roared at that. "What would I know?!"

"You know plenty! And I don't even really know you! I know absolutely nothing about your past ... "

"The past is past ... "

"But ... why?"

"Who cares? Why are there scandals every time we turn around? Why are there always sex scandals, for example? Like this one? That's a more poignant and interesting question surely. Remember the televangelist sex scandals that shook the nation and began turning the tide on Christian growth because of the loss of faith that resulted. And that in turn resulted in the loss of revenues and eventually the loss of churches. To us no less! Is that destiny? Or a self-wrought fall from grace because too many were preaching one thing and secretly doing another? You can fight natural impulses all you want, but in the end, repression will destroy you. And now they want to throw this absurdity on us! What a joke! Too predictable! I think that it's time to shed this delusion like a winged serpent sloughing its skin. Sex and spirituality are not mutually exclusive forces in our human natures. They are really at one as basic impulse. It's just that it's a wide spectrum we are necessarily living with. The forces of the psyche are vast! And pit that vastness against the vastness of the celestial psyche! What are we dealing with here? God is a marvel. And the common man and woman are going to change what happens on this planet. Our whole destiny! With a little help from certain friends, of course!"

"Who? International bankers? Politicians? Aliens? The Illuminati Conspiracy? Who are these friends?"

"The Dream Illuminati!" Kelby shot back. "And you are already one of them!"

21

THE PHONE rang and rang. Neither Jack nor Tamara could be roused from their sleep to answer it for what seemed like interminable minutes to Aaron.

Finally, Jack woke enough to get a hand on it. "If it's morning, you'll have to prove it to me," he muttered. He had gone to bed late and wanted no part of giving up his sleep yet.

"Jack, it's me, Aaron. Listen, buddy, we need you up here early today."

"For what?" He sounded grumpy.

"Could be trouble."

Jack snorted sleepily. "Don't worry, trouble will wait."

"If we're lucky . . . "

"Why? What happened?"

"Didn't you watch that show last night, with the evangelists?"

Jack thought for a moment, then he remembered about it. "Uh uh. No. I forgot."

"Well, it got nasty."

"How so?"

"We'll tell you all about it when you get up here. No time now. We're prepping for a news conference, and we need you to organize security. We're going to be bringing in reporters. We'll be showing the dream chambers."

191

"What!"

"I know . . . but it's necessary."

"What's going on?"

"Just get up here! You can replay a tape of it and see for yourself."

"Okay, I'll get it moving!"

"Talk to you later then."

"Hi-dee-ho."

Jack hung up and rolled over a moment. He rubbed his forehead and massaged his temples slowly. He was focusing thoughtlessly on the dragon statue which Aaron had brought back with him from Hong Kong. It sat on the mantel of the bedroom fireplace beside all of his other dragon statues and pictures. He was acquiring a large collection.

At last, he rolled back over and on out of bed. Tamara slept on, completely undisturbed. He thought about waking her, then decided to leave her a note if she wasn't up by the time he left. But he knew that he had better hurry.

When he got to the living room, his kids were already up watching cartoons. They all grinned to see their father, but quickly looked back at the screen, all in sleepy trances. Jack went to the kitchen and began making up some breakfast.

Then he heard it. It was a newsbreak, and the anchorman gave the story lead, describing the situation with characteristic flair. "Christian leaders across the country today are in an uproar over alleged accusations that there are men and women sleeping together in the so-called dream chambers at the Order of Vimana. The leaders denounced such practices as 'the worst form of immorality imaginable' and also placed allegations against the Vimanians for what they term 'cultist brainwashing.' They are now demanding the ouster of all Vimanians from churches owned by the notorious flying Order and the return of those buildings to Christian congregations.

"In other news . . . "

Now it was Jack's turn to be stunned. He could feel the fury rising up through his sleepiness. His mind began racing to make sense of the allegations, but the puzzle would not fit. He could not decide what to think. Then his body took over, and his pace quickened. He began gulping his eggs but let the bacon sizzle longer in the pan. The coffee went down with a burning. His eyes throbbed with anger.

Another five minutes, and he was in his flysuit. He went to his children and gave hugs and kisses all around. "Tell Mommy that I had to fly."

He waved his arms like a bird, and the kids giggled. "Tell her I'll call."

Amid the volley of *good-byes*, Jack hurried through the kitchen and grabbed his four pieces of bacon with a fork and napkin and began chewing as he headed for the back room to get his XRK-4. He was strapped in and ready to fly in less than two minutes. He moved so fast that he was still swallowing bacon when he rose up like a brawny astronaut over the creek and pines and up into the sunny Almaden sky.

The flight north was smooth as he passed over San Jose suburbs and on toward Palo Alto. He followed a very moderate diagonal toward the coast and was finally in view of the ocean. The blue waters sparkled in myriad patterns in the new morning rays. Jack always loved the views when he flew to San Francisco, but this day a pall had been cast over his mood and his mind cluttered with thoughts of crusades and the Inquisition. He had not grown up in a Christian home and so had never acquired a special endearment to that faith. Now the newscast rattled in his mind as complete provocation.

Up ahead lay San Gregorio, Half Moon Bay, Pillar Point. It was all resplendent in morning mist with sea birds sailing on swift currents of air.

But further on, he could see clouds. At first, it didn't alarm him. Pacifica was often misted-in like the City. But as he got closer and closer, he could see that he was approaching rain clouds. It was not a vast squall but sizable enough to disturb him. There would be turbulence, and extremely dense rain might even mean temporary grounding. Still, he felt that he had no choice: he would push on no matter what.

Then a fork of lightning streaked through the thick cloudbank out to sea. Jack began weighing his alternatives if a coastal flash should strike out. He did not want to get caught between the hills behind Pacifica in a heavy rainsquall full of deadly, fiery discharge, trapped like a helpless bird in an electric cage.

But soon he was in darkness and drizzle. It was cold on his back despite the insulated flysuit. His helmet pattered with increasingly fat droplets of rain, and the plastic face shield bore tiny rivulets and deltas across its curved surface. Visibility decreased measurably.

Then, without warning, it struck him. It was a wide flash, brilliantly illuminescent, and it crackled like a sonic whip. Jack had no idea if he was plunging as he rolled. It had been a quick, furious lashing, and his radio control unit went dead. Suddenly, the full reality began impacting, and Jack could make out general forms with accelerating clarity.

It was happening. He was plunging.

□ □ □

"But I was only joking! You know how I am!"

Rachel Rarick knew how he was, but she was not very amused by it all.

"She's such a prissy straight! I got tired of her poodley eyes and dumb questions. She bugged me!" Eric was flashing his hot temper with a rising burst of ferocity. He felt deeply offended by Rachel's interrogation, but he knew that it had been inevitable and that he would just have to suffer through it. "I hate being at the center of this thing! It's so stupid!"

"And you can't keep your mind off other women! You joked about sex with her because that's what you were thinking about!"

"Rachel!" He was whiny and still offended. "This is ridiculous!"

"Well, Aaron is going to expect you to take the fall."

"He never said anything about that! If anything, he was glad to have found out so fast. And relieved. They won't have to use my name at the press conference."

"I'm so humiliated!"

"You're humiliated! What about me? Think how I feel!"

"Lusty as usual, I'm sure!"

"Stop that!"

"You stop it! You say that you love me and then go off and prove your loyalty like this!"

"I do love you! I was only joking with her!" He was gritting his teeth like a mad dog, then he looked hurt. "I do love you . . . "

Rachel shook her head again angrily. Neither spoke for a time. "Let's cool out and try to figure out how we can help get us all out of this. Maybe I should go down there . . . "

"And do what?"

"I don't know! Just be there. Talk to people. Explain."

Eric was suddenly pointing at the television. "Look at this! They're outside Vimana Cathedral again."

"Turn it up."

It was a live telecast. Some reporter was talking with people near the front of the cathedral. " . . . in a little over a half-an-hour, Vimana leaders will be speaking here on the church steps. How do you think they will defend themselves on these allegations?"

A young woman began answering, but Eric and Rachel were all at once completely disinterested in her words. Behind her, they saw something shiny flash, and it startled them both when they realized what it was: a very large aluminum ladder in the hands of a dozen people.

"Where are they going with that?" Rachel shrieked.

"Oh no . . . " Eric droned.

The ladder was being hoisted up the front of the cathedral as a great cheer swept over the crowd.

"Can you tell us what's going on here?" the reporter asked, turning from the woman and moving very excitedly forward.

"They're going in!" the man said, grinning.

"For what purpose? Can you explain to our audience exactly what the plans are here."

"I'm not sure, but we know that the doors are open up on the landing platform and it's probably the only way in."

"What about their guards?"

Another man standing nearby had binoculars. "There's only one," he said, "and you can tell that he doesn't see them coming."

Rachel began pacing worriedly. "Eric, do something!" she yelled.

Eric nodded once and hurried to change into his gear.

"It is just a little foggy here now . . . " the reporter was saying, "and it does appear that the Vimanians do not realize that they are about to get company . . . "

"My god!" Rachel screeched.

Four men could be seen hurrying up the long ladder. It had been extended so far that it was sagging slightly in the middle, but the men pushed on.

"First guy's going over!" the man with binoculars yelled. "He's pushing the guard back! Man never saw it coming!"

Then the other three went over. A second man helped subdue the Vimanian while the last two turned and went to the edge of the platform and began waving triumphantly to the crowd. A huge cheer went up, and the men danced and flaunted their jubilation.

Soon Eric was in his flysuit. "I'm going for it!" he told Rachel. "I'll get those son of a . . . "

But suddenly a black figure came whooshing out of the light fog on a Vimana XRK-4. Rachel let out a tiny squeal, and Eric stood stunned looking at the streaking new presence. A telephoto lens was instantly on the figure as the television crew followed him in, focusing in split-seconds.

In a flash, Rachel knew that black Vimana with the bold yin-yang symbol on its underside. "It's Jack!" she roared. "My god! In his dragon suit!"

Eric began grinning like a candy bandit. He whooped loudly and ran forward toward the screen.

Then they saw it clearly. Like some comic book Batman, he plowed, head down, straight into the dancing intruders and landed helter-skelter all over them, his great huge body writhing with muscular determination. One aerial view of the ladder and he had known what he had to do. He came up with fists flailing and all the momentum of a ring boxer. The intruders had nearly fallen paralyzed by the sudden attack and in seconds Jack had the inside track. Now the intruders found themselves backed toward the edge of the landing platform, and they all sensed the precipitous drop at their heals. One wrong move meant death for sure.

Jack knew that he had the upper hand. He could choose to fly at them and bowl them over like wobbly pins. He tore off his helmet and looked them straight in the eye. They were all poised to tangle, the adrenalin of death pumping rapidly through their bodies.

No one below or on television could hear it, but the shouting had started. Jack pushed his wet, blond hair back and moved slowly from foot to foot with hands out.

"If this is your idea of Jacob's Ladder, I think that you've got it wrong fellas." Jack felt cocky knowing that he had the complete edge, even though there were four of them.

"You and your dreams!" one man muttered angrily. "You people make a mockery of everything!"

"No," Jack protested with a wide grin. "We just never lost our sense of humor."

"Yeah!" he spat back. "And you rebuilt the golden idol out of gobbledy-gook and rocket trash. You people are despicable."

Jack nodded his head playfully and smiled. "You wanna talk metaphor, tough guy? Well, how do you like the thought of me kicking your ass from here all the way back to the catacombs!"

The man did not laugh. "Heathen!" he muttered.

"Now, now . . . get ready to fly, guy."

But the four men were in the throes of terror as they feared being thrown from the high Vimana landing ramp. "Let's rush him!" and one of the men was so fast that Jack never even had a chance to rev up the flypack. Suddenly all were on him, and fists flew every which way. But only for a moment.

Eric Harrison hit like a dynamo of explosive fury. He roared in and knocked two unconscious with a flying blow from each fist. They tumbled like bowling pins. The other two leapt up and backed away when they instantly computed bad odds and had decided to escape down the ladder. Jack stood up and grinned at Eric. "Shall we?" he said, with a wink.

Eric laughed. "It's aces all the way. Let's take 'em."

They flipped thrusters on and swept across the ramp like fighter jets taking off for a surprise attack from the deck of an aircraft carrier. They hit the men each with the flying horsepower of a Pegasus. Far below, the crowd screamed out in frantic desperation, awaiting the long, long drop of bodies to the hard ground of death. But it was not to be. Jack and Eric had slammed into their stomachs and knocked them breathless, and they fell humped over their shoulders as the Vimana men rocketed out high over the terrified crowd. They flew on around and had soon deposited the groggy intruders safely into the arms of their comrades. Then they looped back and screeched low over the screaming throng like divebombers. It was a warning to all.

Jack circled again and went sweeping by the great ladder and got a hand on it. His momentum made it jerk violently for a second. The crowd let out a piercing wail as the giant ladder went rattling, long and menacing, across the green Vimana lawn.

Meanwhile, Rachel was giddy with cheering gusto as she watched the live coverage on television. She sat back grinning like a Cheshire cat on the couch, her heart palpitating wildly. While she loathed violence, she thought about the exciting heroics she had just witnessed and wondered to herself why it had made her feel so glad. Then she leapt up and went for her flysuit. She wanted to get on over to Vimana and tell Eric how much she loved him, and be there with Kelby for the press conference and stand firm with her people.

Back on the Vimana lawn, Jack loosed the ladder when the sea of people had adequately parted, and it fell with a loud rattling bang. He then flew on around and landed. He felt exhausted but triumphant, smiling to himself for having perhaps cheated death twice that day. His last-second pull-out earlier in the heavy rain had been a nightmare, but he had managed to land and race for cover under a store awning until the storm had diminished appreciably. The owner had noticed him there and had invited him in, mentioning that he had heard about the trouble at Vimana. Then they both watched a newscast, and Jack wasted no time in getting back into the air while the pipe-smoking store owner cheered him on.

When Jack was later lauded for his heroics, many called it his finest hour. Only Aaron knew of an even better moment, but he said nothing when he remembered how Jack had once dove out an open window at his Almaden home to save the life of a young lady friend who was racing from the clutches of a jealous boyfriend and the long knife he was wielding in total, final anger and despair.

Jack Katz was not a man of fears.

The news conference took place as scheduled, behind a cordon of police and barricades. As the time neared, X. Rex Kelby and Aaron Harrison found themselves agreeing to be joined by two of their companion Vimanians.

X. Rex Kelby spoke first. He grinned charmingly and quickly tried to defuse the tension. "Welcome to Vimana Babylon," he laughed. "I'd say that we're seeing a very successful case here of rumor over reason, so let's talk." He quickly introduced his associates: Aaron Harrison, Rachel Rarick and Peter Varden.

The Vimana Babylon remark had brought a huge round of laughter from the reporters, but behind them were hundreds of jeering protesters.

"Our aim now is to simply clarify our position in regard to the absurd and slanderous allegations made against the Order of Vimana." His voice was deep and steady. "Of course, we deny these false assumptions and will go so far as to prove our position."

"Aaron . . ."

Aaron stepped forward to the microphones. "We are hereby extending an open invitation to the main networks to join us in a tour of our dream chambers. In this case, we will permit a camera crew and one reporter from each of the three major networks and cable news."

"Rachel . . ."

"Yes, and we also invite your reporters to spend the night with us to see what really goes on . . ." Her huge brown eyes flashed with playful humor, and Eric grinned at the side of the platform.

The reporters began cheering and laughing. A few catcalls went up, and Rachel turned her head coyly and smiled at the bawdy hooters. She wanted to slap their faces, but Kelby made it clear that they would handle it all without umbrage or incident. She looked over at Eric and winked.

"Now before any of you get any ideas," she continued, "let me assure you that at no time, ever, has anyone participated in such activities as we're falsely accused."

"Yes," Aaron added, "and our equipment is open for inspection to any scientist that Christian or government leaders may choose. We have nothing to hide."

"But first . . . " Kelby said, returning to the fore, "let me try and clear up our position on religion. It is true that we have drawn from all religions: Christian, Jewish, Moslem, Buddhist, Hindu, Amerindian. We have taken imagery and ideas. We've learned from all. I know that Christians feel singled out because we've chosen to build our Order within their structures. But Christianity did much the same in the old world. They built on Pagan themes and worshipped on sacred Pagan grounds. Any Christian celebration with a solstice tree is evidence of that. But we are not a new religion! We are just devotees of the human spirit and the human mind. We invite people of all religious persuasions to join us."

"Peter . . . "

Peter Varden nervously stepped forward. He hated public speaking, but he had a conviction he wanted to share. "I am a Vimanian," he said. "But I am also a Christian. I, like so many, have had a personal experience of Jesus, and He is at the heart and source of my life. Life for me would be worth nothing without His saving grace. But I am also a man of my times, and this is indeed a new age. Ladies and gentlemen . . . you wonder what this Order of Vimana is all about. I do not speak for my companions here, or for the Order as a whole. But for me . . . for me," he said with a very subtle smile, his blue eyes glinting, "flying means: Christ has risen!"

22

BY NIGHTFALL, the contingent had been assembled. There were two men and two women reporters each accompanied by a two-person camera crew. Two scientists had also been chosen to study the equipment in the dream chambers. And finally, there was an evangelist and a priest.

The dream chambers were behind huge soundproof doors and were made up of a series of smaller cubicles inside a huge basement room. Each cubicle contained beds which were separated by partitions for privacy. The headboards were all back to back around a large circular computer bank, rather like flower petals around its center. They were single beds, and each compartment had a small clothes bureau and a wash basin.

"We call these dream rosettes," Aaron explained like a tour guide. "As you can see, we have sets of two, four, six and eight."

"Why the variety?"

"Experimental," he said matter-of-factly. "We don't have all the answers yet. We're trying to find out about collective dreaming. Can it happen, does it happen, how can we help it happen. As you can see, these are very unexciting, almost sterile sleeping compartments. A far cry from any notions anyone might have of ancient dream temples with a high priestess at each man's beck and call. There is nothing going on here that need cause concern."

"What about the machines?"

"Well, of course, they contain an electroencephalogram for measuring brain waves. We have biofeedback equipment built in also so that each person can gain greater control over their own bodies and psychic processes. Relaxation is necessary to restful sleep and to meditative modes. Yes, we study the yogic mind and hypnagogic states. After all, the real thing we're after here is knowing mind. Dreams just happen to be the purest archetypal manifestations of psychic processes, so we tend to concentrate on them. Know your mind and you know yourself."

"What about the other pieces, Aaron? The ones that supposedly feed . . ." the woman reporter held up her hands and shrugged, "that feed electrical energy to the brain."

"Oh yes, the so-called brainwashing machines." He laughed. "All we're talking about here are these electrodes being attached to our dreamers' heads . . ." He showed them at the computer panel built into a headboard. "These are the Benzon electrodes, more sensitive than any yet devised, which can send a subtle electrical signal through the skull and into the brain. Scientists have pain and pleasure centers fairly mapped out now, and we're striving here to find out how stimulating these centers affects dreaming. We try it on groups and then compare reactions. We've had some fascinating results."

"Will we be hooked up with those tonight?" the evangelist asked.

"I hope so! With your consent, we will work with all of the equipment. The two neutral-party scientists will monitor, of course, and then you all can learn first hand what you've been hearing about."

So it went for hours with questions and answers and more probing, roaming and quoting. Finally, near midnight, it was time for the reporters and religious leaders to take their places on the beds. Attendants attached the electrodes after the guests had changed into sleepwear and climbed between the sheets.

"How do you normally choose who sleeps in which rosette?" the priest asked one of the attendants.

"Normally it's based on compatible dream motifs. See, we record all of our dreams into the computer, and that way we get cross-referencing on motifs and symbols. We've been experimenting with compatibility analyses and trying different people in the rosettes. But all of you are just being put around at random. You choose! None of these rosettes are any different really. You'll see. Our people are coming in now to fill out the rest of the beds."

"Why are these areas above the beds shaped like a pyramid?"

"Well, there have been volumes written about pyramid power, Father Maddox. Again, we're just experimenting."

"Indeed we are, Father!" a deep voice suddenly interjected. It was X. Rex Kelby, and he was extending a hand. "The Egyptians and the Mayans and many other ancient cultures knew about the effects of geometric spaces and shapes on the minds of men . . . " Kelby looked over at the attendant, " . . . and women, of course," he said with a quick nod. "American Indians had a profound sense of spaces and shapes as well. Frankly, I'd rather sleep out in the mountains or the plains than down under a structure like this for the best dreaming. All that clean air blowing through all night. The stars twinkling like diamonds."

"Sounds indeed like you've done it a few times, Dr. Kelby," the priest laughed. "I remember many a fun time in the backyard when I was young, but that, unfortunately, is about the extent of my sleeping in the wilds!"

"Well, perhaps one day I shall have a good wilderness retreat for meditative and dreaming purposes, and you can come visit."

The priest smiled broadly and lay back on his pillow as the attendant placed the electrode skullcap on his head. "Now see how easily it goes on," the woman said. "And if nature calls in the night, just release this band and it pops right off. Okay?"

"Fine," the priest answered. "Oh, Kelby. Will you be sleeping here tonight, too?"

"Wouldn't miss it for anything," Kelby remarked.

"In my rosette?"

"Just on the other side of you, here," he answered, pointing.

"Good. I'm curious to see how our dream motifs compare." The priest seemed pleased that he could be using the jargon so easily.

"You don't seem too uncomfortable with all of this, Father Maddox. Why is that?"

"Well, the Catholic Church has always given credence to dreams as a source of divine guidance. It is true that our mysticism is generally kept far out of view of the ordinary person, but we do nevertheless still have the ancient doctrines very much in place for those of us who wish to study them."

Kelby looked down and thought a long moment before speaking again. "Do you disapprove of what we're doing here, Father? I mean, personally..."

"I dare not speak personally!" Father Maddox said, shaking his head. "I'd like to, but it wouldn't be wise at this time."

"You know we can't really accept this kind of activity in a church. Oh sure, it's fascinating and there's a lot of truth built into your system. But you're not Christians *per se*, and you've taken over a Christian house of worship. I'm afraid that no matter what, I'll have to comdemn you in the morning." The priest's face looked pained. He was a kind man and very much in awe of Kelby's achievements.

Kelby nodded and began turning slowly to go. "Well, anyway, pleasant dreams, Father. I can only hope that deep down you'll come to understand my actions. It's a changing world out there . . . "

"We'll speak in the morning?"

"Sure," Kelby said. "Let's sleep on it all. See what happens."

"Oh, Kelby," the priest suddenly called out again.

Kelby turned and looked back.

"All those people are still going to be out there tomorrow. And they're angry, Kelby. I pray that you come through all of this okay. I can see that you're not an evil man, but a lot of people see this whole thing as evil, and you are the most visible focus of their anger. So please be very careful, Dr. Kelby. Keep your guard up so that all of your followers don't lose their guiding star. This is dangerous now, but it would be even more so without you."

Kelby smiled and said nothing. A deep hurt seemed to flash across his face for a moment as he and the priest locked eyes. Then he was gone. He went to confer with Aaron a few minutes and make a final check to see that everyone was in place. All of the lights went out except in the monitoring stations. At last, everyone settled in to sleep.

But long about the hour of four, the sleepy peace was shattered. The priest had seen an intruder with a weapon. The man had stealthily crept by and put a gun to Kelby's head. When the shot rang out, the priest screamed and Kelby lay dead in a pool of blood, his neat gray hair and beard wet and matted on the pillow. In that instant, the priest knew a truth that he would never, under any circumstances, speak about with anyone, ever. No one. Not ever. And it had only been dream.

At dawn, Aaron Harrison sat at the computer terminal and began typing in his own dream. It had been an exhilarating dream, and Aaron was convinced that it was one of the most profound and mystical dreams he had ever had. He could still feel the imagery flowing through his body in powerful waves of ecstasy and exhaustion. He thought it uncanny that his dream had arisen, built and neatly ended just minutes before the priest had screamed. It had been an odd synchronicity of timing. Kelby had often spoken of what he called "the mystic hour of four." It was the magical dreaming hour when the dark winds of the night blew through in a cool, high peace.

But that peace had been rent asunder, and now his eyes were bleary and red, but he pressed on anyway.

After he had typed in his code and date, he decided to switch over to voice print. He was too tired to type. His hand went out and flipped the switch, and he set the dials on volume. He pulled the microphone down low and leaned back on the chair. Then after a few sips of Darjeeling tea, he finally began to tell his dream.

"I was in a huge space-age building of some sort," he said, "and all those who entered could travel through time there. I was with a young lady friend of mine, and we set off on a long adventure.

"We were instantly in India amid lush mountain vegetation, walking up a long, winding trail then up to a road beside a high stone wall. For some reason, we decided to climb over the wall and go walking in the tranquil, misty forest.

"As we pushed on through, the mist got thicker and thicker until we could barely see. We came to a clearing, and there we found a beautiful cultivated garden. I could feel my heart beating excitedly to be there. It was an earthly paradise! The lake was filled with water lilies, and all around were perfect pine trees and flowers everywhere.

"We wanted to stay there and make love, but as we strolled along we could see the mountain road again, and we became curious to follow it once more.

"So we went on up the mountain and where the road plateaued, we met with a surprise. Suddenly, we were confronted by a band of Indian mystics, all yogis in orange robes, with painted faces! They were giants! Like twice my size. As we passed through, we were afraid we might be trampled!

"No sooner had we passed through the yogis when a band of giant women came along! They, too, were in orange robes and were heavily jeweled. They were all gray haired with faces of intelligence, but their size was unnerving.

"After they had passed, I went near to the stone wall and looked down over it to see where they were going. Far below, I could see an enormous throng of people, and they were all dancing with ecstatic ritual frenzy! Drums could be heard, and I was able to look through the crowd and find the drummers. I could see three. Two were women, and one was a man. To my shock, the young man was someone I knew! It was an acquaintance from my youth, a young man who had died from a drug overdose at least a decade ago. I was totally amazed to see him there pounding out a primal rhythm on a skin drum. The drumsticks were human bones!

"I was overcome by the frenzy and started shaking and dancing there on the road. I happened to see two cymbals lying on the stone fence nearby and hopped up on the fence, grabbed the metal cymbals and began clashing them in time with the drumbeat. In a moment, I was beating so hard that the large cymbals became like wings, and I lifted up into the tropical sky. Soon, I soared out over the valley of dense jungle foliage and swooped on above the heads of the Indian revelers. I darted like a bird for a time then landed right in the midst of the crowd and laid down my wings.

"There was a stone altar there, and when I stepped up to it, I was amazed at what I saw. It was a perfect pile of white excrement! As if it were the gift of a god!

"I was both repulsed and curious, but my instincts overcame me and I thrust my hand deep in the heap, then tasted it. It was neither awful nor sweet, just bland and mysterious. But I raised up my hands and declared that it was nothing less than manna from heaven! I was ecstatic. And the crowd pressed in, dancing like wild madmen and women as the primal beat reached a fantastic crescendo."

That was the end, and Aaron leaned forward and flipped off the switch. He slumped deep into the chair, smiling, and had barely closed his eyes when a voice suddenly startled him.

"What's this about holy shit?" It was Eric, and he flashed a grin, but his expression seemed serious.

"Sorry, Aaron," Rachel said. "We didn't mean to overhear . . . " Aaron laughed quietly. "Holy shit? More like wholly mystifying! What a dream!"

Rachel put a hand on Aaron's shoulder and looked him sadly in the eye. "Have you heard?" There was urgency in her voice.

"About . . . ?" He drew out the word so that she could fill in the answer.

"About the bombing."

"Bombing?" He bolted upright in his chair.

"It's just in on the news. There was a bombing early this morning in one of the wings of Atlanta Vimana."

"Anybody killed?"

"Injured, yes. Killed, no."

"He was a janitor," Eric explained. "Pretty seriously injured."

Aaron shook his head and felt nearly nauseous. "Damn it, why does it come to this!"

"Because religion always demands a sacrifice," Rachel said. "It's always been that way, and it will probably never change." She was bitter.

"This is all getting out of hand . . . " Aaron was almost sing-song in his travail. "For God's sake, the press is just getting their stories filed about last night! Now this!"

"Don't you think that we had better get on the phone to Atlanta? They're going to need some feedback on how to handle this situation."

"Well, for starters, let's get Jack up here, and he can offer ideas to Atlanta security. I'll talk to the Vimana director, and you call their press secretary."

"I'll check on security here," Eric offered. "I know that there are probably still holes we can fill."

"Good idea," Aaron agreed. Then he pounded the table with his fist. "Damn it, why did it come to this?"

An hour later, calls had been made, and the three retreated to the television room to watch the news. Jack and Tamara had joined them, and they sat around talking and listening for any new developments. The anchorman had a story, but it had nothing to do with Atlanta Vimana.

"This just in," the man announced. "Another Vimana-related story. It seems to be a black day, indeed, for members of the Order. For this latest piece, we will switch to our Washington bureau chief, Sam Koorman. Sam..."

"Thanks, Peter. An early breaking story here centers around anti-Vimana fighters, Reverend Donovan Reaves and the lobbyist Daniel Quenton. It appears that they have now successfully managed to get their anti-monopoly legislation introduced into the House. State Representative, Marshal Hoover of Alabama, is the sponsor. The bill threatens to break the solitary hold the Order of Vimana has on single-person propulsion units, the so-called Vimana flying machines. This, in connection with other recent events, might spell more setbacks for the increasingly beleaguered Order. Reaves and Quenton have announced a press conference for later this morning.

"And now, back to you, Peter . . . "

The long, awful day finally ended, and everyone went home except Jack and his security team. There was nothing more to be done. They had all worked and worked for hours on end. The press never let up. When Aaron went home, he felt as if his brain had been stretched out on the rack for days. His only joy and hope by that hour was the huge, cute gummy grin of daughter Ariel, who had just learned to giggle for the first time. Despite everything, those airy little squeals of delight made Aaron practically weep with love and pure joy. Then he kissed her tiny cheek, and he could hold out no longer. He was laughing with tears falling, pressing her little body against his chest.

Meanwhile, outside Vimana San Francisco, the crowd was more restless than usual. Events had been turning in their favor, and public support was growing despite the basically favorable stories the major network reporters had filed which fairly dispelled the original allegations raised on the Hennessy show. Still, the public perception of Vimana was increasingly that of a renegade cult which threatened the long-standing cultural norms. Most Americans felt very unsure of the direction in which its latest rebels were taking the country.

However, the crowd at Vimana Cathedral did not share that ambivalence. They were convinced that the House of Vimana was now perched very precariously on the hill and that they could affect the final changes that would bring it all tumbling down. They cheered and they chanted and they showered the grounds with the confetti of jubilation, so that when the men appeared, very few noticed. But that quickly changed. A wave of gasping voices sounded from the front of the crowd all the way back to its far scattered flanks. Fingers went up, pointing, anxious, worried. The faces were stunned in disbelief. At last, only silence reigned supreme.

The crowd looked on, unmoving. The two were like pure light where they floated high over the heads of the crowd together. Many began to weep, but others simply grew more and more bewildered. They could not believe their own eyes. For there above them, just below the great dark Vimana triskelion, was Jesus Christ and X. Rex Kelby. They each gestured, one to the other, and then they were gone.

Five minutes later . . . five long incredulous, silent minutes later . . . it came down straight at the murmuring crowd like a sudden black cloudburst off the magical trident of Poseidon, complete with thunder and lightning and the ruby eyes of death. Only this was a creature long and luminous, possessed of teeth and a fire-breathing tongue. Its nostrils fumed and its red eyes paralyzed, and it shot forth with a fury.

High above it all, in a darkened spire, it was Jack Katz loosening his ire on a panicked, fleeing crowd. He stood like a madman, laughing diabolically and bursting off great spasms of vengeful joy as he aimed his laser light dragon hologram straight down the gaping mouths of the bolting mobs.

23

THE FOG was thick as ever on Friday, and Eric and Carlos wanted to be nowhere to be found. Eric was still bothered by recent events and since the two had not been out drinking together for awhile, they decided, spur of the moment, to get an early start. They had no plans for Saturday, so they knew that they could sleep it off in the morning and if they decided to fly later that day, maybe Kelby's "watchdogs" would not notice anything unusual and make them go in for testing. Besides, they felt that they deserved a hot night out on the town. They had both truly cut back on their drinking when they had formally joined Vimana, and they were playing it as straight as they could. it was not easy. Swilling cold brews and having fun had always been one and the same pleasure.

So they raced off to Carlos' sportscar and bounced into the sleek bucket seats. They decided to kick things off with a six-pack and a quick spin over the bridge to Berkeley. As always, Carlos said he knew of a great bar with a live band. He always made it sound as if he had already been to every bar in the Bay Area. So they took off and bantered in the usual crazy way. Always kidding, almost cruel, but every jab rooted in friendship.

"Come on, Carlos! Step on it!"

"That old lady is in my way!"

"Well get around her! Can't you drive this thing?"

209

"Better than you, big shot nobody!"

"I doubt that."

"*Jeah . . . yust* you wait! I show you race driver!" He stepped on the gas and roared around through the lanes. It was as if they needed to break some laws to feel like they were still young and on the edge. And the six beers went quickly.

"We've gotta go down to Mexico!" Eric decided. He had been reading about Hemingway and loved the author's macho swagger. He especially loved the fishing stories: going for the *big ones* out of Cuba. "Let's go down and do some ocean fishing!"

"Puerto Vallarta . . . " Carlos said as if he had done it a hundred times. "I know . . . "

"If there's one thing I want, it's a big, blue marlin on my wall. Huge! A monster!" Eric felt expansive again.

"Mazatlan is good, too."

"Geezus, Geezus Chrise," Eric laughed, pretending that he was Nick Adams on the Big Two-Hearted River.

"What are you saying?" Carlos huffed. "Goosey, goosey . . . "

"Eh, you're drunk!" Eric suddenly bellowed. He loved to scare Carlos.

"On three beers? You crazy!"

"Huh!" he yelled, poking Carlos in the ribs.

"Oooo! *Yust* you wàit!"

It was always like that. They raced on to the next beer stop and proceeded to drink like one of Papa's *big ones*.

But in an hour they were bored.

"*Ees* no fun if we can't pick up women!" Carlos complained.

"Yeah, well, you better just be glad you got one."

"I know . . . " He was starting to slur his words. "But *ees* difficult when all the women want me." He cackled high and loud. Eric thought about how Carlos always looked like a jackal when he tittered like that, even though he was otherwise fairly good looking. "I am the new boss," he snickered, and he looked around the bar with slitted seductive eyes. "*Mi amor!*" He was ruminating over an underdressed gamine in high heels with lush, painted lips and great swirls of blond hair. "Let's go talk to her!"

"She won't talk to us!" Eric laughed, as if it were sheer folly to even consider it.

"Hey!" Carlos objected. "I am the King of Cool!"

"Yeah, you and every other half-wit in the bar. Come on, let's get out of here."

But Carlos was gone. He bobbed rhythmically across the floor and sauntered up to the buxom blond. Eric watched wide-eyed from the dark corner. He was suddenly full of admiration for his gutsy drinking buddy. But when Carlos returned five minutes later, he was quick to be mean.

"Haw! I knew you couldn't get anywhere with her."

"*Jeah*, but at least I have guts to talk."

Eric shrugged. "Okay, I'll give you that one. Now let's get out of here! Move!"

They quickly hit the street to ogle at all the loitering Berkeley girls outside the cluster of bars. Eric was totally taken aback. "These women are weird!" he said as if disgusted.

"*Beezarre* . . . "

"Do they all dress like this here?"

Carlos shrugged. His features were drooping from all the drink, and he felt more than a little out of place. "Let's go back to the City," he suggested with an unabashed beer burp. "This *ees* crazy."

Driving back over the Bay Bridge, they each finished another beer than cut off onto Fifth Street downtown, weaving warily through the crunch of traffic. It was dark, but still early.

"Let's go back to my house awhile," Carlos decided. "I've got some whiskey . . . " He fluttered his eyebrows up and down.

"Sure," Eric answered wearily. The alcohol was dulling him instead of perking him up as he had hoped. He fired up a cigarette then threw the empty pack down on the floor. "Need some cigarettes," he said with a slur and a scowl.

Carlos screamed out with a drunken hoot and slammed the gear shift into third and squealed around a corner laughing. "*Jeah!* Boogie!" In a flash, he was pulling up in front of a small market on Turk. Eric slowly climbed out to get his smokes. But suddenly, he stopped stockstill on the sidewalk and looked around. His eyes were nearly glazed. He squinted hard as he turned his head.

Carlos beeped the horn. "Come on man!"

Eric held up a finger for him to wait.

"Don't throw up here, you idiot!"

Eric shook his head solemnly and frowned, then went on into the store, and in a moment he was back with his cigarettes and a new cold six-pack.

"Why you stand there like that?"

"I was just thinking . . . that maybe somebody we know lives right around here." His voice had an ominous ring to it.

"Who! Some hot babe, I hope!" He rubbed his hands together, then stole Eric's pack of smokes and filched one out.

Eric did not reply. Nor did he struggle over the cigarettes. He opened a fresh beer and careened his head around to look back down the street. "No . . . " he muttered. "Somebody else . . . a little prick snitch . . . "

"Not Sara Tynes! Oh god!"

"No . . . Bradley Neiman. Little rat face!"

"Got your ass in deep shit!" Carlos teased, snickering through his nose as he exhaled a dual gust of smoke.

"Yeah, well, I want *his* ass! Drive up the block here. I know he lives right around here. I checked in the files at Vimana. It was something like 3384 or 3385. Damn it! I should have written it down."

"What for? What you going to do?" He drove ahead slowly.

"We're too far," Eric shouted. "Go back. Come on!"

"Why . . . ?"

"Just do it."

Carlos reeled around, and they headed back down the street. Soon, he was told to slow down.

"This is getting close . . . " Then suddenly, "Stop here! Stop! That's his car. I saw it on the file. I don't forget about cars." He was out of the door like a stalking leopard. "It has to be 3385, this is the odd numbered side. Come on!"

"What we going to do? This is risky."

"So what. He deserves whatever I decide to give him. Come on, let's go around back."

"I can't get in trouble, man. I get deported." Carlos was getting more nervous by the minute.

Soon they were alongside the wall in the dark shadows of the old Victorian houses.

"I can't get in trouble!" Carlos whined again.

"Why? What's the big deal?"

"I'm not here legal, man. I use my brother's passport."

"What . . . ?"

"I use my brother's passport. I'm not really Carlos."

Eric stopped cold and turned. "What do you mean?" he whispered brusquely. "Then who the hell are you? Why did you use your damn brother's passport?"

"I get in trouble in Mexico."

"For what?"

"Oh, *yust* nothing! We blow up some monuments. It was stupid . . . "

"What! You're a terrorist!"

"No, no, no! Shhh . . . " He looked back and forth, then burped quietly. "Protest, man. We *yust* protest, but we get caught."

"So you came here."

"*Jeah* . . . but I came for Lisa, man!"

"Sure. And what's your name? The Jackal?" This time it was Eric cackling.

"No . . . Hector."

"Hector?" He said it like the word *nectar* and grimaced.

"*Ek-TORE!*" Carlos whisper-screamed with perfect Spanish enunciation.

Eric began laughing maniacally. He had to put a hand over his mouth. "This is too funny! Hector!"

"*Ek-TORE!*" The flat midwest accent irked him.

"And I'm *Air-EEK!* Ya airhead!"

"Shhh . . . " A dog started barking.

Eric suddenly quieted and looked back and forth. "Oh god," he whispered. "This is too strange. Come on!"

But when Carlos stepped forward he tripped against an old bicycle, and a metallic bang echoed down the walls between the houses.

"Shhh . . . " Eric barked. "Watch out!"

"I can't see. Let's get out of here!"

"No, no. Come on . . . "

Finally they were around to the back. Eric slowly climbed the back stairs and craned his neck to see in. The interior was bathed in the colorlight of TV.

"Is he in there?"

"You're damn right he is. I can see the little worm now, watching some dumb show. Oh, I want his ass bad . . . "

"Well, how? We can't just walk in."

"No, so let's get *him* back here. His roommate looks like he's sleeping. He won't notice." Suddenly, Eric scraped the metal blade of a pair of weed shears across the old wavy-glass window. It squeaked out in a high, awful noise. Carlos immediately clutched his ears and bent down in a nerve-crawling fit.

"Stop! I hate that!"

"Shhh . . . he's looking!" Eric ducked down and chuckled deviously. "Get over there!"

Carlos jumped up onto the steps and kicked into a tangle of clanking old metal car parts, then lost his footing on a blob of oil. He cursed and spat and wobbled up onto his feet, then reached down and picked up a greasy aluminum rod, ready to beat on the junk heap in a fit of drunken hysteria. But just then Brad Neiman came bursting nervously out the back door. Eric slammed a board to the bare lightbulb Neiman had switched on as he pushed out onto the porch, and Carlos, in his frenzy, brought the aluminum rod down on his head. Now it was Neiman wobbling on his feet, and his legs went rubbery. Then a rock-hard fist slammed into his eye, and Eric had his revenge. They were far away in the car before either dared cackle through a breathless, beer-wetted throat.

"Now let's go get that whiskey, Hector."

"*Ek-TORE!* Gringo!"

"Yeah, yeah." Eric laughed like a wildman as Carlos squealed up the hills of Twin Peaks, hooting in total drunken reverie. "Geezus Chrise!" he wheezed. "Geezus Chrise!"

24

THE REVEREND Donovan Reaves
was in a fury. The major network journalists, he felt, had been too easy on
the Vimanians and, in fact, had offered up fairly positive stories two days
before. To make matters worse, the scientists had completely debunked
the brainwashing allegations and then the priest and the evangelist had
dispelled any notions of prurience in the dream chambers. On the one
hand, he had felt relieved and on the other, he knew that it would make his
mission just that much more difficult. But the hologram projections had
renewed his fervor. He had been rightly outraged and had even grown in
his conviction.

As he sat on the plane, enroute to San Francisco, he felt a great relief
wash over him. He had never been at ease with the smear campaign. The
allegations had been thrown in as an afterthought when the Hennessy
show had neared airtime. It had turned out to be the exact kind of tactic
that he himself most deplored. But Hennessy was a showman, and he
knew how to deliver to his loyal audience. Brad Neiman had come along,
and suddenly the whole broadcast had gotten slanted. Now his movement
had a look of fanaticism about it, and Reaves realized how pivotal his role
had become and how in such a brief time he had found himself behaving
precisely as his followers had expected him to act, not as he would have
naturally acted being true to himself.

And, yet, he had to win. There was no question in his mind over the rightness of his stand. Now he was enroute to see Kelby in person, and he had full plans to take the proverbial bull by the horns.

He was met at the airport by a black-eyed Brad Neiman, and the tension between the two was immediately palpable. But they went on to dinner at a seafood place near the marina and set about rebuilding their strategy. Above all, they had their common goal to keep them talking, and they pursued discussions in that direction. The fact that they did not really like each other was made secondary and unimportant.

The next day, the two went to their prearranged meeting with Kelby in his office at U-Star Videos. Rachel wondered about Neiman's eye but quietly showed the two in and after introductions were made, she began to leave. But then Kelby was suddenly adamant that she stay, so the four sat down, and an awkward situation quickly became even more awkward.

Reaves was first to attack. "Dr. Kelby," he said, "the lord does not look kindly on this charade of yours, and I want you to know, here and now, that we intend to put you out on your ear. We cannot permit you to continue to bring sacrilege and Satanic pollution to the House of God!"

"Oh, cut the crap!" Kelby instantly shot back, surprising the preacher with his directness. "You're not on television now, Reaves. Neiman told me that you wanted to talk, so let's talk. But don't waste my time with phrases like 'Satanic pollution.' That offends my intelligence."

Reaves was taken aback but managed to lean forward in his chair and wag a mean finger. Nevertheless, it was a flash of anger he quickly got past. He sat back and mumbled a quiet apology. "I'm sorry, Dr. Kelby," he said. "I'm not really a fire and brimstone kind of preacher, but I have been genuinely upset at this whole thing. It's very distressing to me and seems to truly point to the quickening decadence in our world today. Why do you have to pick on our churches, Kelby? Why did you have to tear a hole in the wall of the last real shelter we have in this day and age?"

Kelby was touched by the sudden sincerity. "Reverend Reaves," he began, "I can see why someone would not want outsiders coming in and taking over their sacred places, but we're not destroying them like heartless conquistadors. We're rejuvenating them! Giving them new life and, I believe, new sacredness."

Brad Neiman stood up, already tense, and began slowly pacing. "I can almost see that," he told Kelby. "I was not just a stooge sent in to try and find sleaze in the Order, you know. I really do love flying, and I had really hoped to make a go of it when I joined. But I was never at ease in that setting!

For God's sake, Kelby, a Christian church is not the place for a club! It's a house of prayer and a refuge from evil. It's a place to purify the spirit!"

"Which is just what we offer at Vimana!" It was Rachel Rarick talking now, and she, too, was now on her feet. "We offer meditation and refuge; and to soar with other flyers in an initiation rite is nothing if not purifying! How more angelic can any act be?"

"Please, please! Sit down, you two!" Reaves insisted with a shake of the head. "You're making us all nervous."

"The thing is," Kelby suddenly said, "is that we are trying to bring higher truths to our people. In the age of the global village, we simply must strive for an eclectic view of religion. So if we see a great symbol which demonstrates a universal truth, we use it.

"Like the Chinese symbol of yin and yang. It's a symbol which expresses the unity of complementary opposites. That makes it a useful tool! We're not necessarily Taoists because we display that symbol. But the way of *tao* is beautiful!

"See," Kelby went on, "man's ideals are a quiltwork of interrelated thoughts, like the fabric of space-time. They are made up of a woven blend of the dualities, part warp and part woof . . . "

"And you Vimanians are just a lot more warp than woof!" Reaves blurted out. Then he laughed. "Oh, I'm just kidding, Kelby. I'm sorry. I couldn't resist that one." Kelby laughed hard, but not Rachel. Brad Neiman frowned and seemed enormously confused. When Reaves saw his face he laughed again, and Neiman glowered angrily.

"Look, I'm really sorry," he said again. "But this kind of philosophizing really misses the point."

Rachel turned her face away, irritated. "It is the *real* point, Reverend Reaves! Can't you see that?"

"I don't mean to belittle your insights here," Reaves insisted. "All I'm saying is that all of us have our own ideas on what life is all about, and that is not our argument here. Sure, I'd love to convert you two to my religious point of view, and perhaps one day you will see things more the fundamental Christian way. But the immediate question is how can we resolve this other issue? Can we compromise somehow? Can you be offered a sum of money to abandon the churches and move your quarters elsewhere? What can we do to change this unacceptable situation?"

Kelby sat nodding and gestured to Rachel to calm down. He realized that Reaves was actually a pragmatist and not at all the bully he sometimes appeared to be. But no sooner had he thought that, than Reaves seemed to immediately jump in with a shovelful of brimstone again.

"Kelby," he said, "what happens on the Day of Judgment? Do you have any idea of your fate? Can you imagine what the Lord will say?"

Now it was Kelby who was taken aback. But he quickly rallied. "Reverend Reaves," he said, "if you want to know what I believe about the Day of Judgment, I'll tell you. That Day does come at the end of time, and it *is* man's last day. But not because God will judge our acts, one by one, and condemn us to Heaven or Hell. No, it's because only man really judges, and he does so because he is cursed and blessed with the knowledge of good and evil. Again, we are just talking the dualities without which there would be no life at all. When man ceases, so do such notions. And without any minds to comprehend time, time ceases, too. We won't go to Heaven or Hell. Those are just two more dual notions which have taken on a life of their own over the millenniums. Heaven and Hell are in any plane where there is consciousness. The mind is all, Reverend Reaves, and that is as true for the here and now as it is for any next world."

Reaves sat silent for a moment, then very quietly took objection with Kelby's argument. "It is true that good and evil are of this world, Kelby, but God is finally beyond good and evil, and I expect and pray for the day when I am taken by the Lord, and I will remain conscious, but I will never again face evil. The good will win! I believe that. To seek proof, as they say, is to admit doubt. In that there is peace."

"That's some peace!" Rachel quickly argued. "If you have not put your faith to the grindstone of reason, by doubting with everything you have in you, then how can there be peace in that?"

"Because!" Brad Neiman shouted, "we don't explain! We just proclaim! We are not here to question God's Word which has been handed down for all time in the Bible! The more I listen to all of this mumbo jumbo, the more angry I become. Remember that Jesus, Himself, cursed the figs and lost His temper at times of injustice. It's obvious to me that you will not listen to the voice of God as delivered here through an anointed spokesman. You argue arrogant gibberish, and now you leave it to us to drive the money vendors from the temple!"

"Brad! Sit down!" Reaves yelled. "You're getting out of line here!"

"I will not sit by and watch this man make fools of us!"

"Neiman, sit . . . down!"

But Brad Neiman had suddenly snapped. He brought a gun out from under his coat and pointed it at Kelby. "Now you will die for your sins!" he yelled as he cocked the trigger.

In a flash, Rachel was there in front of Kelby, but Kelby threw her aside and she went hurling over a coffee table. The gun sounded with a metallic pop, and a fiery spark propelled the killer bullet. But it was Reaves who leapt forward and took the lead piece in his side. And Reaves who managed to lay a fist across Brad Neiman's eye. They both fell as Rachel grabbed the pistol from the thrashing youth as he quickly struggled to rise.

Several states away and in a very different state of mind, far above all the anguish and rages of the changing world, Oriana Zevallos was humming a quiet song to herself. It was an old Hollywood show tune, and she gently rocked back and forth on a high pinnacle overlooking a sparkling green lake. Her mother had died only a month before, and she was thinking back to when the family had been in full bloom; how her mother had always been the center; how her own life had always revolved around that pivotal, powerful woman. It had never been less than an extremely complicated relationship, often demanding to the point of exasperation, but there had never been anyone Oriana had admired more. Now her mother was gone, and it would never be the same.

The night of her death had begun understandably in anguish, but then when sleep had finally come, she had had a dream. She had found herself in the huge basement of a building, walking down a great, long corridor, where she had seen a man looking down through a high window, and it scared her, so she grabbed a long rod and busted out the window. But the man only smiled. He was a famous poet, and he had just continued looking in. Finally, she had gone on into another huge room where she had encountered a beautiful ballet scene: a hundred dancers in pastel pinks and blues, all in the throes of a gentle sensual ecstasy, leaping into pirouettes and bending to gracefully plie. Oriana had suddenly found herself joining the dance, and soon she had been lost in the reveries, too. But at one point, the dancers had set up two lines and then had leaned into one another to form a tunnel of arms. Oriana had found herself dancing down through the tunnel of bodies, and when she had gotten to the end, she met there a prima ballerina in a soft blue costume with a glittering tiara of diamonds atop her short, dark hair. She was young and smiling, and she had held out her hand to Oriana as she dipped into a perfect plie. Then Oriana recognized her. It was her mother, young and radiant, and from that moment forward, Oriana did not anguish for her worldly passing.

But now Oriana was high up on a Teton peak with a small climbing party, and they were all resting on a precipice. She slowly edged around the rock wall to have a moment alone. As she quietly ran her fingers along the length of a crampon, she was struck with a new realization as the bright sun poured down on her face. She saw in her mind a vision of Artemis, the ancient Greek Goddess of the Hunt, Virgin of the Moon and sister of the sun-god Apollo. Suddenly, she knew why she was alone. She rose to stand on the edge of the ledge and thought to herself how easy it would be to simply leap off into forever, because she did not now fear death and because there could never be a fuller moment than this. The climbing party had turned to see her long, black hair blowing just above the stone that was hiding her. As one of the men edged round, sensing a sudden danger, Oriana made her move. The man gasped and called to her, his voice breaking with terror. But Oriana only smiled. She had shed the safety belt which connected her to the life-saving crampons. Now she was scrambling up toward the peak alone, and she knew that she would make it. She knew that she would one day climb beyond the earth, but she would never really die.

Back at Vimana, the crisis continued. The attempted assassination of Kelby immediately became a front page headline across the nation, but Kelby did his best to defuse the situation by not pressing charges. Nevertheless, Brad Neiman remained incarcerated pending complete medical testing. He pleaded stress and explained his weapon as a necessity to his own protection once it had become known that he had betrayed the Vimanians. But he had used the gun with aggression, and the police assured Kelby that he would be locked away for a very long time.

The Reverend Donovan Reaves had survived the night but was still listed in critical condition by morning. A copy of the day's news was beside him on a chair, but he was not able to read about the ill-fated incident. Powerful painkillers had been administered, and he would awake and talk for only brief minutes. Police tried to question him, but he was not able to respond. Meanwhile, a crowd of reporters waited impatiently in the wings, all anxious to ask the same question: Why did Reaves sacrifice himself to save Kelby?

Reaves did not know the answer to that question at first, except that, of course, killing was forbidden in his religion and he could never consider such a heinous, sinful act. But a few nights later, Reaves had a dream that changed everything in his mind. He had rarely paid attention to dreams, but his wife Jennifer had arrived, and they had talked off and on and Reaves had agonized over the incident to an unbearable degree. Then he had a dream that he was unable to ignore. The imagery had been too powerful and the message too poignant. Finally, in the dead of night, he sat up in a sweat and when Jennifer heard him stirring, she went to him.

"What is it?" she wanted to know. "Should I call a nurse?"

Reaves waved a hand and told his wife to sit beside him on the bed. "I'm alright," he told her.

"Well, what is it then?"

He was not pleased to tell it. "A dream . . ." he stammered. "A nightmare."

"Do you need to tell it?" She took her husband's hand and then grabbed a washcloth with her free hand and brought it coolly across his forehead.

"I don't want to tell it but, yes, I guess I do need to tell it. It took place like in medieval times. It's a long one . . ."

"Go on . . ."

"Well, we were living in an old European city, see, and our home was a great huge castle. We were waiting for friends to come over, but they didn't show, so I went to bed. As I was sleeping late in the night, I heard a commotion and woke up and heard you arguing with someone. There was a fight and when I got up and went out to investigate, I found that you had killed a man."

Jennifer's face contorted for a moment in confusion, but she decided not to speak.

"This gets strange . . ." Reaves warned her. The sweat was returning to his forehead.

"Go on, Donovan!" she insisted.

"Well, you placed the dead body in a tub of water," he blurted out. "And you . . . brought the body miraculously back to life!" Reaves eyes were wide. "The man was very angry, of course, for having been killed, and he ran off to call the police. I feared for you suddenly, and I took your hand and we fled into the city. Soon we were at a cafe, and we met a man that was in some sort of secret league. We all sat together whispering like conspirators. Then I took off . . . dare I say it? Flying!"

Jenny raised an eyebrow and smiled subtly out of one side of her mouth. "Was that so awful?" she asked.

Reaves flushed slightly, then asked for a drink of water. "Now this next part . . ." he warned his wife, "I can't explain, but . . ."

"Just tell it!"

"Well, I flew around the city, then eventually returned to the cafe. You and the man were gone and, instead, there was some mysterious woman there. I have no idea who she was, but . . ."

There was a long pause as Reaves struggled to admit something. But

Jenny already anticipated what he was trying to say and bent down and kissed him on the cheek. "Don't worry," she assured him. "The woman is an anima figure. She represents your own soul."

Reaves looked astonished.

"I've been reading, Donovan. I'm trying to understand . . . "

Reaves held up a hand. "Okay," he said. "In that light maybe I can say this. When I met that woman, even though I couldn't really even see her face, I knew that she was my one true love." Reaves flushed again.

Jenny smiled. "It's all right!" she said. "Go on, Don!" She felt very maternal and loving.

"Well . . . this woman possessed a secret, and she soon revealed it to me. She told me that she could murder! That was all! That was her secret! I felt such sadness, like I've never known. And yet, I was so happy to be with her.

"Then my father and mother were there and they led me to a huge banquet hall where a great fabulous feast was all laid out. We sat to eat. My father pulled out a lute or some instrument like that, and he played one of the saddest, most beautiful songs ever. I could have cried. But, instead, I leapt up and I raced out of the hall and I hurried back to the castle we lived in. I knew that you were inside, and I wanted desperately to be with you. The door was guarded, and a great long line of animals was there, each awaiting their turn to be admitted. I had to stand in line to get into my own home! And there were these large birds in front of me. Swans, I think. They tried to fly over the high castle wall but failed. They just couldn't fly anymore. Then I tried it, and I couldn't fly anymore, either. And it depressed me. I've never felt so depressed! So I went off in the tall grasses to find a long limb. I was determined to pole vault over the wall! But again I failed! So I wandered off sadly with my long stick, and I just poked around in the tall grasses feeling miserable and forlorn. At one point, I hooked on a snake with my stick and threw it out into the open. As I looked at the snake, I just wondered aloud why I had lost my ability to fly and why I couldn't get back into the castle. Then I said aloud, and I remember this very vividly, I said 'Maybe I've lost the power to fly because I once actually considered murder.' "

"My God!" Jenny whispered, her eyes wide in wonderment. "Like a parable . . . a fable!" Reaves nodded and raised a final finger. "More?" she asked.

Reaves shook his head no. "Only this . . . " he said cautiously. "There was a phrase I kept thinking over and over as I began to wake. It was strange, as if it were meant to sum up everything. Same words over and over . . . "

"What words?"

"I kept saying to myself, 'This is the secret.' "

"What secret?"

"The secret of paradise lost."

25

IT WAS A WEEK before Aaron and Phoebe could get away for a break. They had arranged to meet Jack and Tamara at a favorite camping spot near Mt. Tamalpais. There was a small creek that ran down through a lush ravine where they had hiked back through the redwoods and the pines together several times before. It was a perfect hide-away, and they would only rarely see other hikers passing through. They all needed the brief solitude. Events had reached a feverish pitch, and they each had a tremendous yearning for some simple restful recreation. So they made their plans, and they packed their cars. Ariel was given to grandparents for the weekend, and exodus from metropolis began early, before the heavy rush hour.

But other hours rushed by, and they were all finally in back packs, setting out through a fragrant twilight wind with the birds and other creatures of the leaves chattering softly about the impending sunset. They were soon by the creekwaters, following it upstream and watching its clear ripples break against stone and fallen timber, all with a pleasant gurgling and a whooshing sound. It became very easy to let their minds drift, to relax and forget their problems. They trekked on up into the thickening darkness of the forest and made camp on a tiny flowered meadow with a fine view of the brightening stars. A great crackling fire was lit deep in a circle of stones. Food and drink passed over hungry, thirsting lips and then finally, at last, there was nothing left to do and nowhere left to go. The stars grew more and more brilliant, as if a billion other worlds were pressing down with searchlights, hoping to find any trusting friend anywhere out there across the vast void of endless space.

"And to think that one day my boys will travel up through that . . . " Jack sighed.

"What about your daughter?" Phoebe quickly asked with a sly glance.

Tamara laughed and shook her head. "And *your* daughter!" she added, thinking of Ariel.

"But not me," Aaron said. "I like looking from here just fine."

"That surprises me!" Tamaraps eyes were glistening in the firelight, and she grinned. "I would have thought that you of all people would want to go to other planets."

"I do, but . . . there's too much to see here yet. Besides, the real excitement of the stars is their unfathomable distance. I don't even bother looking through binoculars or telescopes very often. I just like to walk or lay out under all the billions of lights and feel the whole incredible miracle moving like a rapture over me. There is no greater fulfillment possible if you just open up to it fully here."

"Yeah," Jack agreed. "But I'd still like to go up. Even to the moon before I die. It's still really possible. And I know for sure that my . . . children . . . will go." He smiled at the women.

"Can you imagine what it must have been like for our ancestors to look out on this and only feel its power and grandeur, and never even think about distances and travel and hydrogen and helium? Just . . . awesome grandeur."

"And then a spaceship flies over!"

"Vimana! The gods!"

"Coming back . . . overseeing everything forever."

Tamara laughed, then looked serious. "Do you really think that they dreamed it all? The spaceships I mean."

"Who? The Indians?" Aaron asked.

"Yes. In the old books."

"Maybe . . . " he answered. "The psyche certainly has the archetypal impulses for it. But in the end, I have to believe that they were once really here. The giant stoneworks all over the planet make it near impossible not to believe. How could ancient men cut massive stones like butter and then transport them to boot?"

"Impossible," Jack laughed. "Unless a whole great civilization rose and fell before this epoch. Either way, they were our ancestors, and they knew space and flight."

"I can feel that in my body!" Aaron said excitedly. "And I dream it! We all dream it!"

"Not me," Phoebe joked. "All I ever dream about is buying clothes. Unless, of course, some creep is chasing me to put a knife to my throat. Those kind are always fun."

"Why do you dream about flying all of the time?" Tamara asked Aaron. "Is that normal, or is that just you?"

Aaron thought a moment. "Well, it is normal, but still I'm sure that not many dream-fly as often as I do."

"Was it always like that?"

Aaron nodded. "Yes. It all began when I was still a kid. The first flying dream I remember took place at my parents' home. Our front porch was a ways off the ground, and I used to try to walk off it and not touch the lawn. It was such a struggle at first! I would float and bob up and down on thin air, trying to walk clear across the yard to the road. At first, I would end up falling to the ground, but as the years passed, I just kept gradually staying up longer and longer and getting further and further across the yard. It was a very recurring dream. Then as I got older, I started rising up higher. I remember that for years I kept trying to fly over the telephone line out front of the house. But the real impetus to fly higher was always fear. Somebody chasing me and I had to get away. There's nothing like fearing for your life to make you get your butt moving!"

"Hey!" Jack suddenly pondered. "If the fear of God is supposed to be the beginning of wisdom, then maybe the fear of death is the beginning of the wisdom of transcendence. Maybe they're the same thing, really."

"The Buddhists say that suffering and death are what drives humans to be spiritual. Without death, there would be no religion at all. When we suffer and begin to fear death, our attention turns, and we begin to pray very hard that death is not as final as we fear it to be."

"So we pray for a savior."

Aaron nodded, then grinned. "I remember when I was in Australia one night. Oriana and I had gone out to dinner at a friend's house. We were drinking wine and having fun, but my index finger kept swelling more and more from an infection I had. I had gotten a bunch of wood splinters in there when I had run my hand hard across the top of an old antique picture frame. I was just brushing off dust. But it got very infected and worse as the evening went on, and finally I just had to go to the hospital even though I was half drunk on wine.

"Anyway, we get to the hospital and they take me in to the emergency room and lay me out on a surgical table. Then they pull out a sideboard and lay my arm out on it and a young medical intern comes and looks things over. Suddenly, he pulls out a huge needle and tells me that I had better not watch. So I look up toward the ceiling and what do I see just as the needle goes into the raw, infected finger, but Jesus Christ on the crucifix hanging above the door! And it was excruciating! Then he probes and probes with pins and tweezers and has to re-stick me two more times with a painkiller and all of the time I'm lying there writhing looking at Jesus on the cross! I could have screamed! But I began to really understand what Jesus is all about. See, Jesus is everything they say He is. He is the perfect archetypal image of the whole spectrum of what it means to be born of two natures: the physical and the spiritual. When we face true suffering, it is pure torture, and that image of Christ on the cross shows that to its unbearable extreme. And if we suffer, there is always one great impulse: to be free of that suffering. The impulse is to fly! To be out of body. To soar! To be beyond the torture which the body endures. The spirit wants to break away from physical existence. So, it's at that point that we realize that we are both body and spirit. And, of course, eventually we do die. The Christ myth tells us that the reward for compassion is ascension. When we care that we suffer and that all people suffer in this bodily existence then we have found the love at the very heart of all life. God goes out of Himself, so to speak, because God is life. And life is always some form of energy, which means that there must be a flowing of positive and negative forces. That basic duality creates all dualities: good and bad, pleasure and pain, self and other. So wherever there is life, there is body and spirit and the eternal tension that brings with it. The only way out is to get off what the Buddhists call the Wheel of Life. Christ ascending into Heaven is the same as the Buddha entering Nirvana. It is a place that is nowhere because it's beyond the physical Wheel. We won't know what that is until we die."

"So how do we deal with that now?"

"By dream flying!"

"Really?"

Aaron looked very serious. "The secret of dream flying is that it provides a way of learning how to exist beyond the body. The more conscious you are of departing the body at death, the greater control you will have over what happens from there. The Tibetan Book of the Dead talks about a series of *bardos*, or planes, the spirit goes through after death where we see all kinds of phantoms, some friendly and some ferocious. There is usually a guide of some sort, a light-being or an ancestor. Still, it is up to each of us how we respond to what we see. If we know nothing of the mind and its archetypes, then we will most likely spook and race off trying to hide. They say that most souls at that time flee back to earth to be reborn into this familiar world where they take a nice unconscious rest as a baby. Back to unknowing and total dependence. Others go on into different levels of existence: purgatories and karmic realms. But if you're enlightened, you can push on undeterred, straight on into the highest purest light, whatever that is. God, I guess. Pure energy. What happens there is anybody's guess. Maybe they choose to go back out again."

"Like the *bodhisattvas*," Jack added. "Give up your own total peace to go back into the world and help enlighten others. It's the ultimate gesture of compassion."

There was a silence as the four each turned to their own thoughts a minute and gazed off into the roaring fire.

"So how do we learn to fly in our dreams?" Tamara wanted to know. "I've never done it before. Can you make it happen?"

"Flying and the thought of flying are really the same," Aaron explained. "If you just become more and more aware of your dreaming, you will set the thing in motion. Keep a dream diary so that you force yourself to pay attention to the events in your dreams. Soon you'll find that your conscious mind becomes watchful even while you're dreaming. Then at some point, you'll be in for a surprise. Maybe some shadowy figure will be following you and you'll be trying to get away. But instead of feeling like lead, and barely moving, struggling with everything that you have in you, you'll simply *will* yourself far away and presto! you fly like a bird escaping the claws of a pouncing cat! As this happens more and more, you'll feel more secure in yourself because you know that you can get away to safety. That security will then allow you to move on into higher realms of dream learning, which is really learning Mind."

"And Mind is everything," Jack laughed. "Lucid dreaming lets you know Mind."

"Everybody can fly then?" Tamara asked. "Even somebody as down to earth as me?"

"Everybody!" Aaron assured her. "Anthropologists have found that to be true in every culture, whether primitive or modern. It's a universal truth that every human psyche possesses the instinctive ability to fly or, at least, desire flying. All through the ages this has been true. Every culture has myths or legends about ancestors or gods who can fly and who ultimately call to the rest of us to join them. This, of course, takes many forms. It may show up in virtually any kind of tale. The most poignant are the tales of men and women who actually physically fly, like the old divine kings, the yogis, the sages, the mystics. Then, of course, there are the shaman and the sorcerers, the witches, the alchemists, the genies, the magic carpet riders, the saints who levitate, the fairies, the sun-gods and on and on. It never stops. The ancients saw vimanas, we see UFO's. Both may be real, both may be archetypal projections."

"Don't forget about Superman and all the comic book heroes!" Jack laughed.

"The list is endless, and it goes right on into the future. Which is why the Order of Vimana will survive. We're striking an ancient nerve deep in the modern psyche. I won't begin to suggest that we can make anything like the impact Christ had on the world, but we just may be the next evolutionary step in the growing spiritual impulses of the people of this planet."

Tamara gave Aaron a mischievous look. "You're not getting a messiah complex are you?"

Aaron raised his head and chortled. "Messiah? No, too messy! I wouldn't begin to play with all of that."

"Where do we go from here?" Jack wondered. "How do we win over our enemies?"

"Well, Jack, for starters, let's quit scaring the bejesus out of them with dragon holograms!"

They all four laughed maniacally about that. The story had made national news, and Jack had become both a Vimanian hero and a Christian villain. He had thumbed his nose and nearly caused riots.

"I think, in all seriousness," Aaron went on, "that we should go ahead with the full demonstration in Washington. But we've got to stay non-violent and win both legally and morally. Let's just show them who we are and why we're here to stay. Then we'll let time and every dreamer take us deeper and deeper into the national psyche."

"And then the world!" Phoebe yelped like a mad cheerleader. "Yippee-ki-yay!"

They all laughed again, then settled into less fantastic flights of fancy. When the conversation came around to Ptero Boa and the band's impending U.S. tour, Jack had a thought that he wanted to float by Phoebe.

"What is it?"

He began by gesturing with his hands. "Well . . . it's just a little idea to promote the band . . . "

"And make you money!" Tamara laughed.

Jack grinned through his rascal mask. "Yeah, okay, that too . . . "

"What is it?" Phoebe asked again.

"Lyrics, symbols, pictures . . . "

"Say it . . . "

"You could be the High Priestess . . . "

"What are you talking about?"

"Oh, just a little something we'll call Ptero cards!"

"Tarot?"

"No, Ptero! As in Ptero Boa! Only Ptero tarot, see?"

"Ptero tarot?!"

"Ptero tarot. That's it!"

26

AS MAURICIO Manza spoke to the vast crowd in his distinctive accent, he breathed a very charming excitement into his mysterious and ethereal subject, and everyone sat back rapt as if listening to poetry or myth or fable. As he smiled through his dark beard, the listeners found themselves floating on a sea of lulling words, each imagining a scene all their own. He was talking about out-of-body experiences.

As Aaron pondered the grand mix of ancient and modern ideas, his mind drifted on wave after wave of fascination and probability. It was all fantastic and enigmatic, perhaps only because he had never actually experienced it. He had never astral projected.

But he thought about his closest people and they had experienced it. Oriana was the first. It was back after they had first moved in together. Oriana had gone out of town to a research facility in another city while working on her doctoral thesis. When she had returned after the week ended, she came back excitedly proclaiming that she had had an out of body experience. Then to Aaron's surprise, she told him that she had come to him on a certain evening and even described which room he had been in at a certain time of night and what he had been doing. When Aaron thought back, he realized that she had been absolutely correct.

The second person who had described such a personal experience to him was his brother Eric. Eric said that he had been under a lot of stress from his job at the local newspaper, and in fact he had been dangerously close to a nervous breakdown from the pressure. One night, he went out to the backyard of his parents' home and lay down in the grass to gaze at the stars and relax. Before long, he fell into a sort of semi-trance and then suddenly found his viewing perspective changing drastically. All at once, he was hovering above his own body looking down on it! He rose up higher and higher until he was able to see over all of his parents' property, and there he hovered in a mysterious silence for a time he was not later able to measure.

The third was Phoebe, and she had described how one night she had rolled out of her body and floated up through the ceiling and roof where she had hovered looking out on the golden stars. She believed that given the right frame of mind that she could do it again, but she had said that she was in no hurry. It was an experience not to be taken lightly, and she wanted to be sure that she was more ready for it next time. She wanted more control.

But Mauricio had studied with the yogis in the far recesses of the Himalayas, and his stories had everyone spellbound. For thousands upon thousands of years, the adepts of the mystic East had pursued this arcane phenomenon and had passed down knowledge from master to disciple in an unending chain reaching back into forever. Now, the audience was rapt in tales of Bon-po priests flying on their drums, and trance-runners racing at inhuman speeds across impossibly rugged terrain, their feet barely touching the ground at all. Taoist sages were stepping off misty ridges onto thin air as astonished followers stood watching in disbelief, only to see their master return later, acting as if nothing extraordinary at all had occurred. And then there were the stories of holy men being in two places at once; perhaps quietly reposed in meditation at a hermitage, but also seen far away at the wedding or funeral of a close friend.

So the tales went on, and eveyone marveled and wondered. Aaron, like so many others in the audience, was marveling and laughing to himself, too, about something different, something which had nothing to do with words. It concerned Mauricio's fine features: his long, shaggy brown hair, full beard and bright blue eyes. All the talk of holy men brought back a memory, going back only a brief few weeks to an infamous night in Vimana history, when Jack Katz had set a dragon loose on an unsuspecting crowd. When Jack had projected the hologram of Kelby and a holy man. When Jack had electrified with an image of Mauricio Manza, and everyone had taken it to be Jesus Christ.

By the time Aaron took the stage, his audience had been well primed. Two days of conferences and seminars had preceded him, and he could feel their excitement as the end approached. Rachel Rarick had opened the conference with a fine talk on the growing Vimana movement and had organized a step-by-step manual for new members. She offered her services to anyone who needed information on procedures, then continued on as master of ceremonies, introducing all of the speakers and telling about their backgrounds. Atlanta Vimanian, Simon Cody, had talked about his Order's handling of the unfortunate bombing which was never resolved. Each side claimed that the other had done it to score propaganda points, and it had finally just died in the press. But they had all learned the necessity of improved security, and Simon finished his speech with suggested measures. Then Chicago's Justin DeWitt lifted the proceedings with an inspired, stimulating talk on the benefits of hypnotism in reaching the subconscious, and also cited the benefits of biofeedback and deep breathing exercises. He was followed by Peter Varden, who in his medical studies had learned of the use of ascension imagery, including flying, in the treatment of various psychological problems, especially fears. He then went on to speculate that perhaps Vimana was to be a great boon to the increasing paranoia of the national psyche and that one day the tide might very well turn and tension subside as more and more Americans join, or at least get inspired by, the flying Vimana. For all signs, he explained, point to ascension imagery as beneficial to regeneration. Therefore, he concluded, crime may in time show significant decreases and a whole new sense of well-being pass over the American psyche. Perhaps, even the world psyche.

When Peter had finished, the talks ended for the first day. But when the new day rolled around, Damon Burke immediately kicked things off with an exciting update on hologram research and how the mind may in fact use a similar means to create its images, which apparently transcend time. As with any hologram, in which any part can be used to recreate the whole, so with mind which, as part of the great emanation of intelligent energy of the total cosmos, may in fact at any time reflect past imagery of what once was, or offer precognitive flashes of what may one day be. Hence deja vu and likewise prophetic dreams, all in the great mystery of Mind flowing through eternity.

After Damon, there was a new face. Her name was Shana Capella, and she was from London. She had bright, long red hair and a mischievous smile, and she immediately dazzled with a long talk on the relation of dreams to alchemy. She wove a great tale of imagery drawn from mythology, fable, religion, psychology, secret societies, history and even UFO research. It was all, she said, a spiritual quest for an ever-changing grail which humans always and everywhere had sought and that alchemists through the millenniums had uncovered the secret of, only to hide again and again because it is too sacred for profane eyes to see. To turn lead to gold was as nothing compared to turning the base soul into a light of Eternal Gold. She was often cryptic and left much unsaid, but she did hint that future revelations would follow as she herself pursued the elusive elixir of immortality. She promised to return again soon to describe her progress in the search.

Then it had been Mauricio Manza's turn, and he had delivered his stirring tales of the astral fantastic.

And, finally, it was Aaron at the podium, pushing beyond his initial trepidations and into the subject matter of his obsession: dream flying.

"We have all come to Washington for the same reason," he began, "because we love flying!" His audience cheered wildly, and Aaron smiled coyly, then brought a hand up to hush the huge crowd. "Now here in this place our time has come to pass and indeed, in a great show of unity and determination, as you all definitely know, we will fly! The nation and the world will see that we are many in number and long on resolution. We are sweeping across this country and growing at a pace that makes us a true phenomenon. We will not be stopped!"

When the cheering diminished, Aaron was still beaming. Something new was stirring within him. A new courage and a new passion such as he had never known. Suddenly, it didn't matter that all eyes were on him. His self-consciousness had simply evaporated. Now his mind bent to the task at hand, and he wanted only to share his genuine vision of a hopeful future.

"And where does this motivation come from? Where does the heart of this drive spring from? From within, of course! That is why Vimana is built on the deepest dreams of man. We are earthbound creatures, wedded to the gravity of a giant sphere lost in space. We, too, are lost until we have found the inner vision, a glimpse of the spirit that animates this whole miracle. When we go with that vision . . . when we fly that vision, then it all grows clear beyond the struggling days of each of our own lives.

"So permit me to quickly share two dreams I've had in just these last few weeks. The first occurred on a recent camping trip I was on, where we slept in the shadow of Mt. Tamalpais under the soaring stars. I dreamed that I had a tape recording of some of my own songs and I thought that the songs were good, but when I played the songs for an audience, I got a very unfavorable reaction. Worst of all, they seemed completely disinterested! I felt crushed at the reaction and began cursing at the crowd.

"Then a professor stood up and began handing out special awards to the best songwriters. In a very obvious manner, he passed me by, and this infuriated me even more. I cursed the professor with a venomous tongue and screamed at the crowd as they booed me. I was so angry that I challenged them all to a fight, and several men jumped up and came at me!

"I took off running to save my life, and the men were in hot pursuit. As they closed in on me, I suddenly lurched forward and took off flying up near the ceiling of the great hall. I flew around a few times, then saw an open window and went straight to it. In a flash, I streaked out of the hall and up into the bright blue sky. Strangely, all at once, I had my guitar between my legs, with neck forward like a witch's broom! My speed instantly doubled! It was fantastic!

"Eventually I circled back around and flew on into the great hall again. As I circled over the crowd, I felt a new exhilaration, but also a moment's sadness as I saw the crowd cheering for a new performer there on the stage. But then I noticed an Aborigine man dancing out in the audience. He was naked and joyous, and he danced with such utter abandon that I immediately knew what it meant to be free, and I realized what a fool I'd been to get so distressed over the disinterest in my own ego songs. In that realization, I was able to continue my exhilarating flight with total joy and abandon and soar back on out and up into the free blue sky.

"In a second dream a few nights later, I found myself by a river in the wilds and I was walking with a friend. Huge logs floated by, and I marveled at the great weeping willow trees which hung drooping along the riverbank.

"Then we came to a large building and went on in. There we found another great hall, filled with people, and an orchestra played at the front of the crowd by the stage. I suddenly realized that I was supposed to get my guitar and play, so I went backstage and found it. But when I went on stage, I did not play. Instead, to everyone's shock, I began smashing the guitar to pieces! The audience went into hysterics and again I went fleeing for my life!

"I quickly found an elevator and got in and went up and down, but I was getting nowhere. So I got out on a high floor and ran for a window as my pursuers closed in on me. I leapt with all of my strength and tried to fly. At first, it was a struggle, and I felt leaden and uncertain of my abilities. But then slowly but surely it got easier, and I felt lighter and lighter. Finally, I was soaring like an eagle over trees and houses. A great exhilaration set in, and I realized that I was only as free as I thought myself to be and that there was no limit to how high we can fly!

"Suddenly, I shot straight up through the sky, rising higher and higher. My speed kept increasing as I jetted upward like a rocket. Then it happened . . . I burst through the atmosphere and on out into space! I had gotten beyond the planet, and I felt a great peace there. I just floated along on my back, looking out at the glittering stars. I actually saw satellites fly by and all was clear. The whole great Milky Way hovered there before me, and I knew that all the far celestial starfields are ours forever and forever.

"So now say what? The dreams have said it all, and our lives are not something from which we seek to escape. Our lives are a challenge, and we seek only to overcome obstacles and expand ever inward and ever outward, like the universe itself.

"There is precious little time for wasting on battles of the greedy ego and on people that strive to shackle us to the tortures of narrow-mindedness. Death is not an end! We go on . . . our dreaming tells us that. We live that truth! And we will take it all with us! Every pain and every ecstasy, every incredible memory will fly away with the spirit and move on again, to see, to learn, to know. And to love . . . to love it all for what it is, as it is, and share that love forever and forever."

The audience roared, and they all began leaping to their feet. If Aaron was surprised at the standing ovation, he understood at once as a sprite, gray-bearded man walked quickly out to him at the podium. It was X. Rex Kelby, and he was smiling and waving. He held in his hands a Vimana for Aaron who was already clad in a flashy purple flysuit. Kelby, himself, wore gold, and he was ready to fly!

As Aaron quickly donned his helmet and strapped on the Vimana XRK-4, and as scores of hands passed out other Vimanas to the huge audience, all suited up and ready, X. Rex Kelby stepped up to the microphone and let loose with only one great cry, screaming "Let's burn wind!" So it began, Kelby at the lead, crossing out over the great cheering throng and on out the wide doors of the conference hall. He circled the building four times as scores of new fliers joined the sky ranks on each soaring pass, until they were all airborne, every one of them: Kelby, Aurora, Aaron and Phoebe, Eric and Rachel, Jack and Tamara, Mauricio Manza and Shana Capella, a cackling Carlos, Damon Burke and Katerina Markovich, Justin DeWitt and Simon Cody, and Richard Getz, who had hosted Aaron and Phoebe in his Washington home . . . all the Vimanians . . .

each streaking forth like the greatest aerial dreamers of all time. Kelby led on a lofty fun flight, circling the marble edifices of the Jefferson and Lincoln memorials, around the vast rotunda of the great capitol dome and then finally to spiral the awesome obelisk of the Washington Monument, round and round and up the pillar of freedom.

As the innumerable cameras scanned and jostled and jousted to bring the sudden fantastic flying show to the eyes of the millions who were sitting in the bright glare of television screenlight . . . watching, waiting and wondering where such bravura and bold flights of fancy and freedom would finally lead, X. Rex Kelby brought the whole great flying Vimana to circle the soaring spires of the great stone structure dedicated to all free spirits of the world, with the beautiful stained-glass rose above its open doors, the Washington Cathedral. He held his arms high in triumph and laughed hard as he flew by. The new era was in full flight. Man had finally, really gotten his wings.

THE END

WAYNE SAALMAN, novelist, poet, futurist, is a dedicated syncretist who has traveled extensively throughout North America, Europe, Asia, Africa and Australia. A native of Ohio and a graduate of Bowling Green State University, he has been intensely researching dreams for over twenty years. He has lived in San Francisco since 1981.